NICOLE CAIN

Crier's Peak

Where the sins of the past ignite the fight for the future.

*To the quiet moments and the loud dreams that
brought this story to life.*

Contents

Acknowledgments

This story has been five years in the making. It began with *Star Wars* and a daydream to escape reality. Seeing it come to life on paper is truly indescribable. I am deeply grateful to the many people who supported and encouraged me throughout the journey of writing *Crier's Peak*.

First and foremost, thank you to Mittens, my orange, velcro cat, who never once left my side. Your constant presence kept my lap warm and my writing position uncomfortable. You were there for every late-night edit, every frustrated sigh, and every small victory. You reminded me to take breaks... even if it was just to fill your bowl.

To my parents, thank you for instilling in me a love of reading and stories from an early age. You surrounded me with books and never questioned my need to stay up past bedtime to finish just one more chapter. Your love and support laid the foundation for everything I've created. Look, Mom—I wrote a book! Thank you, Dad, for introducing me to *Star Wars* so young that I don't remember the first time I watched it. It's what started this whole thing.

To Colten, my best friend, my boyfriend, and my biggest supporter. Thank you for (lovingly) bullying me into dreaming bigger. Your encouragement and terrible jokes during this journey means everything. Thank you for standing by me through every doubt, every rewrite, and every meltdown.

Endless thanks to my beta readers. You brave, brilliant souls who dove into messy drafts and came out mostly unscathed. Your feedback was sharp, your patience saintly, and your ability to spot plot holes truly terrifying. This book is better, and less confusing, because of you.

A special thank you to Laë Proofreads for your guidance, your encouragement, and your insight. You helped shape this story into its final form, and you were an absolute blast to work with. You saw the heart of the story and helped me bring it into focus. Thank you for your patience, your honesty, and for making the developmental editing process something I looked forward to.

And to Gillian Baines, my copy editor, thank you for making me realize that I may not actually know what punctuation is. You approached my chaos with kindness and made the final stages of this book feel polished. I am truly grateful for your steady guidance.

A huge thank you to Pamela Cone, my high school English teacher and my proofreader. Working with you brought everything full circle, and your help made *Crier's Peak* that much better. Thank you for catching all the little things that slipped through the cracks. I'm incredibly grateful for your support, both then and now.

Finally, thank you, dear reader, for taking a chance and reading this book. Your time, imagination, and willingness to journey through these pages mean more to me than words can express. I hope this story stays with you, and that its message gives you something to carry with you. Thank you for being part of it.

With love, Nicole.

The Hero of Strife

In the age of shadows and souls grown weary,
A man born of strife with eyes of fury,
Shall journey into the heart of ancient stone,
Where slumbers a dragon, in depths unknown.
With courage as his sword and wisdom as his light,
He shall awaken Aarth from his long, dreamless night.
From ashes of old and tales untold,
The dragon shall rise, mighty and bold.
Through fire and storm, they shall forge a bond,
As fate intertwines their paths beyond.
Together they'll soar, with power unseen,
Where the whispers of fate weave a timeless dream.
Yet heed this warning, Hero of Strife:
Those who seek power may lose their life.
Plunge too deep, and let the beast arise,
And the soul within you will fade into the skies.
For this power is a seductive call,
It is in this greed that the mightiest fall.

1

Greyson

Killing *Father will have been worth it in the end.*
Greyson's contemplation turned to memories of Malric Hawke, his father, the ruler who had left the kingdom in shambles. After conquering Navaria's outer regions, Malric had looked to the seas for further expansion, escalating worldwide tension. And then he made the mistake of attacking Marella, the bustling coastal city across the sea, while unprepared and vastly outnumbered. Though over a decade had passed since the Two-Day War, its impact was still fresh in Navaria's collective memory. Despite Malric having the benefit of surprise, most of his men had perished in Marella's counterattack.

My father was a fool. A dead fool.

It had been three months since Greyson's coronation, and he sensed the growing unease among the nations across the seas, anticipating an act of aggression. Suspecting this apprehension would drive other nations to infiltrate his ranks, Greyson conducted an exhaustive investigation in his first weeks as king, but found no one of suspicion.

The winter wind lashed at his face, whipping loose tendrils of black hair against his forehead, leaving his cheeks pink with windburn.

Alongside the Grand General, he rode through the night, flanked by two battalions trudging through the snow behind them. Overkill for the task at hand, but this was what the Hawke bloodline was renowned for—might, ferocity, no mercy.

A black flag billowed overhead, a striking blue drake at its center, its wings spread wide as it snapped in the wind. The insignia was recognized and feared by many nations. To see the blue drake was to look suffering in the eye.

Bound tightly by the weight of his armor, the thick fur pelts he wore offered little respite against the biting cold. Navaria was in the grip of its most unforgiving winter yet, with heavier snowfall, relentless winds, and a scarcity of food making the odds of survival drop even further.

The tall pines creaked overhead as he led his men along the main road. His steed's hooves clomped on the cobblestones as they came upon the remnants of a long-abandoned village, its name forgotten. It was one of many settlements that had died under his grandfather's reign. The wind howled and whistled as it whisked through the destruction, charred remnants of houses looming just beyond the reach of their torchlight; its eeriness raised the hair on the back of Greyson's neck.

His albino elk stopped, snorted, and shook his head. Jericho's white fur rippled. Greyson signaled his men to halt and peered through the ruins, into the darkness. Five pairs of eyes glinted back at him.

Though prey was scarce and packs were small, wolves in the area had little trouble feeding themselves. Attacks on humans weren't uncommon, but he doubted this pack would dare prey on a group of men this large.

"Tighten the rear," Greyson commanded before clicking his teeth to coax the elk onward. Jericho snapped his jaw and pushed forward, his breath rapid though they passed without incident.

"Easy, boy," he murmured, stroking Jericho's neck.

The flickering light of a fire danced among the trees, casting a warm glow through the forest. Greyson tugged on the reins, signaling his men to halt. Grand General Eden brought his steed to a stop beside him.

"We are here peacefully," he said to the general. "Do not engage unless I give the command."

"Yes, Your Majesty."

As they neared the village, Greyson's hand instinctively found the hilt of his sword, weighing the potential outcomes of their journey. There were two ways this trip could end, and he hoped to Aarth that the people of Wimborne would accept his offer.

Shabby structures came into view, weatherworn and ancient. It was a miracle that the cabins were still standing against the wind. There were no watchtowers, no fences, no guards, nothing to warn the villagers of Greyson's arrival.

Distant chatter echoed in the night. Townsfolk braced themselves against the cold, huddled together around bonfires, passing around pints of ale.

But the calm was soon shattered.

Panicked villagers scattered as Greyson's presence became known. Some dropped to their knees in fear, while others retreated into the safety of the shadows, hoping to avoid his notice. Shame surged within him, further adding to the flush in his cheeks, and his heart felt heavy as he internally cursed his ancestors.

In the village square stood a stone platform with a statue atop it, the founder of Wimborne, who had lived among dragons long ago.

Greyson dismounted and stood atop the memorial, his gaze sweeping over the crowd until he locked eyes with Eden who stood tense at the structure's base. As the villagers gathered around, their frail figures huddling together, their gaunt eyes fixated on Greyson's gleaming white armor and the image of a frost drake engraved on his chest plate. Fear radiated from their gaze, lingering on the scabbard tied to his belt.

Navaria had declined over the centuries, each king ruling more cruelly than the last, until finally it had been crippled by Malric's rule, and now it was up to Greyson to mend this shattered kingdom. The dwindling population of Wimborne, a once-thriving livestock town, was now a mere two hundred souls, and served as the prime example of the kingdom's decline.

Holding tight to his vision of an era of peace after generations of conflict and turmoil, the urgency to gain the trust of his people grew more intense with each passing day.

In the streets beyond the crowd, a cloaked figure dashed between buildings, and Greyson might have believed he imagined it, but he knew better.

On time as always, he thought as the figure faded into the shadows.

The crowd whispered among themselves. Resisting the urge to grab the hilt of his sword, a nervous habit he'd developed in his teenage years, Greyson cleared his throat, silencing the crowd.

4

"Vanya Lockwood." His breath clouded into the frigid air.

"Here." A woman emerged from the crowd. Her face weathered with crow's feet around her eyes and streaks of silver through her dark hair. Meeting Greyson's gaze with resentment, she stood her ground, a revolver secured firmly in her belt.

Firearms were a technological wonder in this part of the world, one that Malric had shunned and all but outlawed, and was responsible for Navaria's defeat in the Two-Day War. Firearms were another avenue where the world outside had progressed, but Navaria had not.

"A man who lacks the talent to fight with a sword is a coward." His father's words came to him.

"You will kneel when addressing your king," General Eden commanded.

"Why have you come?" Defiance gleamed in Vanya's eyes. Every bit a warrior as much as a matriarch, she carried herself with a grace and power that Greyson could not help but admire.

Eden charged forward, drawing his sword, the silver blade glinting in the firelight. "I said kneel."

Unfazed by the threat, Vanya met the pointed blade without flinching, further deepening Greyson's admiration for her.

"Stand down," Greyson commanded, quelling Eden's aggression, but only just, before addressing Vanya. "As your king, I am here to make you an offer. Consider relocating your people closer to Beckinsdale."

"Have you gone mad?" she exclaimed as chatter rippled through the crowd. "My family has lived on this land for centuries!"

"As have mine," Greyson countered. "But with you being

5

so close to The Barrens, you're all at risk of starvation if the jaws of frostbite don't kill you first."

"We've managed thus far."

"At least speak with me about this, we can negotiate."

"No," Vanya said. "Wimborne is our home. We settled in this valley long before your bloodline came to be."

"Please, do not force my hand." Greyson swallowed, his mouth bone-dry as dread reared in his stomach and swirled like thick fog. "I'll escort you to Beckinsdale and show you myself if I must."

A shake of her head was her only response.

"Very well," he said. "General, arrest her."

As Eden charged, Vanya swiftly drew her revolver and fired. He raised his steel bulwark, deflecting the bullet with a sharp clink. With each shot fired, the bullets ricocheted off Eden's shield until there was the click of an empty chamber.

"No, wait!" Greyson said as Eden thrust the blade through her neck, the sickening squish of flesh cut through the air and the gurgles of Vanya wheezing for breath.

General Eden ripped the blade from Vanya's throat, and she collapsed—dead.

"Mother!" A woman shrieked as she darted from the crowd.

The sword's magic took hold as soon as it had pierced Vanya's skin. Her neck, purple with frostbite, quickly froze, and the icy crystal essence spread to her face and chest like growing cracks in a window. Blood, the consistency of slush, oozed from the wound like thawing snow.

The young woman kneeled. In vain, trying to dress the strange wound. When her attempt failed, she choked on a sob, her shaking hands soaked with gore and finding no pulse.

Eden's eyes swam with excited malice as he dropped his

6

shield and pulled the distraught woman up by the fur collar of her coat. She screamed and flailed as she was ripped away from her mother's corpse. He dropped her into the snow at the base of the platform.

It had happened so quickly that Greyson scarcely had time to move. His face burned. Not just from the cold, but with an unsettling wave of rage.

"Looks like you're in charge now, darling." Eden said. "Let's hope you're more cooperative." He leveled his sword at the girl's neck.

Shock and terror rippled through the crowd of onlookers, their unease almost tangible in the air. Greyson knew he had enough men to quell a potential mob, but his concern lay with Eden's unpredictable actions. The crowd held its breath as General Eden prowled around the woman like a hawk, tension mounting with every step.

"State your name," Eden commanded.

The woman's shoulders trembled as she continued to wail into the snow, her cries echoing through the tense silence. Greyson's hand found its way to his sword hilt, his knuckles whitening as his grip tightened in anticipation.

"Stand down, Eden," Greyson said through gritted teeth.

"That was an order!" Eden planted a boot in her ribs, ignoring his commander.

The anger boiling beneath Greyson's skin erupted in a burst of fury. Before he could stop himself, he lunged down from the memorial, grabbed Eden by the collar of his tunic, and shoved him into the stone foundation of the platform, knocking Eden's white, perfectly combed hair askew.

"I said stand down!" He shouted in Eden's face. Somewhere in the swift descent, Greyson had drawn his weapon and was now holding it mere centimeters from Eden's neck.

"Your tactics are weak." Eden spat out as his free hand gripped Greyson's wrist, his touch ice-cold, even through Greyson's gauntlets. "You don't hold a candle to your father."

"And you should be grateful for that. *Fall in line.* Disobey me again and you will not see the night's end."

"Yes, Sire."

Greyson released him and sheathed his sword before turning to approach the girl who remained hunched over in the snow. "Please," he whispered, crouching in front of her. "Your name."

"Terra," she said through tears and gritted teeth. "Terra Lockwood."

2

Greyson

The moment he and the Grand General were alone in the tiny cabin, Greyson could no longer contain the fury boiling inside him. "You made me look weak!" he shouted, his voice echoing off the wooden walls, sharp as shattered glass. His fists clenched at his sides, knuckles white.

"I did what was necessary," Eden replied, each syllable dripping with venom as he stalked closer, his shadow stretching long in the lantern light.

The embers in the fireplace had yet to melt the snow clinging to their fur coats. The cabin hardly had room for a fireplace, a dingy table, and chairs, much less two large men with opposing beliefs.

"You disobeyed a direct order." Greyson slammed his fist onto the table, causing quills to roll across the surface. "You were to *arrest* her."

"She fired her weapon."

"That's not an adequate excuse. You're the Wolf of the North, *a war general*. Do you expect me to believe you felt threatened by an old woman with a gun?"

Beads of sweat trickled down Greyson's back as the atmosphere grew more heated by the second, unsure if it was from the fire or flaring tempers.

"You've complicated the situation," he added before Eden could defend himself. "I now have to compensate Terra for her mother's death."

"You have no obligations to that girl. If she's smart, she'll yield to you. As we both witnessed earlier, stupidity kills."

Greyson's fingers curled, knuckles cracking. A pit of rage swirled deep within him, snarling and pacing like a caged beast. Despite his efforts to keep it buried, Eden had a talent for drawing it to the surface at will. Yet, that very anger fueled his success in seizing his crown. Greyson had feared that the nobles would challenge him, but the brutal murder of his father had done its job in silencing them.

But I need the people's support, not the nobles'.

"You didn't need to come all the way out here," Eden pointed out. "You should have sent an officer, as I suggested. You're the king, your presence is not required in small matters such as these. If one of our own is leading the town, you have complete control."

Placing commanders of his choice in positions of power across nearly every town governed by the Hawke regime had ensured his father firm control. Wimborne stood as the last village untouched by this.

"That is not what I want. Our ties with Wimborne were already delicate, and you've utterly shattered it," Greyson countered. "I seek allies, yet your actions have only widened the divide between the crown and the people!"

"I understand your concerns, Sire, but your desire for unity can only be achieved by ruling with an iron fist. Why not appoint one of our own to lead this waste of a village?"

"If this village is such a waste, why bother?" Greyson challenged him.

"Navaria will not respect you if they do not fear you. You must have total control, just like the kings of old."

He held Eden's frenzied stare for a moment and shook his head. "You and these kings of old are getting in my way."

"If I am such a nuisance, then kill me."

How I would revel in that.

But death seemed too merciful a punishment. Eden, having served under Greyson's father as a commander, swiftly ascended through the ranks due to his unapologetic cruelty, earning him the moniker "Wolf of the North." Lawfully, Eden would retain the position of Grand General until he retired or died, a result of the grandfathered laws Greyson despised.

"I wouldn't stoop so low."

"Your father—" Eden began.

"I am *not* my father."

"Unfortunately."

Silence descended in the cabin. Eden's black eyes bore into Greyson, a silent challenge echoing in the air. The scars on Greyson's back throbbed, dredging up nauseating memories. Malric was a cruel king as well as a cruel father. Violence and bloodshed stained his lineage, haunting Greyson like looming storm clouds, casting shadows wherever he went.

There was a knock at the door.

"Enter," Greyson said.

A soldier stepped across the threshold with Terra in tow, his gloved fingers coiled around her arm. Her eyes were red and swollen, as if she had wept for a lifetime. Greyson averted his eyes, biting the inside of his cheek.

11

The soldier pulled her deeper into the cabin and prodded her into the chair at the makeshift desk. Though she refused to meet his gaze, Greyson forced himself to look at her and see the distant, somber emotions swirling in her watery eyes.

I've been in that abyss.

"I searched her," the soldier said, handing Vanya's pistol over. "This was the only weapon she possessed."

Greyson's brows shot up. He hadn't seen her take it from Vanya's body. "Thank you, officer. Leave us," he said, securing the revolver inside his belt. "You as well, General."

Eden hesitated for a moment, then followed the soldier outside, glaring the entire way out. The cabin's windows rattled as the door slammed shut, and Terra glanced around like a caged animal.

Greyson settled into the chair opposite her and tidied up the mess of quills and parchment. This conversation would lay the groundwork for their future relationship. Vanya didn't trust him, but she complied. Until recently.

I want her to trust me.

Wimborne was dying, and the only solution he could offer was one that had been refused multiple times before.

"How are you holding up?" he asked, trying to catch her eye. Fresh tears welled up and fell down her cheeks, a release he never had the luxury of. He couldn't recall the last time he cried, and he wasn't sure his body remembered how. He almost envied her. Malric would have punished him if he displayed such a behavior, deeming it a weakness.

"I'm sorry for your loss." Greyson leaned against the desk. "I lost my mother when I was a boy. I know that the loss of a parent is difficult."

Terra's head snapped up, her nose scrunched. "How dare

12

you say such a thing to me," she exclaimed, her lips trembling as she glared at him through hot tears. "You don't understand how this feels. You *murdered* your parents."

He let the accusation roll off him. Terra, like most people, had heard the stories and already condemned him.

"I truly am sorry. I didn't want it to happen the way it did, but now the leadership of Wimborne passes to you and we have business to attend to." He slid a quill and a hastily written contract across the desk.

"You're not going to make me call you 'Sire' or 'Your Majesty'?"

"No," he said. "Titles aren't important at the moment. I failed you and your mother. 'Your Majesty' is not a title I deserve right now."

Terra opened her mouth as if she wanted to say more but decided against it, stopping to wipe away tears with the sleeve of her coat. With her attention drawn to the parchment, brows furrowing deeper as she read, she could've been a younger version of Vanya with her black hair, serious eyes, and passion for her people.

"I can't agree to this," she sniffed. "What my mother didn't tell you is that a large portion of our crops didn't survive, and our remaining bison are too young to slaughter. We can barely feed ourselves. If I sign this, my people will starve. There will be nothing left of Wimborne."

"There's hardly a Wimborne as it is… It's in your people's best interest to relocate, please."

She scoffed. "You don't care what's in our best interest, you just want us under your thumb."

"That was my father's intention. If I wanted to control you, I would have forced you to relocate, but instead, I'm allowing

13

you to make the decision," he countered.

Her face changed, emotions shifting into something curious and hopeful, and reality seemed to set in. For the first time since Greyson's arrival, she grasped what he was offering her people.

"No," she whimpered. Bowing her head as defeat rushed in and shattered whatever was there before. "They'll think me a coward for giving in to your demands."

"Leadership comes with impossible decisions, and sometimes, what's best for everyone is the last thing they want."

He let his words hang in the silence as her feverish eyes darted around the floor.

"I have made this offer multiple times," Greyson continued, "and I offer it to you once more. Relocate. Move your people closer to Beckinsdale. With so few of you remaining, integration into a larger, more stable town would be feasible."

"This is our home," Terra asserted, summoning all the authority she could, weakly holding to her mother's stance. "We've lived here for centuries."

"Your people don't need to suffer this way. I want to help."

"Only the Raven can—" she stopped, suddenly interested in the sleeve of her coat.

"The Raven?" he asked.

"It's nothing."

"I don't believe you."

She fell silent, fidgeting with the sleeve of her coat. Then, shaking her head, she murmured, "It's only a legend."

"I know the legends, but nowhere do they mention a raven."

She leveled her gaze, seemingly unsure how they had gotten to this subject and why the king of Navaria was interested in a local ghost story.

14

How much does she know?

"We heard rumors of it from passing travelers," she began, shifting in her chair, "and then we started seeing it here. It leaves food, clothes, and blankets. Sometimes medicine."

"What does the Raven look like?"

"No one has actually *seen* it, only glimpses," she explained. "Some say it's a man. Many have claimed to have seen a shadow darting through alleyways just before dawn."

A shadow darting through alleyways. Greyson recalled the cloak he'd glimpsed just before Vanya's execution.

"Do you put your faith in this legend?"

"What do you care what I choose to put my faith in?" She folded her arms. "We have needed something to believe in since the dragons vanished from this world."

"Old texts speak of the Aarth returning one day—"

"—to right the wrongs of traitorous bloodlines," Terra finished.

He understood more than anyone the implications of the ancient texts. That Aarth, the father of dragon-kind, would return to smite the bloodlines that had slaughtered his kin.

The great lizards had been extinct for centuries. Were it not for his dragon steel sword and the massive, dry bones left behind in deep, remote caverns, Greyson might have doubted the existence of the magnificent beasts.

Reaching behind his back, he revealed Vanya's revolver. "The craftsmanship is impeccable. Your mother was truly talented. If I were my father, I might have chosen to destroy it, but," he said, placing the gun on the desk, "it belongs to you."

Fleetingly, her eyes darted from him to the gun. She reached for the handle and ran her thumb over the sleek steel barrel.

Though it was unloaded, it was still a hefty weapon, and he was certain Terra knew this. If she felt him responsible for Vanya's death, she had ample opportunity to act on it. If she was looking for a chance, this was it.

"I understand," he began in a whisper, "that you are grieving, feel cornered, and are frustrated beyond measure. I, too, am weary of the suffering this nation has endured, but I refuse to continue as my father did. Furthermore, I cannot continue without my people's support, without *your* support."

Greyson's insides sagged with relief as she holstered the revolver. He knew nothing could ever compensate her for her mother's death. There wasn't a thing in this life that he could give her to make up for it. Still, she needed some glimmer of hope, some assurance that he would keep his word. Greyson reached into his coat, withdrew a small bag, and placed it into her hand.

"It's not much, but it'll buy a decent number of supplies for the village."

As she opened the bag, her eyes widened at the sight of the glittering gold coins in the firelight. He had captured her attention, and he had one more offer up his sleeve—a secret.

Would she even believe me?

Though she had already condemned him, Greyson dared to hope. For his conscience, the sake of Wimborne, and his newfound reputation.

"Terra," he said.

Their eyes locked, and he hesitated, opening his mouth, then closing it again. He swallowed, reluctant to speak it aloud and terrified not to.

"I know who the Raven is."

Her eyebrows shot up, a mixture of surprise and disbelief.

16

Her mouth dropped open as understanding settled on her face, and he waited for her to challenge his claim, to dismiss him. Greyson felt compelled to say something to break up the silence when Terra slid the contract across the table.

"Two months," she said, "give me two months to think this over."

"Granted," Greyson dipped his head.

"Don't make me regret this… Your Majesty. Don't let us starve."

Greyson rolled the contract and tied it neatly with twine. His shoulders feeling a bit lighter than they did minutes before, he stood to leave.

"And one more thing," Terra added as he walked past.

He paused, his hand on the doorknob. "Yes?"

"Promise me that one day I'll get a chance to take a swipe at General Eden."

"I'll hold him down for you," Greyson replied with a smirk.

3

Lavine

Lavine darted down an alleyway, finding cover from the wind and the Navarian soldiers that patrolled the area. Navigating the maze of streets, she tracked the signage hanging from above until she spotted the tall wooden building of an inn, standing like a beacon in the night.

Crouching behind barrels, she yanked her mask down, the wool no match for the gusts of icy wind. She ran her tongue across her dry, flaking lips, craving Marella's salty, warm summer breezes which seemed a world away.

Footsteps crunched from behind. She snatched a dagger from her waistband, shifting her stance to the right, listening to the intruder's gait with her good ear. There was a subtle but unmistakable weight to his tread, hitting the cobblestones with purpose. Despite the tension in her body, her heart thumped steadily, her composure unwavering.

With the dagger gripped close to her chest, he closed the distance, the faint metallic clink of armor. He was just feet away. She drew in a breath and—

A stream of liquid splattered against a wooden surface.

Peeking over the barrels, she spotted the man relieving himself on the opposite side of the alley, oblivious to her presence. After a few awkward seconds, he hastily zipped himself up and continued on his way. Lavine's shoulders dropped, and she chuckled at herself.

Since when are you so jumpy? Get back to work.

Straightening her cloak, she gathered herself and strode onto the sidewalk, blending in with the passersby. The wooden doors of the inn opened with a heavy thud, and she was greeted by the warmth and light from an enormous, roaring fireplace. The air was alive with laughter, the cheerful clinking of glasses, and the faint scraping of spoons against wooden bowls, the last dregs of soup being savored. Navarian soldiers took up the bulk of the room, none of which turned to look at her. To them, she was just another citizen seeking relief from the weather.

Seating herself furthest away from the hearth, where tables sat vacant, she observed the room. The sea of patrons congregated near the stone fireplace, drawn in by its warmth. She tallied every soldier and citizen, noting every face, scar, and shade of hair, as well as the array of weapons, accents, and clothing.

"Want anything, lass?" inquired a burly man, his apron smudged with grease. "Perhaps a hot drink or a bite to eat?"

"Only warming myself, thank you."

"Suit yourself." He shrugged and continued his way back to the kitchens.

She checked the comm strapped to her wrist.

He's late, she thought, looking around the room for his face.

A group of cadets were gathered around a table near the bar, engaged in a spirited card game. Among them, a young soldier slipped a card from his boot, his sleight of hand leading him to winning the game. As the game concluded, ten minutes had drifted by.

Beginning to worry, she traced her thumb up and down the handle of her dagger, counting the grooves on its hilt.

Down. One. Two. Three. Four. Up. One. Two. Thr—

An unsettling shiver crept up her spine. Feeling as though she was being watched, she surveyed the room and caught sight of a Navarian officer eyeing her from beside the fireplace, his dark skin clashing with the muted grays of his uniform. Their eyes locked. He abandoned his place by the fire and sauntered toward her.

"What's a gorgeous girl like you doing sitting here all alone?"

"Nothing that concerns you."

"Why don't you join me by the fire?" His voice dipped. "I could use some feminine company."

"Shove off," she snapped, dismissing his advances.

"I can't believe you would treat a serviceman with such animosity."

"Well, one of us has to be a decent actor." A playful grin spread across her face. "Got anything for me?"

"I have something worth the lives of an entire civilization," he whispered. "We'll need privacy. It'll have to look like I'm taking you to bed."

She nodded, allowing him to take her hand and help her rise from her seat. His hand trembled in hers as they ascended the stairs, traversed a narrow hallway, and climbed another staircase. Finally, she found herself in a cramped, dimly lit room, heavy with the scent of dampness and mold.

As the door clicked shut behind her, Lavine surveyed the room, her mind already looking for potential escape routes.

One door. One window, two-story fall. Two escape routes. One that could result in a possible injury, one that would not.

"What do you have for me, Theo?"

"It's *Corporal* Theodore now." His chest swelled with pride. "How is everything in Marella?"

"A little tense. Things have quieted down since Malric's son took the throne, the council thinks he's up to something."

"They may be right." Theo buried his trembling hands in his pockets. "There's been rumors about a weapon."

"What kind of weapon?"

"They call it '*Mundicar.*' I'm not sure what it is or where it's being kept, but it's capable of wiping out entire towns at a time."

The notion of a weapon with such catastrophic potential struck her like a physical blow. Even the Marellan military had nothing compared to this level of devastation, leaving her mind spiraling into what 'Mundicar' could be. "Are you sure?"

"Yes. Two months ago, I was sent to Beckinsdale to report on the mining progress here in Alain. I was early and wasn't to be expected for another half hour, so I waited outside my colonel's office. I heard voices coming down the corridor, and it was General Eden."

"Grand General Eden?"

"Yes, I don't know to whom he was speaking, but he said that Navaria wouldn't need to plunder their own towns when they had the means to expand further south than ever."

Eden was a legend throughout the world, and tales of his bloodlust spread through the Academy like ghost stories. He almost didn't seem real.

Classified information conveniently spoken at the right moment?

The Grand General wouldn't be so careless.

"Theo, this feels like a setup."

"Promise me, Beckett. Promise me you'll look into this," he pleaded. "If it does exists, it's not just Marella that's under threat."

"Mundicar…" she echoed, her voice barely above a whisper. The thought of such a devastating weapon being wielded was chilling.

A heavy fist pounded on the door, startling Theo who flinched at the intrusion. Lavine drew her dagger, her stance poised and ready for whatever awaited on the other side.

"Corporal!" a man shouted through the door. "Commander Johann has called for a meeting."

"Remember, *Mundicar.*" Theo took the dagger from her grip and tore at the front of his new uniform.

"What are you doing?"

"You have to find out what this weapon is."

The man beat his fist against the door, the sound like thunder in her bones. "Corporal, are you alright?"

The door handle shuddered.

Theo drew the blade to his face and slashed his cheek. Blood spilled from his dark skin as Lavine lunged forward, gripping his wrists, and shoved him into the dresser.

"Have you gone mad?" She hissed.

The door crashed open. Theo wrenched his wrists free from her grip, his eyes wide. "Assassin!" he cried, pointing the stolen dagger at her. "Arrest her!"

The soldier rushed into the room. Lavine drew a second dagger from her boot and sprang forward as the soldier brought down the silver blade of his sword. He swung down as she careened to her right and kicked. The soldier stumbled and fell, his body slamming to the floor. She slashed his neck open as she slipped through the doorway.

"Assassin!" Bellows rang down the hall.

Dammit, Theo!

With heavy boots pounding on the floorboards overhead, Lavine raced through the halls and down stairwells, her mind working furiously to calculate her next move.

Sprinting down an adjacent hall, she fled to the nearest room and slammed into its door. Her eyes dropped to the rusty lock. She dug her finger behind the crook of her ear, retrieved a hairpin, and fidgeted with the lock until there was a click.

The door flew open, startling a disheveled woman within who let out a piercing scream and scrambled to hide under a blanket, shielding her face from the intruder. The soldier this woman had bedded instinctively reached for his sword, his expression red with rage and alarm.

Always with the swords, these guys.

Lavine hurled her dagger at the shirtless man before he could reach his weapon. He cried out as the blade impaled his muscular sternum. She dashed across the room and yanked the blade out, blood spattering onto the wall. A flurry of cold air rushed in as she heaved the window open.

Her head snapped to the bed where the girl was still huddled under the blanket, sobbing. Lavine's hand gripped her dagger. Distant shouts of soldiers reverberated down the hall.

I don't have time. She never saw my face.

She pulled her hood up and sprang out of the window. The sting of the landing shot through her shins like lightning strikes. Without a moment's hesitation, she bolted down the alleyway, her heart racing, not daring to look back.

The town buzzed with activity as she weaved through Alain's winding streets. The shouts of Navarian troops grew distant, and buildings became fewer and further in between as she reached the outskirts of town. Keeping to the shadows, she crept along the side of the largest of the lonely buildings, a sign bearing crossed swords hanging from the porch.

A blacksmith's shop.

Lavine pressed her back against the rear of the building, closing her eyes as she panted. Imagining the warmth of a forge on the other side of the wall, it reminded her of how cold she was. Her fingers stung and the frigid air burned her lungs. A moonlit field stretched out before her, and beyond it stood a pine forest, its dark silhouette etched against the canvas of the starry night sky.

Two hundred yards.

Squinting into the darkness, Lavine spotted a sad excuse for a shed at half the distance, the only cover on the barren field. With a deep breath, she blew warmth into her cupped hands and rolled her shoulders, bracing herself for the grueling sprint.

"You can do this, you can do this, you can—"

Lavine staggered as something slammed into the left side of her face. Her vision blurred. Agony reverberated through her head as it collided with the wall.

A meaty hand clamped around her throat, crushing her windpipe and pinning her against the rough wooden wall.

"You're the one they're looking for," the man whispered.

Lavine's hands flew to his tightening grip. The man, wide and brawny, held an unfinished weapon in his free hand, the metal glinting in the moonlight.

"You... must be... the... blacksmith," she gasped, her words

24

strained as she struggled for breath, shifting on the tips of her toes in an attempt to ease the pressure on her throat.

"They'll pay me a fortune for turning you in," he said through his wild, ungroomed beard.

As his hand clenched tighter, her vision blurred, and her mind raced to find a way out. Each passing second seemed like an eternity. Her lungs felt ready to burst if she didn't get oxygen soon, and her only weapon was tucked into her boot, out of reach.

Feeling herself on the brink of blacking out, Lavine's arm moved without her command, as if it already knew what to do. She pulled a pin from her hair and jabbed it into the man's eye with all the force she could muster.

With a howl, the blacksmith released her and swung his weapon in a wide arc. Before she could fully catch her breath, she reached for her boot and dove between his legs. Rolling away from the wall, she spun on her knee and drove her dagger into the blacksmith's fleshy thigh.

He hit the ground screaming, and her blade cut off his cry with a single, swift motion. He became still, his eyes staring into nothingness.

After taking a moment to catch her breath, Lavine cursed herself for not being more careful. Being deaf in one ear begged for more caution, and she hadn't been thorough enough in her observation. Her gaze drifted to the black-smith's corpse.

Did he have a family? Who did I just orphan?

Before the guilt could take hold, she turned and sprinted across the field. Only when she reached the cover of the shed did she dare to look back. The field was clear.

The toll of the day's events were beginning to settle into

her bones. Her lungs burned and the ache of bruising was already creeping up on her neck. She looked out to the piney woods, her safety net, and raced across the clearing, pushing away the fire in her lungs.

"Dragons above, I hate the cold," she muttered to herself.

Her calves joined the symphony of bodily aches as she reached the forest, slowing to a walking pace. Adrenaline drained from her veins. Within the refuge of the trees, her heart returned to its normal rhythm. Yet, beneath the calm, anger simmered at Theo's actions, recklessly blowing her cover to save his own skin.

It was for the greater good.

The blacksmith's face resurfaced in her mind, joining the many other faces forever burned into her memory. Despite being just a citizen of Alain, not necessarily loyal to the Hawke Empire, he had still attempted to turn her in. Yet, she couldn't hate him for it as he was just trying to survive, like all villagers under the Hawke rule.

Passing a familiar tree with a notch carved into its bark, Lavine turned left into the darker depths of the forest. There, where little moonlight shone through the canopy overhead, she spotted the ship hovering silently above the ground.

Piper.

Lavine whistled, and the side hatch of the small ship opened, revealing a figure who leaned out and lowered a rope ladder. She climbed, her limbs aching in protest.

4

Lavine

Lavine braced herself as *Piper's* engines roared to life. The airship shuddered as Kace pushed the throttle up. Snow whirred around the small airship, a funnel of winter glittering in the night. With steady hands, he guided *Piper* into the air, setting course to the south.

"Well, Beckett, was this trip worth it?" Kace shouted from the cockpit, his hands flipping switches across the console.

"I hope so." Lavine tore off her winter gear as the warmth in the cabin pressed in on her. She slumped onto a crate in the compact cargo hold, loosening the laces of her boots.

"Any useful information?" Ivy asked, stuffing Lavine's winter clothes into a nearby crate.

"I hate winter," she grumbled as she turned a boot upside down and shook it. Flecks of snow fluttered to the floor.

"That's not very useful considering you've told us a thousand times." Ivy crossed her arms. She was well accustomed to Lavine's routine complaints about weather below seventy degrees. "I know you've had to deal with the cold, but I've been stuck here with *your* brother."

"I've had to deal with him for over ten years," Lavine retorted. "I think you can handle a couple of hours."

"Speak of the devil…" Ivy said as Kace strode into the bay.

"The devil never looked this handsome," Kace quipped, leaning against the wall. "Piper's on autopilot. We'll reach Marella by morning."

Ivy turned back to Lavine. "So, did Theo discover any leads?"

"Hawke's soldiers interrupted our rendezvous, and I had to take out a few to get away, so they'll be on high alert for a while," Lavine explained. "But, yes, he has a lead, though a suspicious one."

Ivy's brows furrowed. "What do you mean?" she asked, her tone low and concern, eyes narrowing as she waited for a response.

Lavine unsheathed her dagger, now crusted with blood, examining it as she repeated what Theo had told her about the weapon he'd called Mundicar.

Both Kace and Ivy's eyes widened as she spoke. Their expressions shifted from curious to concerned.

"A weapon like that could end civilization as we know it," Ivy said, handing Lavine a rag. "How did he come by that information so easily?"

"Suspicious, isn't it?" Lavine said. "Theo's always been resourceful, but this feels too convenient. Like it was dropped in his lap."

"Agreed. We'll see what the High Council thinks about this. I'm sure they'll send us back to look into it," Kace added.

"I'll make sure we're sent back… I *need* to go back. Theo has my other dagger."

"Why does he have your other blade?" Ivy tilted her head,

her tight brown curls shifting.

"He took one when he blew my cover," Lavine said, the memory of Theo's actions in the heat of survival fueling the angry scrubbing of her dagger.

"He what?" Kace gaped. "He's defected!"

"No, he blew my cover to keep his." Lavine explained how Theo had cut his uniform and slashed his skin open to imply an assassination attempt. Content with the shining blade, she sheathed the weapon. "I don't blame him, but I want my dagger back."

"I don't think you understand the danger he put you in," Kace continued, sternly. "You are Marella's best-kept secret, and he just exposed you!"

"No one will believe him. He's just a corporal who's been attacked by a stranger. They'll think he's just flustered."

"Do you think he'll get close to Eden and Hawke?" Ivy asked.

Lavine knew the chances of that would be slim. High-ranking officers, especially the Navarian king himself, were incredibly difficult to get close to. If Theo did manage to get that close to the notorious duo, he'd be in a useful yet deadly position.

"I doubt it. He's too low on the food chain." Lavine fidgeted with the empty sheath at her hip, feeling bare without her second blade.

Though her mission had not gone flawlessly, she could already hear Tallulah's praise of her success.

I'm one step closer to earning a spot on the High Council.

Palm trees whirred by as *Piper* approached the outer walls of the place she called home, the warm summer sun beaming into the cockpit.

The outer wall gleamed brilliantly in the sunlight, its towering white concrete shimmering against the lush green foliage surrounding the port city. Curving gracefully around Marella, a sprawling metropolis that functioned as an independent nation, the wall embraced the coastline in a protective arc.

Lavine craved the warmth of the sun, delicious food, and current technology. How Navaria had refused to push their engineering further, or at least embrace the world's current tech, was beyond her understanding. She theorized that Hawke must be deliberately holding them back to keep better control.

If every Navarian had an airship to flee in, there would be no one for Greyson Hawke to rule.

"Let's get this over with." Kace sighed as *Piper* landed with a slight shake on the platform of the entry terminal.

Lavine trailed behind her crew to the inspection line, inhaling the warm air tinged with citrus and salt. It made her long for the secluded beaches she grew up on. Blocking the sun with her palm, she stared straight up at the white wall, a wave of vertigo nearly making her stumble.

Kace huffed his annoyance at the routine inspection of their gear and munitions. "Do we really have to do this every time?" he complained to the deck officer. "You know who we are."

A blush crept into the officer's cheeks as she smiled. "Standard procedure, Captain. You of all people should know this is necessary."

The officer had fancied Kace since their first meeting, and Lavine couldn't fault the young woman for her unrequited crush. Kace was the kind of handsome that was rare in Marrella, one that caught people's attention. His green eyes and loose, curly black hair made him stand out, and his strong nose and sharp jawline showed off his roguish smile.

"We're moving as quickly as regulations allow," the officer assured him. "Regulations are getting stricter each year."

With *Piper* locked down for docking, they boarded a private train car and sped along the track, passing through the outer wall.

The outer district, with miles of fields and thriving crops, whizzed by in a haze, farmers working in the foliage, stopping to watch the passing train. As Marella's second district blurred past, a jungle of housing and concrete, Lavine prepared her report for the High Council, hoping Theo's intel would prompt them to send her back to Navaria.

Feeling more than capable, Lavine aimed to be the youngest to make it onto the council. She'd make sure of it.

The train seamlessly curved into the inner districts of the city, heading straight to the Capitol Building. As the train drew nearer to the city's center, the buildings became grander and more elaborate in design.

The Capitol Building stood as the epitome of Marella's architectural brilliance. Its intricate coral arches glistened in the sunlight, complemented by the vast blue ocean behind them. The stone masterpiece was perched perfectly on the curved coast—timeless and elegant.

The ocean breeze tousled Lavine's hair as she and her crew climbed the stairs. Bursting into the lobby, she paused to gaze out of the floor-to-ceiling window, looking out over the sea and an endless blue horizon.

"Scenic views never fail to mesmerize you, do they?" Kace teased.

"My only weakness." Lavine chuckled.

Sandals clacked on the glossy marble floor. Lavine whipped around to find Nereida approaching, her strawberry-blonde hair framing her severe, narrow face.

"We need to see the council." Lavine advanced on her.

"You'll have to make an appointment." Nereida smiled with fake politeness, her teeth shades brighter than the silken robes that clung to her body. "We can't have you barging in all the time. The council doesn't have time for bad manners."

"Nonsense!" Kace threw an arm around Nereida's shoulder. "They can clear the next hour for us. This is important."

"Zale and Nesrin—"

"—will also be present." Lavine sidestepped the frazzled woman and marched to the tall, pearl-crested doors of the round room with Ivy and Kace at her heels.

Lavine knew her intel was worth the High Council's time, and with how much trouble she went through to get the information, it had better be worth it. She pushed the polished doors open to find three figures standing in a semicircle, whispering feverishly among themselves.

Nereida hastily pushed herself to the front of the group and bowed. "I apologize, Your Honors. They wouldn't listen to me."

"It's alright." Tallulah, long-legged and graceful with golden hair coiled into an elegant bun, raised her hand. "They're not interrupting anything of importance."

Positioned in front of a wall of glass sat three regal chairs. All decorated with colorful shells and authentic pearls. The entire coast of Marella was brilliantly displayed as natural light poured into the room. Each member of the council took a seat.

Tallulah watched from in between Nesrin and Zale. Lavine and her team approached the threshold of the platform, placed a hand over their hearts, and dipped their heads into a bow.

"Rise," Tallulah said. "Was your mission a success?"

"Yes, Your Honor," Lavine confirmed, keeping the council members on her right so she could hear. "I received urgent intel."

Being deaf in one ear was a secret she'd keep from the High Council at all costs. She had been struck in the head with a cast iron pan the day she met Kace on the streets. Starving and alone, he had stolen a loaf of bread, and Lavine stepped in to protect him.

Being homeless and penniless, she didn't have access to vindeca. By the time Gavriil adopted her and Kace, years had passed, and it was too late.

"Proceed."

"Theo learned of a weapon, and he claims it has the capability to level entire towns at a time."

The council's expressions tightened, brows furrowing.

"Did Theo get visual confirmation?" Zale asked.

"No, sir. He heard of it accidentally from Grand General Eden."

"Interesting," Tallulah began. "Did he say where this weapon was located?"

"Somewhere inside Beckinsdale Castle."

"How do we know this isn't a false lead?" Zale squinted at Lavine and her team. "That's convenient information to come upon."

Lavine repressed a sigh. Zale had always grated on her nerves. Something about his mannerism got under her skin, and she gritted her teeth to suppress a smart retort. No matter how insufferable Zale was, his term on the High Council was coming to an end.

Soon, I'll be sitting in your place.

33

"I had the same theory." Lavine couldn't blame him for being suspicious. "But Theo was adamant that this was serious, and it's our only lead." *Maybe Theo had been in the right place at the right time. Or...* "I think the Grand General let it slip on purpose to get a reaction from us," Lavine said.

"Hmm," Tallulah mused, shifting in her chair. "That is a possibility, but that would imply that he knows Theo is not one of them."

"I don't know about Malric's son," Zale began, "but General Eden would have killed Theo the moment he learned that a threat was within earshot."

"We must leave no stone unturned," Tallulah reasoned. "This could be why Hawke has kept to himself since taking the throne. It's been quiet these past three months."

"Yes, seeing as his father successfully took Haverlisle before he was killed," Nesrin added. "I have a feeling the young king will try to cross the sea and invade our lands."

"Theo mentioned that Eden wanted to push further south, do you really think he and Hawke would risk it?"

"I wouldn't put it past them," Nesrin replied, her expression grave.

"That didn't go very well the last time they tried that," Kace added. "I doubt they've forgotten the Two-Day war. I know I haven't."

While Lavine had no family from the beginning, Kace was among the many hundred children orphaned during Malric's siege on Marella. His family owned a farm in the outer districts and were among the first to be killed.

The Council conversed among themselves, deliberating over what actions they must take and considering the potential repercussions of Marella and the surrounding countries.

Who knows why Hawke hasn't made a move to start a war? If Theo's information is true, I need to get into that castle as soon as possible and find the weapon and maybe... that's it!

"We can get into Beckinsdale Castle, Your Honors." Lavine interrupted, drawing their attention. "I can carry out an assassination and put an end to their reign."

"The Hawke bloodline has ruled the north for centuries." Zale scoffed. "Greyson, the young brute, slaughtered his own father to wear the crown."

"A heart of steel, that one." Tallulah shook her head. "No, killing the young man would create a vicious power vacuum, and Navaria is in enough chaos as it is. He has no family and no heir, which leaves the Grand General to take the throne. There will be other challengers to remove Eden, and the cycle will continue. The north will extinguish themselves to take control."

"They can sort out the infighting for themselves." Lavine pushed on, her heart hammering in her ears. "Once they're done fighting each other, they'll be at their weakest. During which, we can put someone trustworthy on the throne."

The High Council sat in stunned silence, astonished looks on their faces. As the silence lingered on, Lavine worried that she had gone too far. Then the corner of Tallulah's mouth turned upward, offering a glimmer of reassurance that her boldness had paid off.

"My, now that would be something to see," Tallulah remarked.

"We can find Mundicar if it does exist. My team and I have the skill set to succeed." Lavine dared to push further. "But I feel it would be best for the world if the Hawke reign ended. The people of Navaria are suffering. I've seen it."

"Please wait outside while we discuss this in private," Nesrin requested.

The doors closed, leaving Lavine to pace back and forth, muttering to herself.

Why do they need to discuss this? The solution is so simple.

"Relax, Beckett. They'll send us back," Kace reassured, combing his hair with his fingers as he studied himself in the reflection of the window.

"We are the most qualified." Ivy nodded. "And you seem to have impressed Tallulah."

Lavine smiled at her confidence. Best friends since the Academy, Ivy always had her back.

Minutes passed in agony. Lavine was ready to pull her hair out when the doors finally opened and Zale beckoned them back inside.

"There's only one way to know for certain if what Theo says is true," Tallulah said. "Your team will return to Navaria."

As the High Council outlined the specifics of the next mission, Lavine's mind wandered back to that fateful day. She and Kace had chosen the wrong time to pickpocket the wrong person. Homeless and hungry, they adapted and survived the best way they could. Until Gavriil, head of the High Council at the time, caught them digging in the pockets of his silk robes. That moment had set her on her current path. The brief war with Navaria had orphaned so many children, and she wanted retribution for Kace's sake.

"Then it's settled." Tallulah stood, yanking Lavine out of her memories. "Beckett, you and your team will go to Navaria and infiltrate Beckinsdale Castle, find proof of this weapon, and assassinate Greyson Hawke. And if possible, Grand General Eden as well, but know that they are deadly and will not hesitate to kill you. Beginning tomorrow, you have thirty days to complete your mission."

"It will be done," Lavine declared, placing her hand on her heart and bowing.

"Do not disappoint me."

They were dismissed, and Lavine felt as if her heart would shake right out of her chest. A fierce determination was brewing within her soul, so potent that it would take the entire Navarian military to rip it out of her.

I'm coming for you, Hawke. Your blood will be on my hands.

5

Lavine

Packed with merchants and delicious aromas, Market Street was one of Lavine's favorite spots in Marella. It was a culinary melting pot, where flavors and dishes from all corners of the world converged. With each visit, Lavine delighted in trying a new dish.

Wooden stalls and colorful tents lined the beachside streets for blocks, and people of every nation were cooking, selling, and eating in the same streets. The aromas of Market Street could be smelled for half a mile, the breeze carrying scents of exotic spices and meat. A food lover's paradise.

Here, she wasn't a spy or an assassin. In these streets, Harley Beckett didn't exist, and she didn't have people's blood on her hands. Here, she was just Lavine, and she savored the feeling of freedom before the guilt set in, before the faces of those she'd killed flashed through her mind. Her tally had soared into the double digits long ago; she could no longer pinpoint the exact number, but she could remember their faces. All of them.

She pushed the somber thoughts aside as a merchant

handed her a paper bowl full of pulled pork, her stomach growling with anticipation. Juices quickly dribbled down her chin as she bit into the meat that she had folded into a slice of bread. The perfectly tender pork, marinated with a sweet but spicy sauce, lifted her spirit with every bite.

"Hurry up," Kace urged. "I want to check out Morrison's leather jackets."

"So much food, so little time." Lavine sighed, trying to finish her meal as they quickened their pace. She hoped she wouldn't have a stomachache by the time they arrived at Morrison's.

Merchants bolstered their wares, holding out silken robes, leathers, and jewelry. As they walked, a pair of women in the street approached Kace, caressing his arms and fluttering their eyelashes as they tried to sell themselves to him. He quickly waved them off and grabbed Lavine's and Ivy's hands, pulling them through the congested street.

"It really is a shame," Lavine said with a chuckle. "Those girls tried their best."

"It gets worse every year," Kace grumbled, releasing their hands. "I swear, I'm going to start smacking them with sticks."

"Fancy that." Lavine laughed. "Kace, the woman beater."

"Wait!" Ivy called, yanking her hand from Kace's grip. "Look over there."

Lavine spun on her heel and followed the direction Ivy was pointing in. There, under a gazebo in the middle of a plaza, a band of musicians played. The slow melody of guitars and violins filled the air. Lavine's gaze was drawn to a white banner hanging from the arches of the gazebo.

"'Come one, come all,'" Lavine read, "'to the Beachcomber's Ball. A place for fun, food, and wine. Where friends dance and lovers intertwine.'"

"Is it that time of the year already?" Kace groaned.

"It's a little over a month away," Lavine exclaimed, grabbing his arm and shaking it excitedly. "We'll be back just in time!"

Every year, the Beachcomber's Ball was held on the sands of Marella's finest beaches and thousands of people from all over the world attended.

"I'll get to see my parents!" Ivy squealed. Her parents were the wealthiest people in Kallistar, the small, landlocked nation in the east. Another nation that kept a close eye on Navaria.

The girls locked fingers, jumping and giggling. The musicians' song changed, the beat of the drums becoming livelier and more energetic. Lavine pulled Ivy into the plaza, spinning her around in time with the music.

Mid-step in the dance, Lavine turned to find Kace still in the street, trying his best to look annoyed at the diversion.

"Come on!" Lavine called to him.

Kace crossed his arms and shook his head stubbornly.

"Please!" Ivy sang, giving him a pleading look.

"Fine," he huffed with a smirk. "I swear, it's like I have *two* sisters," he mumbled.

After a half hour of dancing and twirling around the gazebo, Kace wedged his way in between the girls, breathless. "Let's get a move on. We don't want to keep Gavriil waiting."

The group arrived at Morrison's, where Kace settled on a brown leather jacket. After purchasing supplies for *Piper* and having them sent to the dockyards, Kace suggested, "I think it's time to head to Gavriil's."

"I'll be along later," Ivy said. "I need to send a letter to my parents. They'll want to know I'm still alive."

* * *

Lavine trailed behind Kace as they strolled down the cobblestone pathway, meandering through sparse palms. The path curved, giving way to a familiar, cheerful cottage with more wind chimes than anyone could possibly need. Nestled just a stone's throw away from Switchback Beach, the cozy home offered a breathtaking view of a long, empty stretch of sand and shimmering blue water.

Home.

Before they had a chance to knock, the door flung open, slamming against the wall of the cottage with a bang.

"My little *scelestos!*" Gavriil's raspy voice boomed before pulling them both into a long, tight embrace.

The tenseness in Lavine's body seemed to melt away in the warmth of his hug, the weight of the world lifting with each second he held onto her.

Her eyes moistened seeing her father for the first time in weeks, her heart aching at having left him alone for such a long stretch of time. With one last squeeze from Gavriil, Lavine's ribs ached for relief.

Good, he still has some strength in him.

"It's been so long since I've seen you two!" His eyes bloomed with joy as he pulled them inside, the nostalgic scent of citrus and salt wafting in the air. "What have my children been up to?"

"We're not children anymore, Pops." Kace laughed as he sprawled onto a sofa. "We've been busy working to get Lavine a seat on the High Council. She's just as bullheaded as you." He leaned back, cupping his hands behind his head, a stupid grin on his face.

Emotions Lavine couldn't name swelled within her, having missed Gavriil and the nickname he had given them, what he

41

had called them the day they first met. He once told them that 'scelestos' meant 'thieves' in a language that had gone extinct a millennium ago. How he knew this, or whether it was even true, she didn't know and didn't care.

"I knew I should have left you on that street," Gavriil teased. "You were always the cheeky one."

Lavine chuckled. "It's not too late to throw him back out," she said, casting a playful glance at Kace before taking in the familiar living area of her childhood home. The ocean breeze blew the white curtains that hung from the window, seashells that she had brought to Gavriil as a child, and a bright, beautiful coral-blue shag rug lay in the middle of the living room.

"Where's Ivy?" Gavrill asked, glancing toward the windows leading to the patio.

"Sending a letter to her parents." Kace picked at his fingernails.

"I'm sure they miss her. Will she be back in time for dinner?"

"Of course, Ivy wouldn't miss it for the world," Lavine assured before plucking an apple from the fruit bowl sitting atop an end table. With a twist, she detached the stem and took a bite.

"Good," Gavriil sighed with relief, a satisfied smile on his face. "I'm happy to hear it."

Having never married nor having had any children of his own, he opened his heart and home to two orphans, giving them not just a home but an education as well. Along the way, he had unofficially adopted Ivy, extending his paternal care to her as well.

"Is our picnic blanket clean?" Kace asked, still lounging on the couch.

Gavriil opened his mouth to answer but stopped, a crease forming between his brows. He turned to Kace once more. "Another assignment? Already? You just got back..."

Before every mission, Lavine and her crew had a beachside picnic just before sunset. It was a tradition dating back to their days in the Academy. In their line of work, tomorrow was never guaranteed, so they made a promise to set time aside to be together, to share laughter, stories, and a meal. To savor the fleeting tranquility before plunging back into the dangers of their jobs.

"The High Council has assigned us an urgent mission," Lavine announced. The wrinkles in Gavriil's face shifted from concern to a deepening sadness. Despite the lingering hints of brown in his short beard, his once chestnut-colored hair was now silver, thinning with each passing year. "We ship out in the morning."

"You could stay a few nights."

How I would love to.

"Just one night, Pops," Kace said. "We'll only be gone a month. We'll be back before you know it."

Lavine watched Gavriil hesitate, watched the hurt swirled in his eyes. She could see the struggle, how he wanted nothing more than to remain with his family, but he knew their work was too important.

After a moment, Gavriil relented. "One night it is then," he said with a faint smile. "Make the most of it, and come back to me safe."

Lavine nodded, her eyes shining with a bittersweet gratitude. "We will, Father. You can count on it." She moved toward the kitchen. "What's for dinner? I'm starving," she asked, steering him away from the heavy topic.

"Your favorite!" Gavriil exclaimed, rubbing his hands together as he hurried to the icebox. With a flourish, he pulled out a massive fish and presented it to her.

"Baked swordfish?" Kace popped into the kitchen, an excited gleam in his eyes.

"With peppercorn butter," Gavriil confirmed with a smile.

Kace pumped his fist with a whoop and pulled potatoes from the pantry. Planting himself at the kitchen table, he began to peel them, his gaze shifting between his handling of the knife and the view of the coast through the window.

Lavine grabbed a clean knife and cutting board, diving into the task of preparing the fish, all the while filling Gavriil in on the details of her last mission.

"There's something you're keeping from me, my dear." Gavriil prodded. "What's going on in that head of yours?"

A coy smile spread across her face. "I don't know. I may have been assigned the mission I've been busting my ass for since day one at the Academy."

"No!" Gavrill put a hand to his mouth. "They're sending you to Navaria? Again?"

He knew all too well how long she had waited for this mission, how she had trained until her bones ached and her fingers bled. How she ruthlessly climbed to the top of her class with honors, making enemies and losing friends, all to be here, serving on this mission.

As skilled as she was as the council's personal spy and assassin, she hoped this would be the last run. After Gavriil's heart failed him five years ago, he stepped down from the High Council, making way for Zale to take his place. Lavine couldn't shake the worry that gnawed at her whenever she thought of her father's frail health.

What if I come back to find him dead?

"What if something goes wrong?" Gavriil asked, his concern resurfacing.

"Are you doubting us?" She teased him in response.

"I believe you three are capable of anything you set your minds to, but there's always a chance for error."

"Nothing will happen, Father," Lavine assured him, though she knew safety was never guaranteed. This mission was undeniably deadly and their lives hung in the balance, yet they had danced on the edge of danger countless times before. "I've been preparing for this since the day I graduated."

"You've come so far in life. It's okay to stop when you're ahead."

"I *have* come far, and all my hard work will have been for nothing if I stop now," she continued. "If I do this one last job, Tallulah will have no choice but to consider me as a candidate."

Having made herself one of a kind, she had rendered herself indispensable and couldn't help but crave more. Gavriil had set her on a path to success, and she had clawed her way to the top to follow in his footsteps.

As if he had read her mind, he said, "You don't need their approval, my dear. Forgive me, but I believe you hold them in too high regard. They can't give you anything you don't already have and can offer you no happiness."

"I don't want anything from them. I'll be happy when I have a say in this city, when I have the power to help people," Lavine huffed, swiping away a stray hair as she rearranged the fish on the cutting board. "And Hawke is the last person in my way," she added under her breath.

Gavriil was long past his prime when he'd adopted them. With time running short, the idea of being away for an entire

45

month made her queasy. Her fingers tightened around the knife. He might not have been her biological father, but that's what made him so special. He had chosen her.

The wooden knife handle snapped, a shard slicing into her palm. She winced and clutched her wrist as blood gushed from her hand, moving away from the food.

"Great dragons above!" Gavriil rushed forward with a clean towel.

Kace swiftly abandoned the potatoes. "I thought I was supposed to be the clumsy one," he said, wrapping a second towel around her hand, the white cloth turning red. "Pops, do you have fresh vindeca?"

Gavriil nodded, guiding them to the living area as he grabbed an empty vial along the way. In the fireplace, hanging just above the flames, was a small cauldron. Its iridescent blue-green hues glittering like sunlight on the ocean. Gavriil carefully dipped the empty vial into the steaming water.

"Be careful, it's hot," Gavriil cautioned, his shaking hand offering her the vial.

Lavine brought the tiny glass flask to her lips, threw her head back, and drank, the scorching concoction burning the back of her throat as she swallowed. Already, she could feel the pinpricking sensation of her skin stitching itself back together.

Though the dragon steel cauldron wasn't the purest, its magic was potent enough to heal anything from colds to open wounds, such as the one it was currently healing on her hand.

As the elixir worked its way into her blood, the pain in her palm vanished. She removed the blood-soaked towel and flexed her hand. The skin on her palm was as it was before, and not a scar in sight.

"There you go, right as rain," Gavriil chirped. "Stay here and rest. We'll finish up with dinner."

The dragons that once ruled the sea were believed to possess the ability to heal through the very water they commanded. Their massive, slender, iridescent bodies shimmered with magic, drawing from the depths of the oceans to mend wounds and cure ailments with their watery breath. After their extinction, Marellan healers discovered that by crafting cauldrons from the dragons' scales, still pulsing with the remnants of their magic, they found that the scales could channel the same healing energy when heated. As the water within the cauldron simmered, the magic transferred into the liquid, creating a potent elixir capable of healing even the gravest of injuries.

The past ten minutes stirred memories of her first day at the Academy when Headmaster Winsdor had offered her vindeca. Another student had picked a fight; Lavine's face had been slashed with a knife, the blade slicing through her left eyebrow. Preferring to allow it to heal naturally, she kept the scar as a souvenir. The hair never regrew, leaving a noticeable notch in her eyebrow.

A knock at the door announced Ivy's arrival, and the four of them gathered around the table to eat as the evening sun shone through the windows.

* * *

Lavine picked up a pink conch shell from the sand, admiring its color as she settled onto the blanket spread out on the beach. She carefully stowed the shell in her pack, planning to give it to Gavriil later as a parting gift.

47

The sky was a blaze of sunset orange, and the rhythmic crashing of the waves against the shore was the most comforting sound to reach her ear. She much preferred it over the biting chill of the mountain wind.

"After this mission, I'll be a perfect candidate to replace Zale," Lavine said. "They won't be able to turn me down. And I'll make Gavriil proud."

"You already make him proud," Ivy said. "You're his daughter."

"I know, but this is different."

"After this, we all need to rest," Ivy urged, peeling a banana. "Take a vacation or something."

"Yeah," Lavine agreed, rummaging in the picnic basket. "Some relaxation would be nice."

"I don't know, Beckett." Kace tossed her a persimmon. "There's no rest for the wicked."

"We're off the clock. You don't have to call me that."

"Where's your sense of humor?"

"At Gavriil's house, would you like to go back and get it?" Lavine said as she peeled the fruit and popped a slice into her mouth, allowing the sticky sweetness to melt away the stress of the past few days.

He laughed and tossed a grape into the air, catching it in his mouth. Lavine leaned back against a boulder as they watched the sun kiss the horizon.

"He's right, you know," Kace said, a little more seriously. "You hold the High Council a little *too* high."

"They'll be my colleagues one day," Lavine shrugged. "I should have a positive opinion of the people I help govern a city with. Besides, Gavriil has known the High Council for two decades and he respects them."

"He respects everyone, even gutter rats like us."

"Speak for yourself! I was born in a mansion," Ivy said playfully.

"And yet, I landed the same career you did," Kace countered.

Lavine smirked as they bickered back and forth. Their playful rivalry began the instant they had locked eyes. In good humor, they prodded at each other just like an old married couple. While Kace could outwit anyone in his path, Ivy could beat down anyone in hers. If Lavine had to bring one of them to a fight, it'd be Ivy.

"I'm astonished that anyone could love you," Ivy teased, "seeing as *you* don't love anyone."

"I love *Piper*."

"*Piper* is an airship," Ivy argued. "Machinery doesn't count."

"I don't need anyone but you guys, and between the two of you, I've had enough of women in my life. *Piper* is all I need."

"Typical."

"What?" Kace shrugged. "All women do is make things more complicated."

"Kace Ryker!" Ivy leaned forward and punched Kace's arm; the water dragon tattoo that spiraled down hers seemed to glimmer.

"Ow!" He laughed, rubbing his arm.

Lavine tilted her head back and chuckled, catching a glimpse of the first evening star. Her gaze lingered, thinking of the bedtime stories Gavriil used to tell.

"Do you think the dragons are really up there somewhere?" she mused, her voice carrying a hint of wonder.

They all looked up at the pinks and oranges streaking the evening sky.

"I don't know," Ivy replied. "I'd like to think they are."

49

"Gavriil used to tell us that the last dragons flew into the heavens, saving themselves from extinction," Lavine reminisced.

Kace sat up eagerly. "Tell us again," he asked, leaning forward and resting his head on his hands like he did when they were children, when Gavriil would spin tales of magic and ancient dragons just before bed.

"Well, Gavriil was always better at telling stories, but it is said," she began, "that the last dragons to roam this world, on of each element, flew into the heavens to live among the goddesses of the night sky, never to be seen nor hunted by humankind again."

"But…" Kace whispered, the story ingrained into his memory.

"But," Lavine continued, "Aarth, the Great Drake who breathed fire, the last of his kind, chose to remain on earth, believing humans to be redeemable. One day, a son of strife will awaken the Great Drake and put an end to traitorous bloodlines, and dragons will be safe to live in this world once more."

Kace sighed, his eyes alight with intrigue. "Can you imagine finding Aarth and unleashing him to wreak havoc in the north?"

"Finding Aarth would be the easy part," Ivy said. "If you're worthy or not, well, that remains to be seen."

"You don't think I've had enough hardship to wake up a dragon?"

"Absolutely not," Lavine laughed.

"Ah yes, being orphaned and homeless at six isn't much of a hardship," Kace retorted.

"We had each other," Lavine argued. "I took care of you just fine."

"I'm pretty sure you fed me a rotten orange."

"I didn't *know* it was rotten!"

"Lavine," Kace said, tilting his head, one brow furrowed, "it was mush. You might as well have fed me a jellyfish. You know I didn't deserve that. I could've died and you two would never have seen my handsome adult face."

Laughing as she stood, Lavine dusted the sand from her pants. "You really are full of it, aren't you?"

Kace hopped to his feet and rammed into Lavine's side, tossing her onto his shoulder.

"Put me down!" Lavine screamed, kicking her legs as he ran across the bank and into the shallow waves. "Don't you dare!" she yelled as he spun around in the water.

Ivy circled around, laughing and splashing water at the two of them. Kace stumbled and reeled forward, sending both him and Lavine plunging into the clear, salty waves.

Lavine sat up in the knee-deep water, pulling her sopping wet hair out of her face. The gentle tug of the tide swayed her back and forth as she glanced around. Kace sat in the water nearby and Ivy was soaked from the splash, the three of them shrieking with laughter as the sun sank beneath the horizon.

6

Greyson

The high ceilings of Beckinsdale Castle loomed overhead. A grand chandelier hanging above the entrance foyer, lavishly draped and decorated. And at the forefront, two members of his personal guard stood waiting.

"Your Majesty," they greeted in unison. The twin brothers, identical in all but personality, bowed with perfect synchrony.

Greyson dipped his head in acknowledgment. "Calix. Jesper."

In response, they fell into position, flanking him as he strode toward the grand staircase, the light above glinting off their polished white armor.

Members of the court scurried about, their conversations filled with nothing but gossip. The same elitist chatter echoed from high-ranking military officials who were far too comfortable in their positions. Each bowed as Greyson moved through the room and up the grand stairwell, acknowledging every "Your Majesty" with a nod.

"What's our next move, Sire?" Eden marched a step behind.

"If we spend the next year gathering our forces, we could cross the seas."

"And do what? Invade Marella? That didn't go very well last time. For now, we'll refrain from acts of aggression. Focus instead on tracking down this assassin. You're dismissed."

Eden's shoulders dipped a fraction, his hand briefly clenching into a fist before he tucked his arm behind his back and bowed. "Yes, Sire."

Greyson proceeded to the upper levels of the castle. To his left where a rug ran the length of the hall, he walked down the torchlit corridor. Natural light poured in as he walked into another hall and looked up at the sheet of glass that should have been the west wall. Beckinsdale had stood for centuries, but when Greyson's great-grandfather brought war to the mountains, the battle blasted away segments of the castle. Thick sheets of glass had artfully replaced pieces of the building, providing views of the mountainous, snowy landscape beyond.

Striding down the hall, he spotted a large red stain in the rug. Remnants of the bloody mess where Greyson had forced the life from his father's body. The servants had tried, in vain, to scrub the stain out but with little success. He squared his shoulders with a deep, satisfying sigh. His father had desired a ruthless killer, and so a killer Greyson became.

As he made his way to the royal hall, he felt the suffocating presence of the portraits that lined his route. Severe eyes bore down on him, the fixed gazes of his ancestors scrutinizing his every step as he walked toward his chambers. He despised every one of them.

All but one.

He paused in front of the portrait at the end of the hall where he read the inscription underneath: *Josephine Ann Farley*. His mother. It was the only portrait Greyson could stand to look at.

With somber blue eyes and a strained smile, her heart-shaped face framed by curtains of black hair, she sat in the portrait with a toddler in her lap. The child's own black hair was neatly combed back, and his clothes were impeccably ironed.

Even in the stillness of the portrait, the atmosphere was charged with unease, as if a lurking beast stood just beyond the frame. It was the man standing by his mother's side. Furrowed brows, pursed lips, and a hand clenched onto her shoulder, Malric's cold cobalt eyes glared with a sour sense of supremacy.

How horrid it must have been to be married to a man like Malric... and to have a child with him.

Josephine's life having been cut short almost gave Greyson a sense of peace, as he could imagine the suffering—he had endured it. Burying the memories he wished to forget, he continued toward his chambers. The two men guarding his door snapped to attention as he approached.

"Good evening, Your Majesty," proclaimed Silas, the sturdy captain of his guard.

"Evening, Brandr." Greyson nodded. "Evening, Thorne."

"Good evening, Your Majesty," the young guard whispered, his ginger hair spilling over his eyes. He stood stiffly with his head bowed. Greyson glanced at Silas questioningly, who shrugged in response.

"Thorne," Greyson prodded gently, "look at me."

The man held his breath, his shoulders tense. He balled his trembling fingers into a fist.

"Wesley."

The guard let out a breath and slowly lifted his head, revealing a fresh black eye. Purple bruising smothered the emerald green of his right eye. Greyson moved nearer, examining the wound more closely.

"Who did this?"

Wesley clenched his jaw and looked down, redness creeping up his neck.

"I can't help you if you don't confide in me," Greyson urged gently.

Wesley remained silent, his breath rapid.

"Go see Sterling, she'll have something that will ease the swelling. You're dismissed until morning."

"I can still do my job," Wesley argued.

"That's an order, Thorne."

"But I—"

"This isn't a punishment. Report back first thing in the morning."

Wesley's shoulders fell. "Yes, Sire."

When the echoes of Wesley's footsteps had faded, Greyson pushed open the large wooden door that led into his chambers. Silas followed, while Calix and Jesper stationed themselves outside.

"Send Adelaide in when she arrives."

"Yes, Sire," they replied in unison.

Greyson draped his cloak on a cushioned settee, a comfortable distance from the fireplace. Above the mantel hung an impressive tapestry depicting Aarth, the Great Drake, his fiery breath descending upon the earth, teeth bared and eyes aglow with burning wrath.

"I failed miserably."

"If I may speak freely, Sire…" Silas began. "You can't expect yourself to run things perfectly in the beginning. You must learn to forgive yourself."

"How am I to forgive myself when Vanya was killed because I was too afraid to act?"

"Then honor her death by doing better."

Silas opened the door to the office, bowing as Greyson moved through. Seated behind his polished oak desk, Greyson replayed the event in his mind. The memory of Vanya's frightened eyes as she realized she was about to take her last breath, and how the situation had gone horribly wrong in an instant.

Although he wished to change what had happened, he knew Silas was correct in moving forward. He didn't have time to feel sorry for himself. "What news is there?"

"Warith has discovered a new mining location and requests your presence."

"Very well, we will travel to Warith in three days."

Silas continued, detailing the various packs of vultures stalking the outskirts of Navaria's territories, the escalating food shortages, and the urgent needs of citizens that Greyson was ill-prepared to address. His father had failed to prepare him for such things.

"There's the matter of the King's Banquet," Silas added.

"Don't remind me." Greyson grumbled, laying his head on the table.

"It's important to maintain appearances, Your Majesty," Silas continued with a sympathetic smile. "The banquet is an opportunity to reassure the nobility and the people of your strength. And to remind them of who you are."

Greyson leaned back in his chair, staring at the flickering

snow outside his window. "Appearances," he muttered bitterly. "Sometimes it feels like that's all this is about."

"Try to see it as an opportunity for them to see beyond the throne and glimpse the person who will lead Navaria into its future. Let them see their new king."

Greyson's initial aggression in seizing the throne had led Eden and his court to believe that he'd carry on as his father did, and to shatter that belief without looking weak would be difficult. And he dreaded Eden's persistent attempts to influence his decisions with unwavering ambition and desire for control. It fueled the almost instinctual desire to put a blade through the Grand General's chest.

Greyson sighed heavily, rubbing his temples. "Very well, Silas. Prepare for the banquet as you see fit. Just... make sure everything is in order."

Silas nodded, relieved that Greyson had finally relented. This banquet was supposed to take place a fortnight after Greyson's coronation, but he had pushed it off for as long as he could. "Of course, Your Majesty. I'll ensure everything runs smoothly."

Greyson glanced up, meeting Silas' gaze with a hint of resignation. "Thank you."

As Greyson's trainer from adolescence and current guard captain, Silas always seemed to know just what to say to reassure Greyson and turn his uncertainty into confidence. Despite the silver flecks in his black hair from the long, hard years of serving, Silas remained as fierce and powerful as ever.

"There has also been a report of a Marellan assassin in Alain," Silas continued.

"Marellan?" Greyson had caught wind of rumors of an assassin but was unable to confirm the information, and so he didn't believe it to be true.

"That's the speculation. She killed two of our own and a civilian before disappearing into the wilderness."

"Marella doesn't *have* assassins. Spies, yes, but assassins? If they do, they've kept this information buried deep."

He ground his teeth, feeling his pulse quicken with frustration. Despite sending dozens of letters to the High Council pleading for aid, the lack of responses led him to suspect he was being ignored.

Not only have they been allowing my people to suffer, they're now sending assassins.

Greyson shot up from his chair, his movements quick and sharp as he sifted through the extensive bookshelves lining the wall. He retrieved a rolled parchment tied with twine. Unfurling it carefully, he spread the map over the surface of his desk, securing its corners with stone paperweights intricately carved in the likeness of dragons. His jaw clenched slightly, a hint of anger suppressed beneath his outward composure and fueled by the frustration of his unanswered pleas.

"She was attempting to kill one of our corporals, Theodore Ashford, when she was discovered," Silas said, explaining further. "A summons from his commander interrupted the attempt."

"I doubt a corporal would attract the attention of an assassin. Was he injured?"

"His wounds were superficial, nothing life-threatening."

That doesn't make sense.

"They're not after anyone in that little town," Greyson mused aloud.

"Then why would they bother sending an assassin?"

"Information," Greyson concluded. "We have a traitor in our ranks."

Silas' brows furrowed, the wrinkles on his forehead pinched. "Are you sure?"

"I've heard rumors of a spy who can slip into any fortress, and I suspect this spy and the assassin are one and the same."

Silas' brows jumped up, understanding donning his weathered face. "You're talking about Harley Beckett."

Greyson nodded as he studied the map, his eyes darting from Alain to Beckinsdale. "This corporal must have been feeding her information and staged an assassination attempt to cover himself after getting caught. It's the only explanation."

"If this is true, she's coming here next, and your life is in danger."

"Respectfully, I've been in danger since the day my mother died," Greyson replied evenly.

Silas grimaced, his posture involuntarily curling in on itself. "My apologies, Sire."

Greyson waved a dismissive hand, his attention fully focused on the map. He calculated his next move. "Bring Corporal Ashford to Beckinsdale. Have Eden interrogate him. He's our only lead to this assassin, and we need to track her movements."

"We don't know what path she'll take."

"But we do. After crossing the sea, there are three routes to Beckinsdale," Greyson explained, leaning over the map. "No one can survive The Barrens, so she could follow the river upstream or she could traverse the eastern mountain range. Normally, she wouldn't risk following the river and going through Warith." He traced his finger along the map. "Our presence is strong there. With her cover blown in Alain, she'll likely be forced to pass through Warith or the surrounding forest."

Silas considered Greyson's assessment before asking, "What will you do if you capture her?"

"I'm not sure, but whatever path I take will be incredibly risky." Greyson slouched over the map, lost in thought. "Share this information only with the rest of the Royal Guard. Keep your eyes peeled for her. She likely returned to Marella to regroup, so it may take her a week or so to resurface. If you believe you've spotted her, do not engage or raise alarm. Report directly to me. You're dismissed."

"Yes, Sire." Silas bowed and quietly left the room, leaving Greyson alone with his thoughts.

His ancestors' rule had crept over the continent with each passing generation. The neighboring nations watched closely, anticipating that he would uphold this long-standing family tradition. It put a target on his back, and with tension rising in the south and with Nerrulth in the east, war was imminent.

Despite the looming threat, Greyson had attempted to pursue avenues of peace. He had even extended an offer to wed the Nerrulthian princess, a gesture of alliance, an olive branch of peace. But the offer was coldly refused, deepening the rift.

The fear of his bloodline was the sole pillar holding him on his throne, yet ruling through fear alone would no longer suffice. The world had changed, and Navaria had stayed behind. Stagnant. With their economy stalling and the Marellan High Council ignoring his letters, it would be easy to direct his anger at them.

But Navarian lives were at stake, and Greyson needed an

opportunity, a way forward. Pacing by his desk, an idea struck him. Without dwelling on the potential consequences or thinking too far ahead, he made a decision. It was preposterous. Even worse, it was treasonous. It would jeopardize his very right to the throne. Yet, in his mind, it was the only viable path forward.

I just need to get Beckett into the castle.

Without a knock or a word, a woman strode in, her slight frame draped in a familiar black cloak. She made no sound as she bowed to one knee, and black curls spilled out from under her hood. "Your Majesty."

"How many?"

"Too many for a single trip." Adelaide rose and presented a small piece of parchment, handing it to Greyson. "I have ten of the most threadbare."

Greyson read through the list, committing every name to memory.

"You weren't seen," he said, more a statement than a question.

"No," she replied from behind her mask.

"Very good."

* * *

Under the light of the stars, Greyson's breath furled into the air as he crept through the dark, winding streets, shifting the heavy sack slung over his shoulder. The scent of smoke reached his nose. He had expected Wimborne's fires to be put out during the night, but not this early. It was just four hours after nightfall, and his mission drove him deeper into the dark, unfamiliar alleyways.

61

As he prowled through the streets, Greyson pulled out the parchment Adelaide had given him, carefully reviewing each address. The first few houses were simple. Mostly unlocked doors and windows, and no large animals to guard the premises. A starving village could never afford to have such pets. He proceeded to break into house after house, his pack growing lighter as the night wore on.

Just a few blocks from where Eden had executed Vanya the night before stood a house that looked on the verge of collapse. Moving toward the side of the ramshackle wooden structure, he discovered a window not visible from the street. Setting the bag down, he peered inside to find an empty living area that opened into a kitchen where a small fire still burned.

Though stiff, he pried the window up. It was halfway open when it screeched, sending a high-pitched echo into the alley. Greyson's heart skipped a beat, freezing in place. After an agonizing minute in the darkness, no one in the house or on the street stirred. Gathering his nerve, he wedged his hands under the window and pushed it open.

He planted his boots on the rickety floorboards and paused, surveying the room. Worn furniture was piled with blankets, and a floorboard squeaked under his weight as he ventured deeper into the room. Wincing at the noise, he moved toward the kitchen, glancing up the stairs as he crept past.

Opening cabinets one after another, all nearly empty, made his stomach twist. Adelaide always chose wisely. From the bag, he pulled out bread, fruits, and cheese. Just as he set the last of the dried meats on the table, the weight on the floorboards shifted.

"Thief!" a woman's voice shouted.

Startled, Greyson spun around, his heart racing as he

62

crouched instinctively to avoid the swinging fire poker. The woman stood before him, her eyes wide with fear and anger, clutching the poker tightly.

"I'm unarmed," Greyson said quickly, raising his hands.

He jolted backward as the woman swung again, narrowly avoiding the sharp metal edge.

"Breaking into my house in the dead of night! Get out!" she shouted, drawing a revolver out from under her night robe. "Get out, or I'll kill you."

"Please, I didn't mean to startle you," Greyson managed, his voice steady despite the adrenaline surging through him. He glanced at the revolver in her trembling hand, acutely aware of the danger he was in.

"Stealing from those who have nothing is despicable," the woman snarled as she advanced, sticking the muzzle of the gun directly in his face. Greyson took several steps back, but his cloak caught under his boot, causing him to stumble and fall over a kitchen chair. The impact reverberated through the small house as he hit the wooden floor.

Gathering himself, Greyson quickly rose to his feet, his hood falling back to reveal his face in the dim light of the kitchen. The woman froze, her eyes widening as the color drained from her face.

"Y-Your Majesty," she stammered, panic in her voice as she dropped to her hands and knees. The fire poker and revolver clattered to the floor. "I'm so sorry! Please have mercy," she pleaded, her words trembling with fear. *"Please."*

"Shhh, I—"

"Mother?" A small voice interrupted from the staircase. A scrawny boy stood on the bottom step, guarding his two younger sisters.

"I'm all they have," she hiccuped through broken sobs, "please spare me."

Greyson felt a pang in his chest at the sight of their fear. "Stand." He gently pulled her to her feet. "I mean you no harm." He gestured toward the food on the table, tore the loaf of bread in half, and tentatively offered it to the boy on the staircase. The boy looked up at Greyson timidly, then glanced at his mother, uncertain.

"It's okay, son." She sniffed.

The boy hesitated for a moment, then cautiously took the bread and tore it into two even pieces, passing them to his younger sisters.

"To bed now, all of you," she ordered.

Their small footsteps trotted upstairs, and soon silence settled over the room. The woman retrieved the revolver and the fire poker from the floor, and with trembling hands, she placed the gun on the table. She prodded at the remaining logs in the fire, coaxing them to brighten the room.

"Will you not punish me?" Tears welled in her eyes. "I almost killed you."

Greyson righted the fallen chair and approached the fire-place. "You were defending your home," he said calmly. "That's not worthy of punishment."

"I cannot thank you enough," she whispered, her voice quivering.

"I'm sorry I couldn't do more," Greyson said solemnly, tossing the list of addresses into the flames. "If you don't mind my asking, where is your husband?"

The woman wrung her hands, a tear tracing down her cheek. "Your father made a summons for the last of Wimborne's able-bodied," she began, her voice trembling. "My husband refused and was executed."

Greyson's heart sank at her words, a mixture of anger and sorrow flooding through him.

He sometimes forgot his kingdom was mostly widows and children and chastised himself for asking such an insensitive question.

I'm still out of touch with my people.

"All I have left are my children and my father... I think. He served under Malric," she whispered. "I don't even know if he is still alive. I haven't heard from him in months."

"Maybe I can find him. What is his name?"

"Silas."

Greyson froze, his blood running cold, and he felt numbness creeping into his limbs. "I know many men named Silas," he lied. "I need a last name."

"Brandr."

His mouth went dry. He swallowed, keeping his expression even. A hint of betrayal threatened to surface in his mind, but Greyson pushed it aside, knowing his guard captain must have a reason and that it wasn't malicious. Silas was one of the few he trusted implicitly: he had practically raised Greyson when Malric had cast him aside. A skilled swordsman with deadly accuracy and Greyson's favorite sparring partner.

Why hadn't Silas mentioned he had a family?

He couldn't fathom that the man who had treated him as a son had a daughter as well as grandchildren.

"I'll see what I can do," Greyson promised.

A hopeful smile bloomed across her face.

Greyson glanced around the sparse kitchen and strode to the door, his cloak rippling behind him. As his hand reached for the doorknob, he paused. "I need a favor."

"Anything," she replied, without hesitation.

"Tell no one of this," Greyson instructed, pulling his hood up. "Not a soul, at least not yet."

"I swear it," she said definitively. "But what shall I tell my children?"

"Their imaginations will fill in the gaps. Children are known for telling tall tales."

He opened the door, and a gust of wind blew snow into the entryway.

"Are you really him?" the woman asked as he moved to leave.

"I'm sorry?" Greyson turned back, puzzled.

"The Raven... Are you him?"

A mischievous smile crept across Greyson's face before he dashed back out into the night.

7

Greyson

Sleep threatening to take him, Greyson stared into the fireplace. He hadn't slept since the night before Vanya was killed. His leg bounced as he sat hunched on the settee—a nervous tick that drove Silas crazy.

The orange flames flickered and danced, their glowing embers rising into the chimney. He silently prayed to Aarth, hoping that confronting the double agent would yield something useful. His people were dropping like flies, and he was running out of options. He had briefly considered offering the palace steeds as food, but he knew it would only be a temporary fix and not nearly enough.

There was a heavy knock at the door. Jumping to his feet, he shook the thought of sleep from his mind and hurried to open it. Silas stood in the doorway. Greyson briefly considered confronting him about his estranged family but now was not the time.

"I've retrieved Corporal Ashford," Silas reported. "Grand General Eden is questioning him in the dungeons."

"Very good," Greyson said, donning his cloak. "Silas, Wesley, stand guard. Calix, Jesper, with me."

Hardly keeping a casual pace, he made his way through the chilly castle halls. Royal appearances were the least of his concerns as he passed the kitchens and servants' quarters and made a right. He whistled sharply, and an answering whistle echoed behind him.

"Are you sure this is a good idea?" Jesper whispered apprehensively from Greyson's left, realizing just what was being set into motion. "We've never carried out a plan like this before."

"Just stay close to me," Greyson replied firmly.

He burst through a massive wooden door and raced down the spiraling stone staircase, descending three stories into the depths of the dungeon. As he passed empty cells along the way, he finally reached the door at the end of the block and paused.

Nearby, a hooded Adelaide silently slipped into one of the cells. They exchanged a brief nod before Greyson pushed open the door to the makeshift interrogation room.

The stench of mildew hit him immediately as he stepped into the cold, damp cell. "That'll do," he muttered.

General Eden's men withdrew their bloodied knuckles and faded into the shadows. Unlike the traditional cells lining the vast room just outside, this one was unique in that it was a solid stone chamber.

Theodore Ashford was tightly strapped to a wooden chair, battered and bloodied, his face swollen beyond recognition.

Eden's voice was rigid. "He's given no additional information," he said, passing a steel dagger to Greyson.

Greyson ventured deeper into the cell, circling the bruised and restrained corporal. His footsteps echoed in the damp, chilly room.

"Tell me," Greyson said, examining the blade intently, "why would an officer of your rank carry a weapon made from common steel? Shouldn't your blades be forged with something more refined?"

"I-I found it," Theodore stammered, droplets of blood sputtering from his mouth, his breaths shallow and labored.

Greyson chuckled darkly, rubbing the grooved handle of the weapon. "I don't believe you. Either you tell the truth, or I separate your head from your shoulders."

Theodore continued to pant, silent either from defiance, fear, or the pain of his broken ribs. Seconds ticked by as Greyson turned away from the faint glow of the small lantern.

"Well then… it is to be death."

"No!" Theodore's breath hitched. "No, please!"

"General Eden," Greyson barked. "Ready the headsman. This traitor is to be executed immediately."

"With pleasure." Eden and his men sprang forth to carry out the command, hungry for the opportunity to spill blood.

Greyson remained, the chill of the air thick with tension. The door shut behind him, and for a long moment, only Theodore's labored breathing filled the silence.

He considered the utility of this prisoner. What good would come from killing him? Would he be the one to persuade Marella to send aid?

I doubt it, but if I kill this rat, I'll have alienated myself further in Marella's eyes.

"I'll cut you a deal," Greyson said, turning to face Theodore. "Answer my questions and I'll let you go."

Theodore's lips trembled. "You mean to kill me."

Greyson shook his head. "I mean to relocate you. I can

69

smuggle you out of here and release you into the Direwoods. After that, you're on your own."

Greyson closed the distance between them, watching Theodore's swollen eyes flicker anxiously across his face. Silence stretched, the tension in the air growing thicker by the second.

"We're short on time," Greyson said, his voice sharp with urgency, his hand tightening around the hilt of his dagger. "Do we have a deal or not?"

Theodore's contorted face twisted in pain as he shook his head, his breaths shallow and ragged, sweat dripping from his forehead.

Greyson leaned in closer, his gaze unyielding. "How long have you been sending information to Marella?"

"Seven months," Theodore admitted through gritted teeth. "The High Council sent me to gather intel, so I joined the Navarian military. I was tasked with finding anything incriminating, anything to warrant an invasion."

"What information have you relayed?"

"Military formations, names and ranks, weapons."

"What else?" Without meaning to, Greyson pressed the dagger against Theodore's throat. "There has to be more."

"That's everything." Theo swallowed, his Adam's apple bouncing under the blade breaking the skin.

"Has Marella sent an assassin after me?"

"I don't know," he replied, his voice strained. "Marellan officials have always kept secrets, even about their own agents."

"You're lying to me, and that is very dangerous." Greyson pressed the dagger deeper into Theodore's skin, blood now trickling down his neck. "I know she's the same girl from

Alain."

"Her name is Harley B—"

"I know her name!" Greyson shouted, desperation gripping his body as he leaned closer to Theodore. "Why did they send her?"

"To get updated information. It was a routine check. I know nothing else," Theodore pleaded, shifting in the chair.

"What does she look like?"

"She has a scar on her left eyebrow. Average build, brown hair."

"That could be anyone." Greyson hissed.

"There's only one way to know for sure… she has a dagger identical to the one you currently have against my neck. They're twins."

"Why did you have it?"

"I took it," he deflated, tucking his chin in, "as insurance. She'll come back for it, she always comes back for them."

"You knew you would look suspicious and needed leverage."

Theodore averted his eyes, sweat rolling down his temples, his shame and silence confirming Greyson's suspicions.

He's a rat.

Yet, he had no choice but to believe him. Beckett would make her way to Beckinsdale Castle, and if Greyson found her, he might have a chance to open a line of communication. There was a chance to help his people.

"Was the information to your satisfaction?" Theodore's tone carried a sharp edge that snapped Greyson out of his thoughts. He swiftly withdrew the dagger from Theodore's throat and secured it in his belt.

"I should kill you right here, right now." Greyson stepped back and drew his sword. The confined space of the cell accentuated the heftiness of the white blade, its glacial blue fuller glowing in the lamplight. Theodore thrashed about, his eyes locked onto the icy mist emanating from the blade.

"You've been in Navaria long enough to know that to die by a dragon steel blade is a high honor. You crumbled under the slight threat of a dagger, and so," Greyson closed in, poised to strike, "you don't deserve that honor." He cut Theodore's bonds with a swift, clean motion. "If I ever see your face in this castle again, I will kill you."

The door flung open, and Eden's men hauled Theodore through the empty dungeon. Greyson trailed behind, giving a quick nod as he passed the cell where Adelaide lay hidden. Theodore was dragged up the stairs and through corridors, his disheveled body shoved across the castle grounds and into the outer courtyards.

The headsmen shouted a greeting when an arrow slammed into the head of one of General Eden's guards. The guard released Theodore, then slumped to the ground—dead.

"Take cover!" Greyson said, pressing himself against a castle wall.

The twins took defensive positions on either side of him. A second arrow loosed through the air, and Eden's second guard fell to the cobblestones. General Eden lunged at Theodore, dragging him into a corridor on the other side of the courtyard.

Greyson ducked as a third arrow slammed into the cement wall where his head had been just moments before. Calix moved in front of him, pressing Greyson against the stone wall.

"Hawke!" Eden bellowed from the corridor. "Stay where you are!" His eyes searched for the source of the attack.

The arrows ceased as suddenly as they had begun. Greyson observed the entire courtyard from behind Calix, seeing no intruders. His focus returned to the corridor where Eden had sought cover and spotted a cloaked figure behind Eden and his prisoner.

"Behind you!" Greyson called before the figure swiftly brought down sacks over their heads and slammed an elbow into Eden's, causing it to bounce against the corridor wall.

A twang of satisfaction coursed through Greyson as Eden slumped to the ground. The hooded figure hauled Theodore out of sight, her cloak and black curls vanishing from the castle grounds. Minutes passed with guards barking orders and securing the area. All was clear. Calix pulled Greyson to his feet.

"Your Majesty." Jesper glanced at the arrow lodged in the cobblestone wall. "She fired that arrow a little too close to you for my comfort."

"Trust me, she knows what she's doing," Greyson said, extending his hand to help Jesper to his feet.

"What if she had hit you? You'd be dead."

"That's what armor is for." Greyson ran a hand through his hair, brushing away the rubble from the cobblestone walls.

"You really should start wearing a helmet," Calix chimed in.

"Maybe that wouldn't be such a bad idea," Greyson replied absentmindedly, glancing around at the aftermath of the skirmish before approaching Eden's crumpled body. He crouched down and, with a steady hand, pulled the burlap sack from Eden's head. The entire right side of his skull was slick with gore, his pristine uniform now dirty, and his normally polished boots now scuffed.

"He's still breathing." Calix joined in on the inspection.

How simple things would be if I drove my sword into his heart.

In the west wing of the castle hung portraits of Eden as a young soldier. In those paintings, he wore the same stern expression but with jet black hair. Sometime in his thirty years of service, his hair had turned the color of snow.

"We should get him to the infirmary," Calix said. "He definitely has a concussion."

Greyson grabbed his arm, Eden's skin icy to the touch, and hastily slumped Eden's unconscious body over his shoulder.

"*Your Majesty,*" Calix said, wide-eyed and exasperated.

"He'll be fine." Greyson proceeded through the courtyard and nodded to the headsman. "Your services are no longer needed."

Greyson retraced his steps through the courtyards and strolled through the castle foyers, opting for the scenic route to the medical wing. His pace was casual, deliberately drawing out the gasps and stares from the courtiers.

With Eden now vulnerable and incapacitated, he would undoubtedly become the center of the castle's gossip. He slid through the door to the medical wing and plopped Eden down on a sickbed harder than he'd meant to.

Calix, ever the concerned field medic, winced at the act, but kept any comments to himself.

"Check him in with Sterling and report back."

"Yes, Sire," Calix replied.

8

Greyson

Greyson galloped into Warith with his head held high, his eyes peeled for any signs of Beckett. The town, just under five miles from Beckinsdale, was firmly under his control, its people well-fed and orderly. Mounted officers approached, their elks whistling a greeting.

Jericho didn't stir, his breathing steady and his ears pressed back. Elks for the royal family were bred for their size. When it came time for Greyson to choose his mount, his attention had been captivated by an albino runt. Despite being marked for slaughter, young Greyson couldn't resist Jericho's unique white fur. Years later, Jericho had surpassed every male in his lineage, towering over the other palace steeds.

"Your Majesty," Avard Corr bowed atop his mount. "I welcome you back to Warith."

The discovery of new dragon tunnels in the earth had spurred dozens of mining expeditions, all led and overseen by Greyson. Such a find was both a blessing and a curse for men like Avard. It meant more work for his people, but it also meant Greyson's return to Avard's inner circle.

"Where is this new dragon tunnel?"

"I'll lead you right to it." Avard snapped his reins. The elk lifted its head and surged forward.

Avard led Greyson eastward, with Silas and Calix trailing closely behind, their steeds' hooves crunching through the snow.

Will this be the one to lead me to Aarth?

According to legend, the Great Dragon still slept, awaiting to be reawakened by a son of strife. Greyson felt he'd endured enough strife in his lifetime to qualify.

They rode the mile into the forest when Avard brought the company to a halt.

"An avalanche dislodged the outer rock and revealed the tunnel," Avard explained, pointing to an opening in the steep slopes of the mountain.

Greyson dismounted and approached the mouth of the vast tunnel. Silas lit torches and handed one to Greyson.

"Keep watch. I'll be back within the hour," Greyson instructed.

"Yes, Your Majesty," Avard replied, standing tall and attentive.

Greyson raised his torch and descended into the tunnel, Silas and Calix on his heels, occasionally stopping to inspect the integrity of the mine. Greyson ran his hand along the walls and brushed against something sharp and cold. Adjusting the torch's light, he discovered a protruding dragon scale.

"Look at this." He gestured toward the crude yet shiny lump of dragon steel.

"That's promising," Silas remarked as he pried more of the ancient scales from the walls. "How far do you think this goes?"

76

"Only one way to find out." Greyson pressed deeper into the depths of the earth.

As they ventured further into the tunnel, the air grew cooler, and the echoes of their footsteps reverberated off the stone walls. The flickering torchlight cast eerie shadows, illuminating more dragon scales embedded in the rock, each one solid proof of the ancient gods who once roamed their world.

Malric had led sixteen-year-old Greyson into a tunnel like this one after he had mastered swordplay and earned the honor of mining the materials for his first blade.

While most Navarian swords had various metals folded into the steel to signify lower rank, Greyson's blade was forged from pure dragon steel—truly one of a kind.

The frost magic infused within was so potent that the fuller had turned a deep, glacial blue, while icy streaks shimmered throughout the blade and turned the edges white.

Mining dragon steel marked a pivotal moment for Greyson. His mother's sudden passing had transformed Malric into someone fearsome and unapproachable. In the absence of warmth, Greyson longed to earn his father's approval. Striving for perfection in battle became the only way he knew how to reach him, yet it never seemed enough for Malric.

"A son of strife shall come into the depths of the earth and wake me from my sleep, and he, of this world, shall call my favor and I shall cleanse all corners of the earth."

With his palms growing sweaty and his heart pounding, Greyson's legs propelled him forward faster than he had intended. A nervous excitement tingled in his stomach.

What if I am unworthy? What if he strikes me down? The world might be better off that way... no, it would give Eden cause to step in.

They rounded another turn in the winding tunnel when Greyson spotted light thirty meters ahead. He halted.

"Is... is that the end?" Calix asked.

Greyson swallowed his disappointment and trod toward the snow-covered pines beyond the mouth of the cave. They emerged into a clearing and surveyed their surroundings. They were still near Warith, on the edge of Direwood forest, a quarter mile from Crier's Peak.

He tossed his torch in the snow, extinguishing the flame. His shoulders slumped as he shook his head. "Another dead end."

9

Lavine

Kace eased *Piper* into a massive cave and brought the hovercraft to a gentle halt.

"Let's go over the mission briefing before send-off," he announced from the cockpit, "just to be safe."

Lavine geared up, pulling her thick winter jacket over her head. Kace beckoned them to huddle by the exit.

"Expected mission completion is one month. You have exactly thirty days to find Mundicar and to kill Greyson Hawke," Kace began. "Because of the importance of this run, your comm will remain on low power mode, sending out only a tracking beacon unless panic mode is activated. Ivy and I will be on standby for extraction. There's a shipment of furs scheduled to arrive at Beckinsdale Castle. It'll stop at Ardor's Tavern for the night and then head out in the morning. You'll catch a ride on that shipment."

Lavine nodded, absorbing the details with a focused intensity. With a yank of her arm, she tugged at her belt, ensuring everything was secure and ready for the mission ahead.

"And you and Ivy?" she asked, her voice steady despite the

fear of this potentially being the last time she'd see her crew if something went wrong.

"We will wait here for seven days and then head to the castle's position," Ivy confirmed. "We'll set up camp on the North Mountain and wait there for your signal."

"They might have decent visibility," Lavine said, apprehension creeping into her bones. "Position yourselves high and out of sight."

Ivy nodded. "Gear check. Comm?"

"Check."

"Weapons?"

"Check." Lavine secured her dagger in its sheath.

"Pack?"

"Check." She pulled a hood over her head, becoming Harley Beckett once more, and she hoped this would be the last time.

Ivy straightened Lavine's cloak. "Are you ready to rock Hawke's world?"

Lavine nodded, a gleam in her eye. "Let's do this."

Kace opened *Piper's* side hatch, the mechanisms in the door hissing, and lowered the rope ladder.

"Don't get caught," Kace called after her as she descended, concern hidden in his playful tone.

"More like don't leave witnesses," she muttered under her breath and started to make her way down.

"Hang on." Kace leaned out into the cold, handing her a small vial of vindeca. "You can't forget this."

She slipped it into a pocket hidden within her boot and continued down. She hopped off the last few rungs of the ladder, landing on the cavern floor. With a final glance at Kace and Ivy, she steeled herself for the dangerous journey ahead, knowing that if she failed, the world would burn under the Hawke reign.

Creeping to the mouth of the cave, she gaped at the vast wilderness that spread in all directions, catching sight of the sun rising in the east.

The cold air stung her lungs as she jogged through the pines, breathing in the crisp scent of the forest. Lavine wondered how long she'd been trekking when she spotted smoke rising into the sky. She sighed in relief and edged closer to Warith.

People bustled through the streets, with merchants stationed in tents selling supplies and food—not unlike Market Street. The people of Warith were noticeably less gaunt than the ones in Alain. Still in need of food but not starving.

Pulling her hood snug around her head, she strode through the town as if she belonged there, following the main road past workhouses and shops, keeping an eye out for Ardor's Tavern.

She watched people walk up and down the street, going about their daily lives. Stepping into Navaria was like traveling back in time, before technology had flourished. Lavine wondered how these people survived without plumbing or electricity and how they managed to maintain such normal lives when their king hailed from such a ruthless bloodline.

The crunch of hooves and wheels on the frozen dirt road made Lavine scurry away from the street. The crowd scattered as a wagon, piled high with furs, made its way through town, pulled by a massive elk.

Marveling at the magnificent animal with its majestic head bearing impressive antlers, Lavine fought the urge to reach out and stroke its neck. The beasts were so much larger than the horses she'd ridden across Switchback Beach.

She followed the wagon to Ardor's Tavern and Inn, quietly

observing as the driver brought the wagon around the back. After securing the elk into sheltered stalls, he disappeared inside the inn.

Leaning against a lamppost opposite the inn, she studied the cart, the surrounding terrain, and the tavern. The nearby streets, the freshly fallen snow, and the looming pines of the surrounding forest.

Two escape routes. The town on one side and the forest on the other.

When she was certain that no one was watching, she crept to the wagon and shifted the furs around, creating a hidden space to stow away. She marveled at how such an old-fashioned mode of transportation could support a functioning society. Engines pushing train carts along tracks were much faster.

Navaria would function better if they focused on progressing their tech rather than weaponizing the only resource they have.

Lavine spun on her heel as shouting erupted behind her. Patrons stumbled out of Ardor's, roughhousing and howling with laughter. She returned to her task, pausing after a few minutes to watch the group of men stumble down the street.

Her head snapped toward the sound of a crack of wood from the forest. She whipped her dagger out, hackles raised and peered into the trees. A fox trotted from one tree to another. Unease settled in her stomach.

Feeling as if something was amiss, Lavine stepped back, hitting something on her left. A rope came down around her neck, and her dagger was wrenched from her grip. Panic surged through her as she thrashed wildly, struggling to cry out, but no sound escaped her constricted throat. A group of men crowded around as she was forced to the ground. She sucked in a breath as one of them bent down to tie her legs, slamming the heel of her boot into his tattooed face. There was a satisfying crack of a broken nose, and he cried out as blood drained from his nostrils. With a grunt of pain, he wiped the blood away with his coat sleeve and slammed her face into the snow.

"Give me a hand!" He said through gritted teeth.

Two pairs of hands held her legs down while someone wound a rope around her ankles. Flipped onto her back, she caught sight of another target and lashed out, her fingernails digging into flesh. A cry of pain followed. A fist connected with her stomach, her eyes watering as the breath was knocked out of her.

Alright boys, I'll play along.

She forced herself to stop fighting, letting her body go limp, and the rope around her neck loosened. Her wrists were then bound, the coarse rope digging into her flesh, causing her skin to sting. She was slung over a man's shoulder.

"I don't have any money," she said, choking through painful gasps of air.

A scoff was her only answer. She counted the minutes as they traveled, noting the direction they were heading and estimating the distance. The trees thickened, and the terrain grew more mountainous and rockier.

Wherever they were taking her, Lavine would not make it a simple task, continuing to flail as they hauled her through the forest. The man carrying her drifted to the back of the pack, and she spotted a hunting knife tucked into his belt. An idea sprang to her mind.

With no eyes from behind to keep watch, she loosened her restraints but kept her hands positioned to appear bound. Using her thrashing as a distraction, she reached down and slipped the weapon from the man's belt, tucking it into her sleeve.

A half hour had passed when they stopped in a thicket. They tossed her onto the ground, and she rolled onto her side. Someone grabbed her pack and yanked her upright, ripping the straps.

"Who the hell do you think you—"

A fist smashed into her ribs, forcing her to double over, gasping for breath. Her cloak was ripped from her body. As she opened her mouth to shout profanities at them, a husky, tattooed man appeared in her hazy vision.

"Aren't you a beauty?" He brushed her hair away from her face. She gagged as his breath assaulted her nose, reeking of fish and decayed teeth.

"Careful, Boss. She's a kicker," warned the man on her right, pulling her arm. "She broke Sabe's nose."

Sabe, his nose still bleeding, handed Boss her dagger.

"I told you I have nothing worth stealing. Cut me loose and I'll be on my way."

Boss sneered. "Darling, we are much worse than petty thieves." He eyed her with an unsettling hunger. "You've got some meat on your bones. You'd fetch a pretty price on the market."

Lavine's heart raced, causing cold sweats as she felt her chest tighten. No longer feeling the ache in her ribs or the dryness of her throat, she replayed the morning's events in her mind, trying to pin down where this had all gone horribly wrong. Though vastly outnumbered, she braced herself for a fight, head jerking around as she tallied everyone.

Fourteen total. Three within striking distance.

Even if she had both of her daggers and a lifetime of training, she couldn't win this fight. There was no shame in running from this. Any direction would do.

I'll kill a few of you bastards before I go.

"But first," Boss said, unbuckling his belt, "I'm going to break you in."

She suppressed the blind, hot panic threatening to flood her veins. The ropes binding her feet were cut. She kicked off Boss' chest, propelled herself over the man holding her arms, and brought her bound hands around his neck. She threw all her weight into her fall and felt his neck break as they hit the snowy ground.

Slipping her hand from her restraints, she readied the stolen knife and thrust it into the nearest thug. Another lifeless body slumped into the snow.

Enraged cries rang out. Two men charged her as she tried to run. A fist hurtled toward her face. Ducking, she sunk the bloody blade into his ribs and kicked his leg out from under him. His corpse hit the ground.

The second attacker landed a weak punch on her jaw. Eyes watering and vision blurring, she grabbed his wrist and drove her elbow in the crook of his arm. There was a sharp pop, and he screamed as his arm hung at an unnatural angle. She swiped the blade across his throat, blood spattering in all directions.

Wiping her face, she made a run for it when Boss' hand clamped down on her arm, ripping the hunting knife from her grip. Whipping around, she slammed her head into his, breaking yet another nose.

Lavine turned and raced through the trees, adrenaline roaring throughout her body like a tsunami. Though her legs and lungs screamed for relief, she forced herself onward, stumbling in the soft, deep snow.

Though she believed she had covered enough distance to escape, angry shouts and sharp whistles grew closer and closer. Soon, boots thundered behind her like a herd of wild mustangs.

Hands seized her once again, air forcing from her lungs as she was slammed into a nearby tree. Her head hit the bark with a crunch, bits of it jutting through her shirt, pricking the flesh of her back. Gasping, she crumpled to the ground, mouth filling with dirt and snow as she struggled to breathe. Ringing plagued her good ear. Spots blurred her vision as she searched for an escape.

"Hold her still."

A hand grabbed the cuff of her shirt, yanking her to her feet. Before she could catch her breath, an arm coiled around her throat from behind, her hands clawing at the man's thick bicep.

"You should have come quietly." Boss wiped his bloody nose with the back of his hand. "You'll pay for that." His putrid breath blew on her face.

He cut her shirt open with her own dagger. Her breath quickened as he traced the point of the blade across her chest.

"Don't—" Lavine's voice broke. It didn't sound like her own. It was desperate and small, she hated it with every fiber of her being.

Her skin stung as the blade's tip glided gently toward her stomach, not breaking the surface but causing an unsettling discomfort.

Her hands clenched around her captor's arm. "Please," she begged, feeling tears well up.

Boss paused at her left side and dragged the blade down the

skin of her abdomen. A scream erupted from Lavine's mouth, a sound foreign even to her own ears—something she didn't think a human could make. Tears burst from her eyes as her blood spilled into the snow.

After what seemed like a lifetime, Boss withdrew the blade. The arm around her throat loosened, and she collapsed to the ground once more, gasping and hiccupping on sobs.

Have the stars abandoned me?

Time seemed to stop. Shapes shifted in and out of focus. With her ear ringing, she tried to find something to distract herself from the agony in her side. Her eyes found her dagger discarded in the snow. Just feet away, covered in her own blood. She rolled over and groaned, feigning a wave of pain, searching for an escape route.

And there it was, a sudden drop in the snow just beyond the trees. The fall could kill her, or she'd live to see another day.

I'm not going to die at the hands of this bastard.

Mustering what strength she had left, she staggered to her feet. But wretched hands shoved her down again, laughter roaring in her ear.

Boss paced two yards away, jeering his men on. The fury broiling in her veins fueled her drive to stand once more. With his back turned, she lunged forward, snatched her dagger and pack from the snow and bolted into the trees.

She clambered through the pines, hurriedly sheathing the bloody dagger. Ignoring the low branches that slapped and scraped her face, she didn't slow when she neared the drop-off. Grasping her wound, she closed her eyes and leaped.

10

Greyson

Greyson's shoulders sagged. "Another dead end."

How many more years must I search?

The quest seemed endless, a relentless pursuit through legends, countless novels, and scrolls that yielded no new information, no hint of Aarth's whereabouts.

He turned to reenter the tunnel, the cool dampness offering a momentary respite from the frustration gnawing at him, when a bone-chilling scream ripped through the trees. It shattered the calm of the forest. The hair on his neck stood on end, and goosebumps rippled down his arms.

Silas and Calix drew their swords.

"I haven't seen a snow cat this far north in years," Calix said, gripping the handle of his silver blade.

"That was no snow cat." Greyson listened for another cry. He couldn't place where the scream originated.

"Don't they sound like a woman screaming—" Calix began, only to be silenced by Greyson's raised hand.

There was a distant sound of whooping and laughter drawing nearer. Greyson spotted a faint trail through the snowy ground leading into the Direwoods. Without hesitation, he led Silas and Calix off the beaten path, weaving through the trees toward a clearing at the base of a sheer cliff. Crier's Peak.

Many residents in the area believed the jagged cliff to be haunted, with numerous infamous tales of grieved lovers jumping from its summit.

As they ventured deeper into the thicket, the chatter grew louder, mingling with the rustling of leaves and crunching of snow underfoot. Greyson's eyes darted around, searching for movement beyond a cluster of pines. Veering off the worn path, he navigated through the trees with his guard close behind, swords at the ready.

They stepped into the clearing, the ground blanketed by fresh, undisturbed snow. Gruff voices echoed from above, growing nearer with each passing second.

Greyson looked up just in time to see her jump.

11

Lavine

Tumbling through rock and snow, Lavine plummeted down the sheer drop of the cliff, a new spike of pain with every impact. The descent was steeper and more brutal than she had anticipated.

When her body came to a stop, she dared to remove her hand from her wound. Her palm was sopping wet, and her stomach churned. A dizzying numbness washed over her, preventing her from feeling the warmth of the blood spilling out.

I'm going to die.

She sluggishly turned her head to see a member of the gang standing at the cliff's edge, a stream of blood soaking the snow she had barreled through.

"She's down here, Boss!" he shouted. "We can cut around. She won't make it far!"

With little strength left to escape, she knew she needed to contact Kace and Ivy. But the thought of returning to Marella having failed the most important mission of her life was unbearable. Tallulah would be furious.

Maybe dying here in the snow wouldn't be so bad. At least it would be on my own terms.

She reached for her dagger as she looked up for one last glimpse of the sun, but her eyes found a man. Wrapped in furs and robes, his white armor twinkled as he towered over her.

She noticed the blue frost drake etched into his chest plate, and realization dawned on her. Hawke stood before her, wisps of black hair dancing in the wind.

Laughter echoed from the pines, heavy footsteps crunching through the snow. With nowhere to go, she had to choose her demise. If he killed her, it would be quick. But the thought of Gavriil's grief upon hearing of her death flashed through her mind.

With one final, desperate attempt to survive, she rolled onto her side, pushed herself onto her knees, and looked up at Hawke.

"Help me," she pleaded, her voice cracking. "Please."

12

Greyson

The battered girl lay at his feet, a tangled mess of mahogany hair hanging over her shoulders, a notch missing from her left brow. Her cheeks were cut and bruised, her bottom lip swollen and bleeding. She clenched a wound through her lacerated shirt, and Greyson feared her insides might spill out if she let go. The slope of Crier's Peak was streaked red with her blood.

A group of men trotted into the clearing, whooping and whistling like hounds tracking game through the forest. They came to a halt when they spotted Greyson and his guards.

"Help me," she begged, tears and terror in her eyes. "Please."

Does she know from whom she pleads?

But her fear was familiar to him, as familiar as the rage that lingered in his soul. In his youth, all he had ever wished for was someone to intervene, to stand as a shield against his father. He positioned himself between the girl and her assailants, his movements precise and defensive, forming a shield with his body and presence.

A hulking man broke through the front of the group, his

arms tattooed with crossed scythes, the mark of the Ice Reapers. Their leader brandished a crude revolver as he eyed the girl with disgusting hunger.

"You must be the Reaper," Greyson said. "I've heard many horrific tales of your endeavors."

"I'm flattered that my reputation precedes me, but it seems you have something I want," he said, his voice greasy.

"She doesn't appear to want you. What business do you have with her?"

"The only business one could ever have with a woman." He sneered, his men chuckling darkly at the crude joke.

Bile rose in Greyson's throat. The nauseating acidic churn made him internally recoil.

Vultures—men who preyed on his widowed subjects. Rabid wolves prowling the tree line, thieving and dragging women into the dark forests like the beasts of old.

"Sire?" Silas stepped forward.

"I'll handle this." Greyson signaled his guard to back away. He had surprise on his side, and he intended to use it. "Do you know who I am?"

"I don't care if you're Aarth himself." He aimed the revolver at Greyson's armored chest. "Hand her over."

The corner of Greyson's mouth curved up slightly, a flicker of amusement dancing in his eyes. He welcomed the challenge with a quiet confidence. Ridding Navaria of filth such as this was an opportunity he couldn't pass. Especially a gang as famous as the Ice Reapers. They were notoriously elusive with their ever-changing hideouts and lack of witnesses. Behind him, Silas and Calix remained poised, ready to spring into action at Greyson's command.

"If you want her," he taunted, drawing his dragon steel

sword with flare, its icy magic misting from the blade, "come and get her."

Realization set in, and the men recoiled, their mouths agape and their gazes darting from the Reaper to Greyson to the sword.

"It's Greyson Hawke," one of them whispered into the silence.

The man's eyes flashed with uncertainty and his revolver dipped slightly as he struggled to remain unfazed. "You think I'm afraid of a sword?" he goaded, his voice unsteady. "I could shoot you and be done with it!"

His companions drew their weapons. Greyson tightened his grip on his sword and stood at the ready. Breathing deeply, he steadied the rhythm of his heart and anchored his boots firmly in the snow.

The Reaper threw his free hand out. "It's ten to one," he warned. "You're outnumbered!"

"Outnumbered, but certainly not outmatched."

As the man fired, Greyson lunged forward, intercepting the shot with his blade. He swiftly cut down the closest reaper, the blade's magic freezing the victim's skin on contact.

One.

Another gunshot rang out. Greyson spun behind a tree, shards of bark flying past his left ear. Emerging from cover, he dispatched two more, spilling more blood into the snow.

Three.

With a twirl of his sword, he advanced deeper into the pack. His sword slammed down on the blade of a hunting knife, the force of the blow driving the knife from the man's grip. Greyson quickly brought down his sword, spun, and impaled another man's chest.

Five.

As he dodged more gunfire, another reaper advanced with a short sword. Greyson parried and sliced through more flesh, cutting them down. Slaughtering them like animals.

Nine.

Greyson slowly turned to face the Reaper, his eyes locking onto the cold barrel of the revolver pointed directly at his chest.

"You've got one shot left," Greyson said, stalking closer. "Make it count."

The Reaper shakily pulled the trigger. The bullet grazed Greyson's neck, the warmth of blood trickled steadily down his collar as he closed in.

"Not good enough," Greyson said, holding the point of his sword to the Reaper's chest. He stood frozen, eyes wide and trembling.

Greyson shoved the blade through the man's heart. The Reaper fell to the ground, ice creeping through his corpse, turning his skin bluish purple.

"Ten," Greyson said.

Surveying the thicket, now dyed red and adorned with corpses, he took a moment to catch his breath. Footsteps approached. Greyson turned to see Silas, his brows furrowed as he held his blade aloft.

"Are you kidding me, boy? He could have *killed* you," Silas chastised. "Are you going to look me in the eyes and tell me that you'd risk your life like that for the sake of intimidation? I practically raised you, so I'm not sure where you get your theatrics from."

Greyson suppressed a smile as his guard captain continued to respectfully scold him about his recklessness.

Silas had always treated him like a son, and while he respected Greyson's rank, it didn't stop him from stepping in when he felt it was necessary.

"You need to wear a helmet, son."

"I've made it this far," Greyson replied, returning his attention to the injured girl, who had planted herself on the ground, supporting her weight against a tree trunk as she shivered.

Calix crouched near her. "You need to let me look at it," he urged. He reached out to her.

"Don't touch me!" she snapped, frightened, angry, and hyperventilating. One bloody hand clamped down on her side, while the other struggled to keep what little was left of her shirt closed.

Greyson approached and handed his sword, still dripping with blood, to Silas. The girl flinched at the sight of him and tried to stagger to her feet. She stumbled and retreated to the opposite side of the tree, clinging to it as if it were her lifeline. Strapped to her wrist was an unfamiliar device.

A comm. She's not a Navarian.

"She'll bleed out if we don't get her some help." Calix stood. "But she won't let me near enough to dress the wound."

Greyson recalled the most intense days of his father's training—the times when Malric was most furious. He knew the terror and anguish in her eyes. A cornered animal, fearing for its life, with nowhere to go but into the jaws of the enemy. She would either come quietly or die fighting for her life.

"You need medical attention." Greyson crouched by her side.

"Get away from me!" She lashed out. "I know who you are."

"You'll die out here. You must know that."

96

The girl's skin was already too pale. Surely, her fear of death would override her fear of him. She held fast to the tree trunk, her eyes staring wildly into his.

"You asked for my help," Greyson said, his voice softening to a whisper. "So let me."

She squeezed her eyes shut, tears streaming down her cheeks, cutting through dirt and blood. She pressed her face into the bark of the pine, hiding behind a curtain of hair.

Greyson unfastened his cloak and draped it around her shaking shoulders. She flinched, studying his face through watery eyes, searching for any hint of deception.

"Can you stand?" he asked gently, wrapping his arm around her shoulders and using his weight to aid her to her feet.

Mid-stride, her eyes rolled back, and she fell limp. Greyson caught her momentum, cradling her body to his chest. "No, no. Don't do that. Look at me," he urged. "You can't give up now, not after everything you've been through."

"She doesn't have long. We need to move," he said, pulling his cloak tight around her. "Now."

13

Greyson

Greyson burst through the heavy oak doors of the medical wing. "Sterling!"

The air was thick with the sharp scent of herbs and antiseptic. With steady arms, he gently laid the unconscious girl on a sickbed.

"We have an injured girl here!" His shouts reverberated off the stone walls adorned with tapestries depicting famed healers in ancient battles.

Sterling, the head healer, rushed forward, worry etched across her face. Her long auburn hair was secured in a tight bun with a leather band, strands escaping as she hurried to Greyson's side.

"She's losing blood fast." He gestured toward the girl.

Sterling wasted no time. She gently pulled back the girl's cloak, her hands moving swiftly to reveal the extent of the injuries. "Great Dragons above," she murmured, a hand flying to her mouth. "What happened to her?"

"I found her in the Direwoods. She was running from vultures."

Sterling peeled back one of the girl's eyelids, a groan escaping her blue lips. Sterling shouted over her shoulder, summoning assistants from all corners of the medical wing, all ready to lend their aid.

"Fetch clean water and bandages," Sterling commanded, her voice steady despite the urgency of the situation.

Greyson lowered himself onto a nearby bench, feeling the adrenaline drain from his veins. "She fought hard," he explained as his leg bounced, and his hands trembled with a nervousness that hadn't plagued his body since his father still lived. "But it seems she was overwhelmed and jumped from Crier's Peak while trying to escape."

"She could've killed herself," Sterling admonished.

When it came to the famous cliff, suicide was usually the goal.

An assistant sterilized a needle over a crackling fire and meticulously minced various herbs in a bowl, their fragrances unfamiliar to Greyson.

"She's lost so much blood." Sterling sighed. "What she needs is some vindeca, but I haven't been able to get a hold of that in years... I don't know if she'll make it," she added, her voice tight as her attendants hurriedly scattered around the room.

"Please, try," Greyson urged, his voice tinged with desperation. He had heard of the healing elixir made from the magic of water dragon scales, but when the world's nations wanted nothing to do with you, acquiring such supplies was impossible. Most of the world had cut ties with Navaria long before Greyson was born, leaving him to imagine what vindeca even looked like.

"I'll do what I can," Sterling promised, pressing wads of minced herbs onto the girl's wound. "With respect, Sire..."

she paused to meet Greyson's gaze. Her eyes full of urgency, softened by their shared concern. She touched his arm briefly, a silent plea for understanding. "I need you to leave."

He nodded and took one last look at the tangled mess of a girl before closing the door. With purposeful strides, he marched toward the royal chambers before the doors had fully closed. Silas and Calix, who stood just outside the medical wing, hurriedly followed suit.

"What's the verdict?" Calix asked breathlessly, matching Greyson's frantic pace.

"If she makes it through, I want to keep her close," he said firmly, his mind already planning ahead. "We need to monitor her wounds closely. Once she heals, she might be our bridge to communicate with her homeland… And after the day she's had, she deserves a place to recover. Have Jesper and Wesley prepare my old bedchamber."

"Yes, Sire." Calix dismissed himself, trotting ahead to carry out his task.

"Do you think it wise to bring this girl in?" Silas asked. "We don't know who she is or where she came from. Aarth knows what brought her here. There are few who willingly enter our nation but to cause harm."

"We won't know if she's dead," Greyson replied. "And if she is a threat, we'll deal with her accordingly. Have Eden tally the officers attending the King's Banquet. I want him out of my way for the rest of the evening."

Once Silas had departed, Greyson slipped behind a tapestry in the south hall, passing through a hidden door. Growing up an only child, he had plenty of time to explore the castle, and its winding secret passageways had proven useful for avoiding his father's wrath. This passage led to the foyer just outside the royal chambers. Lined with torches, it was familiar enough that he could navigate it with his eyes closed.

His mind raced with possibilities. A chance he could contact an outside nation and ask for assistance. A fresh start.

Would they even listen to her? She could be a nobody... still, she could be the key to helping my people.

A feeling he couldn't quite place churned in the pit of his stomach, like lightning surging. An unfortunate situation had pinned this girl between two evils, and she had chosen him—aware of who he was and trusting that he would help her.

This is a first.

His hands continued to shake as the curiosity of the situation overwhelmed him. She had trusted him to get her to safety, and he had done just that.

Emerging from behind a tapestry in the royal foyer, he made his way down the great hall to the bedchamber parallel to his own. He stared at the door leading to his old bedchambers, biting the inside of his cheek. He hadn't set foot in his childhood rooms since his coronation. Haunting memories clawed their way into his mind, snarling and tearing at his heart, begging to be unleashed. A shadowy figure seemed to open a creaky door in the blackness of his memory—a harbinger of a terrible omen and the horrors to come.

His eyes snapped open, breath hitching as his palms grew clammy. With his heart racing, Greyson barged into the bedchamber, finding Jesper and Wesley directing servants as they prepared the space for accommodation. The room was a whirlwind of activity. Dusting mantels, fluffing pillows, lighting candles, and shifting furniture.

The space looked immensely different from when his

belongings had been cleared out and moved into the king's chambers, seeing as his father was no longer in need of it.

His fists unfurled, his shoulders slouched, and Greyson found he could breathe despite the lingering shadows of his memories.

"So," Jesper said, after ordering a servant for a fresh duvet. "What do you think? Is this arrangement to your liking?"

"How exactly did you conjure up all this furniture?" Greyson ran his forefinger over the massive oak four-poster bed frame.

"I have my ways." Jesper shrugged. "If I may ask, what do you expect will come of this, Sire?"

Greyson strode across the room to the east wall, where the top half was made entirely of glass. He gazed out at the afternoon sun streaming down on the mountain pass, a view he'd seen a thousand times.

"She may be able to help me."

"She could be a nobody," Jesper countered.

"I don't believe that to be true… it takes a special kind of strength for an outsider to survive the unforgiving nature of the Direwoods and then to go head-to-head with the cruelty of the Ice Reapers. And besides, I seem to have failed my kingdom, I couldn't bear to have failed this girl as well."

If she perished, it would have been all for naught.

After a beat, Jesper met him at the window and cupped his hands behind his back. "Things will improve soon enough." His mouth pressed into a small line. "It's only been three months after all."

"I don't know how much longer Navaria can hold on. You've seen what it's like out there. It's a miracle the people haven't revolted."

102

"The people haven't gotten to know you yet." Jesper shook his head, his spiked brown hair bouncing as he did. "They don't know you like we do. They don't know what you've done for us," he said, glancing over his shoulder. He leaned in and whispered, "Or even what you're doing for them under the cover of darkness."

"I don't know how to go about telling them the truth." Greyson sighed. "Eden would have a heart attack if he found out."

"If only," Jesper quipped, his thin lips pressed into a smile.

Greyson smirked at the jest as Jesper returned to ordering servants about. Calix and Jesper were the second addition to his personal guard, just months after Silas, and had arrived as gangly, malnourished young men. Their road to adulthood had been rough. Their mother had died giving birth to them, and their father had conscripted them into the army to save them from starvation.

After years of sparring and consistent meals, the twins had grown into stout, brawny men. Jesper, the eldest, had become domineering and fearless, always finding a way to pull through, while Calix was softer and excelled as a field medic. When the news of their father's death arrived, it was Jesper who consoled his younger brother, becoming their protector and bastion of grief. Their bond, once solid, had transformed into something unbreakable.

From time to time, Greyson found himself envious of their bond, but he reminded himself that these men were like his brothers and would walk with him to the ends of the earth. But still...

Why did I have to be an only child?

* * *

The sun dipped below the mountains, and after a restless dinner, Greyson willed himself back to the medical wing alone and in silence, anxiety rising with each step.

Pacing outside the chamber door, he feared he might be walking into the girl's tomb. He pushed the door open and peeked inside. The room was quiet and still as he ventured further and found Sterling writing at her desk.

"Sterling?" he called softly.

She sprang from her chair, scraping it against the stone floor. She bowed deeply, her cheeks flushing with surprise. "I'm so sorry, I didn't hear you come in."

"You needn't bow to me." His gaze fixed on the floor, the old stone worn smooth over the years.

"Force of habit," Sterling said, rubbing her neck as a heavy silence settled between them. The air felt thick and oppressive.

"She made it through," she continued, retrieving the parchment she had been writing on. "But she lost a lot of blood and needed a lot of stitches. She's going to be weak for a while."

"Sterling, you know how vultures treat the women they capture..." Greyson swallowed, his mouth bone-dry. The thought made him sick to his stomach. "Did they..."

"No," Sterling answered, understanding what he could not bring himself to say aloud. "No, she had defensive wounds and skin under her nails. Like you said, she fought hard. They never had a chance."

His shoulders sagged in relief, and he lifted his gaze to meet Sterling's. "Where is she?"

"In here," Sterling said, leading him to the far end of the

104

medical wing. They walked down a long corridor, passing unoccupied rooms whose doors stood slightly ajar.

"I gave her a sedative for the pain," she explained as they approached a door at the end of the hall. "She'll be out for a few days."

Sterling opened the door and stepped aside to let Greyson enter. The girl lay unconscious on a sickbed, looking like a completely different person. Not only had Sterling stitched her wounds closed, she had bathed and groomed her. Thick, dark hair spilled out around her shoulders, and the scrapes that had streaked her face were but faint lines. The gash in her lip was almost closed. The notch missing from her left brow, which he had seen at Crier's Peak, remained unchanged.

Where have I heard about someone with a scar on their eyebrow?

Greyson sat in a chair next to the bed, studying her face, noting every freckle as his mind struggled to recall the information. Though the thought nagged at him, he drank in the sight of her. His stomach clenched at the bruising on her wrists and neck.

"It'll take some time for her side to heal, but her superficial wounds are pretty much gone," Sterling said, reading off her parchment. "Those bruises were nasty, though. Unfortunately, there's nothing I have that can speed up the healing of bruising that bad. They'll need some time."

Greyson couldn't remember a time when he hadn't had a deep purple bruise on his body. Those types of injuries weren't foreign to him. He knew the yellowish purple of her wrists would take weeks to heal. He'd experienced his fair share of nasty injuries from battles, sparring sessions, and from his father.

Looking around the room, he found fault in everything:

the bed was too hard, the room too small, and the walls too dreary. Because of the discomfort, he was glad to put his old bedchamber to use again.

"I'll be moving her upstairs," he said, "into my old bedchambers. She'll be more comfortable there."

"Very well. I can come up occasionally to check on her wounds," Sterling replied. "Oh, and I washed your cloak," she added, producing it clean, blood-free, and neatly folded.

"Thank you."

"I also washed what was left of her clothes, which wasn't very much," Sterling continued, pulling the girl's remaining possessions from the nightstand. "Her shirt was completely shredded, but her boots and pants survived as well as her pack. It took some scrubbing to clean the blood from her dagger though."

Greyson's heart jumped into his throat. "She had a dagger?"

The notched eyebrow, the dagger. It's not the same one. It can't be.

"Yes, it was tucked into her belt. I think it was the same dagger they used to cut her open."

He shot up out of the chair. "Sterling, I need to see it."

Flustered by his sudden urgency, Sterling quickly retrieved the dagger from the nightstand and handed it to him.

Greyson's heart hammered in his ears as he spotted familiar grooves on the handle. He unsheathed the dagger he had confiscated from Theodore and held it alongside the new dagger. His heart stopped. They were identical.

He turned his gaze to the girl lying unconscious on the sickbed.

It all makes sense now—how she managed to get so far into Navaria, how she survived an encounter with the Ice Reapers.

106

Why didn't I see it? It all fits.

He had a Marellan assassin in his custody, wounded and unconscious.

14

Lavine

The ground had spun under Lavine's feet. The trees had whirred skyward, and her skin had felt hot and clammy. Streaks of red. Searing pain. A helplessness she had never felt before.

"No, no. Don't do that. Look at me. You can't just give up, not after what you've been through." The deep, commanding voice echoed in her mind.

She had compelled her body to obey the muffled voice, though she didn't fully trust it. She had fought to keep her eyes open, trying to focus on the tendrils of black hair fluttering in the wind.

Her breath had been rapid and shallow, the scent of smoke and leather swirling in the air. But there was something else, something sweet.

Convinced that she had lost her mind, a crippling panic seized her thoughts and limbs, locking her in a state of terror that she'd never experienced before. Moments later, her world had faded to black.

Soft satin pillows caressed her cheeks as a fire crackled

somewhere in the room, putting off a comfortable heat. She shifted in bed, content to stay there forever.

I never sleep much on missions... Missions... Great Dragons above!

Lavine shot up in bed, her eyes darting around the massive, unfamiliar stone room. A large fireplace sat snugly across from the bed. Despite the room's grand furnishing and lush carpets and curtains, her attention was drawn to a wall that faced east. At least, she assumed it was the east. The wall was a striking blend of stone and glass.

Possible escape route? No, the fall would kill me. One wooden door, one way to escape.

A painful surge in her left side made her hand jolt to the bandaging under her oversized shirt that didn't belong to her.

She checked her wrist for her comm but found nothing but fading bruises. Her skin prickled. Her comm was gone, along with her dagger, pack, and clothes

At least the shirt is clean... Well, I hope it's clean.

Long enough to be a nightgown, the seam of the shirt hit her mid-thigh. She pulled the fabric to her nose, detecting the faint scent of smoke and leather.

And everything came flooding back: the shouts and jeers, being slammed to the ground. Her skin being split open, and her own screams filling the air. Warm liquid drenching her hands. Blood, her blood. Everywhere.

Hawke staring down at her, his eyes as black as his hair. He had looked almost heroic, charging into the fray clad in white-plated armor, looking every bit of a ferocious king, minus the crown.

"Dragons above," she whispered, steadying herself as she swung her legs over the edge of the four-poster bed. Her feet were tucked into a pair of wool socks that also didn't belong to her.

The bedchamber looked like the pictures in Gavriil's fairy tale books, enormous with high ceilings, draped in colorful curtains, adorned with exquisite furnishings, and decorated with ceramic busts of snarling drakes with barbed scales. Vastly different from the slender, benevolent water dragons that once ruled the Marellan seas.

Lavine stood, her legs unsteady, and ambled toward the door, her legs wobbling like a newborn foal. Reaching the large oak door, she twisted the handle.

Locked.

She ran her fingers through her hair, discovering that her pins were missing as well. Her breath quickened and her stomach churned.

I'm not in a cell and I'm not dead, so he might not know who I am.

But she had asked for his help and look where it got her. A fancy prison. Although she wasn't being tortured in a filthy cell, she still felt trapped. A cage was still a cage, no matter how exquisitely furnished.

Lavine examined herself, tallying each bruise and its location on her body. The major wound in her side was likely still healing, and the bruises on her wrists had turned an ugly yellow. She ran her hands along her neck, assuming her neck was fairing the same way.

Nothing a little vindeca can't fix. If it's not too late.

While the dragon water possessed incredible healing properties, it was not without its limits. Delay the treatment too long, and your body would reject it. Just as it had with the deafness in her left ear.

She took another sweep of the room, spotting her pants neatly folded on a table near the fireplace. As she approached the east wall, she couldn't help but marvel at the creative combination of glass and stone, having seen nothing equal to it. The stone portion of the wall reached as high as her waist, while the rest was thick glass, connecting to the ceiling a dozen feet above.

Her eyes wandered beyond the glass and into the skyline. Stars twinkled over the wide, snowy valley nestled between the mountains, with pinks and oranges creeping over the horizon.

"You're awake."

Lavine spun to find Hawke in the doorway, his shoulders draped in thick furs. The sword he'd used to slaughter her attackers was sheathed at his side. She stood motionless, puzzled by her body's instinct to freeze instead of fight. Despite the blinding pain she'd experienced during the attack, she had witnessed how swiftly he had dispatched those men. It was terrifyingly impressive.

He was still clad in a sleek white suit of armor with subtle streaks of blue running through the plating. A snarling frost drake was engraved on his chest plate. Her gaze shifted to his sword, its handle wrapped tightly in white cloth.

Without making a sound, Hawke glided into the room, his rigid posture exuding his royal upbringing. Yet his demeanor remained calm and unbothered, showing no signs of being threatened by her.

Lavine mentally sifted through ways to escape her predicament, but all seemed futile with Hawke blocking her path.

A young guard with ginger hair and a healing black eye followed him with a tray in hand and placed it on the small table. Hawke dismissed the guard, leaving them alone. The silence was deafening and was grating on her nerves. His gaze was like the high noon sun beating down on her skin, and there was nowhere to hide.

He nudged the tray toward her as he sat at the table. "Sterling said you'd be hungry when you woke."

Lavine's eyes darted to the tray, a bowl and bread atop it, and back to him. He removed the lid from the bowl, and the scent of stew filled the air.

In an act of betrayal, her mouth watered, and her stomach gurgled. The lure of food overwhelmed her. She gave in, slowly approaching the table and sitting opposite. The steam blanketed her face in savory warmth as she picked a silver spoon from the tray, ready to dig into the meaty stew, but stopped. She stared at him, still suspicious.

"I've not poisoned it," Hawke said.

"How do I know you're not lying?"

He reached across the table, dipped the bread into the stew, and took a bite. After setting the bread back on the tray, he swallowed and continued to observe her.

Now content with the safety of the food, she began to eat, greedily shoveling the food into her mouth. The stew was earthy, savory, and perfectly salted, while the bread was a delightful mix of soft, buttery, and crisp. With each bite, she was transported back to Gavriil's cottage, with its open windows, billowing silk curtains, and fuzzy pillows scattered everywhere.

"Slow down," Hawke warned, pulling her back to the present. "You'll make yourself sick.

Lavine paused, swallowing as she stared into the bowl, avoiding his intense stare. "How long have I been out?"

112

"Three days."

Twenty-six days left.

Kace and Ivy had no reason to assume she was in danger and in need of extraction. She could still complete her mission; she just needed to kill Hawke. It wouldn't be easy. She would have to be cautious. Lavine had witnessed his sword's magic, how it froze its victims within seconds.

"Who were they?" Lavine asked, her voice softer than she intended. "The men who attacked me."

"The Ice Reapers, one of the last gangs of vultures in Navaria."

In response to her confusion, he explained that they were one of many groups known for kidnapping women and trafficking them into slavery beyond Navaria's borders. She had no idea practices like this still existed. Hawke seemed pleased to have taken their lives, and she couldn't fault him.

"Why are you here?" he asked.

"You brought me here."

"Why did you come to Navaria?" he clarified, a slight bite in his tone

Lavine responded by shoving more food into her mouth, savoring the earthiness of a soft potato chunk as she took a moment to think of an answer. For now, she decided to play dumb.

"Why would I have come here?" she countered. "It's too cold, there's nothing to see, and the architecture is"—she glanced over at the mishmash wall of stone and glass—"questionable. Really, Hawke, the only good thing here is the food."

"If I am to host the most infamous spy and assassin of our time," he said, "I'd like to know her aspirations."

Lavine's hand trembled slightly as she continued to eat, though she tried to keep her movements steady. She could feel the weight of Hawke's gaze crashing into her like a tidal wave. It was a waste of breath to lie about her identity, but she wanted to see just how far she could push it.

"What makes you think I'm capable of assassination?" she replied, forcing a nonchalant tone. "I was just gutted like an animal for slaughter."

"And because of that, I didn't suspect you at first... until I found this in your possession." He gestured toward the dagger tucked into his waistband—her dagger.

Despite the sudden heat in her cheeks, she remained calm. She watched as he drew the blade and rotated it in his hands, his eyes skimming over the grooved handle.

"That proves nothing," she countered, feigning confidence despite feeling uncomfortably defenseless.

"You would be right," he said smugly, "except I have its twin."

Lavine's body tensed as Hawke revealed the second blade, the one Theo had taken from her. Her instincts screamed at her to grab the weapons and flee.

"How did you get that?"

His gaze shifted from the daggers to meet hers. "Your allies are weak. I confiscated this from your supposed friend."

She shook her head. "You tortured him."

"I didn't have to try very hard." His tone was chillingly casual.

"He's dead, isn't he?"

"No, I imagine he's begging a fisherman for a ride to Marella by now. If he survived traveling through the Direwoods on foot."

She glared, her nostrils flaring as she pushed the remaining stew away, no longer hungry.

"He made it out with his life," Hawke continued, "in exchange for information regarding you. Don't waste his sacrifice, I'm sure it was a difficult decision to make."

The realization that this could jeopardize her entire mission, her entire life's work, left her lightheaded. Her mind spiraled as fatigue crept into her muscles.

"Now, Beckett," he said, slowly enunciating her cover name, "you're going to tell me why you're here."

"If you know who I am and have your perceived ideas on my intentions, then why keep me here? Why not put me in a cell?"

"You nearly died," he replied. "You needed a proper place to recover. A cell would be inappropriate, and the medical wing is loose on security."

"Just give me vindeca, and I'll be right as rain. I'll be well enough to get out of your hair. You'll be rid of me, and we can go our separate ways."

"I'm not here to negotiate." Hawke shook his head as he moved toward her, gliding his fingers on the table's surface.

"Why did you bring me here?" she demanded, her voice tight with frustration.

"You asked for my help," he replied, his eyes cold.

"You should have killed me when you had the chance."

He leaned in, his face hovering just within arm's reach.

Give me a reason to strike. We'll see if the monster really does have fangs.

"Some debts demand interest. Lucky for you, your life is worth far more than your death."

Lavine's chest flooded with a rush of adrenaline. She could see flecks of gold in his obsidian-colored eyes, like stars in the night sky. Hawke's proximity once again brought the scent of leather and smoke, that strangely faint yet familiar scent; rich and spicy yet subtly sweet.

The door opened, revealing a grand hall just beyond the threshold where the ginger-haired guard stood waiting.

Hawke's gaze lingered on her for a beat more. "It looks as though you'll be staying with me for quite some time, so make yourself comfortable."

With that, he turned and left the room. The door shut, a lock clicking into place.

Lavine sprang up from her chair, sending it toppling to the floor. Glancing from the chair to the glass wall, she seized it and dragged it across the room, its wooden legs sliding silently over the plush rugs. She heaved the chair at the glass, wincing as the injury in her side screamed in pain. The chair bounced against the glass wall and landed lamely on the floor. Frenzied, she paced the room, running a hand through her hair as she tried to think of a means of escape.

There has to be something in here I can pick the lock with.

While nothing in the room seemed immediately useful, her eyes were drawn to the four-poster bed, its polished wood frame gleaming in the firelight. An idea began to take shape.

Lavine moved to the bed frame and lifted the blanket. Bending down, she slipped her hand under the bed and grasped the wooden railing supporting the mattress. Digging her nails into the wood, she pried off a chunk. After extracting a few painful splinters, she examined the shard. Small enough to hide in her sleeve, but large enough to inflict injury.

As her attention returned to the bed, a wave of lightheadedness swept over her, reminding her just how exhausted she was.

I'll pass out if I continue like this.

Though her body begged for rest, she pulled the chair back to the table and finished her meal as her heart rate gradually returned to normal.

Accepting that escape would have to wait until tomorrow, Lavine forced her fatigued body to the bed and pulled back the plush layers of blankets. As her mind threatened to spiral into tangled thoughts, her heavy eyelids closed, and she succumbed to sleep.

15

Greyson

Sweat dripped down Greyson's back as he swung a wooden sword, the clash echoing in the expansive room. Silas parried his strike and countered with a thrust of his own mock weapon. Greyson intercepted, knocking Silas' sword downward. He lunged forward, halting the tip of his blade mere inches from Silas' neck.

"Three out of five?" Silas huffed.

Greyson nodded. "Let me catch my breath." He lowered his blade and leaned against the stone wall, holding his sword aloft. He ran his hand through his hair, mussing it up further, causing strands to fall onto his forehead.

"You've always had a frightening knack for swordplay, even as a boy."

"Have you forgotten who trained me?"

"How could I forget?" Silas scoffed, sitting on the grimy floor, lifting his arm in the air. "A bit of help, if you don't mind."

Greyson abandoned his spot against the wall. "Old bastard," he teased as he lifted the guard captain to his feet.

118

"Anything new with Beckett?" Silas dusted himself off.

"No." Greyson rolled his shoulders. "Every day is the same discussion."

Beckett proved to be sly, dancing around his questions with more questions and sarcasm—utterly derailing their conversations. She'd been in his care for a mere six days, and he was already losing patience.

"Maybe you should change tactics?" Silas said. "Use her blades against her."

"She'll be no help if I've gutted her."

"And she's been no help thus far. You don't have to actually torture her, just lead her to believe you will."

Greyson shook his head. "I don't want to become my father."

"And you never will. Trust me, you don't have the stomach for that... and I mean that in a caring way," Silas quickly added.

"There has to be a way to get through to her."

"Whatever it is, you'll figure it out. You're a smart lad."

"Alright," Greyson declared. "Round four."

"I'm getting too old for this."

"Nonsense," Greyson said, flipping wet hair from his face. "You're in your prime."

They tapped blades and the match commenced. Greyson struck first; Silas blocked and countered with a low swing, forcing Greyson to sidestep. As Silas readied himself for another strike, Greyson feigned right, then swung left, and pivoted to deliver an elbow strike to Silas' jaw. With a grunt, Silas hit the floor, clutching his chin.

A proud grin spread across his face. "You never lose, do you?"

"I can't afford to." Greyson held out his palm, helping Silas to his feet once more.

They panted in the vast sparring chamber, the strain of training and the crackling fireplace at the far end keeping the chill at bay.

Greyson's thoughts drifted to the grand fireplace in his childhood chambers. Even with a fire blazing in the hearth, Beckett still shivered, clearly unaccustomed to Navaria's climate.

"You're correct in that I need to change tactics with her. But I'm not comfortable laying a hand. It's in my best interest to make her as comfortable as possible. Perhaps she'll be more inclined to cooperate."

"Is that all?" Silas asked, raising an eyebrow and narrowing his eyes.

"What exactly are you insinuating?"

"All I'm saying is that I've never seen you treat someone with such delicacy. Be careful who you invest your care into, and don't forget that she was sent here to kill you."

"It's not like that at all. I can't afford to miss this chance to connect with her and with the rest of the world."

For once, Greyson had made himself out to be the hero and he couldn't bear to shatter that image just yet. That act of humanity might have been exactly what he needed to persuade Beckett to help him. His mind was filled with images of the emaciated people of Wimborne, their gaunt, withered faces, and the many nights he had sacrificed sleep to provide them with stolen food.

"I need her help, and I'm going to ask for it."

"Are you sure you can truly trust her?"

"It's difficult to say for certain." Greyson chewed the inside of his cheek, unable to keep the subject at bay any longer, treading carefully as he was unsure how Silas would react.

"Do you trust me?"

"With my life."

Greyson whispered, "Why haven't you told me about your family?'

The color drained from Silas' face. "How did you find out?" he demanded, his eyes momentarily darting to the doorway. "Who told you?"

"No one did. I met them."

Silas stared at Greyson, wide-eyed, as if he were seeing a ghost. "You've met Becca?"

"And your grandchildren."

Silas' gaze dropped to the floor, dazed and ashamed.

Greyson held his breath, silently pleading for Silas to make eye contact. An ember popped in the fireplace. Greyson remained silent, allowing Silas the time and space to gather his emotions.

Silas drew in a deep breath. "Malric conscripted me into the guard when you were a boy," he began. "He never looked into my personal history, so I had no need to mention them. And..." Silas paused, closing his eyes. "You never asked."

Once again, Silas was correct. A fundamental aspect of the guard was to recruit men who had no family ties—nothing to lose but their own lives. Greyson had assumed Silas fit that profile and never dug deeper.

"They're starving, Silas," Greyson whispered. "You could have told me."

"Thanks to Malric, most of the country is starving," Silas countered through gritted teeth, his complexion shifting from pale to flushed. "I have been sending a portion of my earnings to them for years. They're none of your concern."

"They are now. Silas, I can help them."

"Don't speak a word of this to anyone," Silas snapped, dropping the wooden sparring sword and spinning on his heel. He began striding out of the dueling chamber, but Greyson placed a firm hand on his shoulder, feeling Silas tense beneath his grip.

"Wait," Greyson said. "Take this to them."

Silas turned to face him, furrowing his brows at the sight of the coin bag Greyson held out. He opened his mouth to protest but hesitated. Greyson knew Silas respected the crown too much to refuse the gift.

"Take leave and go see them," Greyson continued. "Return in seven days."

"What of the banquet preparations?"

"Jesper can handle them while you're away."

They held each other's stare for a few beats before Silas bowed deeply. "Thank you, Your Majesty."

Greyson's heart grew heavy as he watched his captain's swift departure. Silas had been more of a father to him than Malric ever was and the first to join his personal guard. A proficient swordsman who captured the king's attention, Silas was brought to Beckinsdale Castle and was soon appointed as a trainer when Malric grew bored of sparring with Greyson.

"Your Majesty." General Eden's voice sifted into the room.

Greyson looked up to see him, his head still wrapped in bandages. Greyson dipped his head in acknowledgment, allowing Eden to continue speaking.

"I've heard you've taken in a *stray*," Eden said, his sharp eyes staring accusingly.

For a moment, Greyson was confused as to what Eden was talking about.

Beckett, he realized. "I fail to see how that concerns you."

"This really is a bad time to bed a common whore. We wouldn't want you *reproducing* at a time like this."

The whole castle knew he had brought a strange woman into Beckinsdale Castle, and Greyson had worried that someone might sniff her out. But they had jumped to the wrong conclusion.

This could work in my favor.

"General," Greyson said, his voice cold and edged with malice. "Do you need a reminder of what happens to those who overstep their bounds. Whom I choose to bed is none of your concern, and I suggest you remember that."

"My apologies. I only wish you success in your time as king."

"Why have you come?" Greyson asked.

"I'm here regarding the Marellan assassin."

"Have you found her yet?"

"Her whereabouts are still unknown. The scent has gone cold."

Furrowing his brow at the news, Greyson strode purposefully toward Eden, maintaining intense eye contact. "Keep searching. She's hiding somewhere," he said, lowering his voice as he circled Eden slowly. "If you don't capture her soon, she'll infiltrate the castle, and by then it will be too late." Coming full circle around Eden, Greyson closed in on him, his towering figure casting a shadow on the general. "Do you understand?" he demanded, his voice echoing in the room.

"Yes, Your Majesty."

"Good. It's the least you can do after letting Theodore Ashford escape."

"That was not my fault," Eden retorted through gritted teeth. "I was ambushed. We all were, and we still don't know who's

123

responsible."

"All the more reason to find her. Bring your sons to assist if necessary—the more eyes, the better. The castle guard will continue looking for the one who ambushed you."

Eden's three sons were his pride and joy. When Greyson enlisted their aid, Eden's focus shifted to ensuring tasks were completed with unmatched efficiency, driven to uphold his family's notorious reputation. This would serve as an easy distraction and keep the general out of Greyson's hair.

"Yes Sire," Eden replied, his chest puffed out. He left as swiftly as he had come.

Fatigued, drenched in sweat, and his sparring partner now on leave, Greyson decided it was time to retire for the day. His feet carried him toward Beckett's quarters, the key to her door dangling from his neck. As he reached to unlock her door, he stopped. Covered in sweat and dirt, with his wet hair plastered to his face, the thought of entering the room in that state felt objectionable.

What does it matter?

He deliberated for a moment, unsure why he felt conflicted. Yes, he was royalty and yes, he was filthy. Yet, as king, he had an image to uphold, even with prisoners. Resolving to maintain some dignity, he turned back to his chambers, deciding to bathe first.

* * *

Snow drifted past the tall, arched windows in lazy spirals, catching the afternoon light and casting shifting patterns on the cold stone floor. All was quiet, save for the occasional crackle from the hearth and the distant groan of wind pushing against the ancient walls. Despite the fire, the chill settled in every corner, creeping beneath every collar and cuff. Beckett stood near the east wall, her gaze fixed on the distant mountains veiled in white.

"The mountains almost look beautiful from here," Beckett mused, standing cross-armed at the east wall and rubbing her hands along her arms in an attempt to keep warm.

"I'll arrange for some extra blankets," Greyson said, setting a tray of food on the table before taking his usual seat.

Beckett sighed, her shoulders slumping as she turned to look at him. "Come on, Hawke. We both know the steps to this dance. Find a new partner."

"What has changed in the past few months that prompted Marella to send you?"

She planted herself at the table and dug into the lunch he had set out for her, struggling to spread butter on her slice of bread with a spoon since he had refrained from giving her a butter knife.

"Well, you did just murder your father a few months ago," she said, tilting her head as if discussing the weather. "That tends to get people's attention, you know."

"That doesn't answer my question."

"Why did you help me?" she said, deflecting and shoving a piece of buttered toast into her mouth. As she chewed, the muscles in her face shifted, and he noticed the genuine curiosity in her eyes.

"Because you asked me to," he countered.

She rolled her eyes as she took another bite of toast. After some silence, she asked, "How did you tie the daggers to me?"

"What do you mean?"

"How did you know I would have twin daggers? You

CRIER'S PEAK

must've known this to ask Theo the right questions."

"I've heard whispers. Once I pieced together that you'd be returning to Navaria, I knew I needed to speak to you. And here you are, albeit not in the way I had expected."

He remembered the terror in her eyes, now replaced by cunning and mischief. He could see now that her eyes were a soft, earthy brown.

"How much did Theo tell you?"

"Just enough to confirm my suspicions: a physical description and the clue about your twin daggers."

A slight furrow creased her brow, her shoulders tensing as she tightened her grip on the spoon.

Sensing an opening, he continued, "He had taken one as insurance, knowing you'd come back for the weapon."

"What?" she blanched.

I have her attention now.

He relayed the highlights of how he had smuggled Theodore out of Beckinsdale Castle. Her expression shifted from bewilderment to confusion and then back to anger.

"This is the second time you've made me lose my appetite."

"My apologies," he replied, his expression softening. "But I need your help, Beckett."

Her brows furrowed deeper, and her eyes narrowed in on him. "And why should I help you?"

"Because no one else will."

126

16

Lavine

Lavine kept her back to him, fingers resting on the windowsill as she watched the snow fall. She could feel his presence behind her. Stripped of armor but still carrying the power of command and a desperation that was impossible to ignore. Part of her wanted to turn, to meet him halfway. The other part remembered who she was dealing with. So when he finally spoke, she braced herself, already feeling a piece of her gravitate to him.

"My people are months away from starving to death," Hawke said, dressed in dark clothing. "You're the only person who can open an avenue of resources for Navaria."

"Tallulah offered you help and you ignored her."

"I've received no word from the Marellan High Council." He shook his head. "I've sent dozens of letters requesting aid and an olive branch of peace. Every one of them has been ignored."

That can't be true. None of this adds up. Lavine mentally went down the list of possible hidden motives, but none seemed plausible.

Though Hawke was unarmored, he still seemed to take up so much space. With his height and bulk, any attempt to confront him head-on would be nothing short of suicide. The wood shard tucked in her sleeve grazed her arm.

I'll have to get him from behind.

His broad shoulders were draped in a cloak adorned with black and gray furs, which only accentuated his large frame as he leaned over the table. His strong nose and high cheekbones made him seem wolfish.

If someone had told her a week ago that she'd be eating lunch with Greyson Hawke, she'd have thrown them from the Capitol Building's balconies.

"Why me? Why not Theo?"

"You have something that he does not—status."

"Stop stroking my ego and get to the point."

"This isn't about your ego. It's about my people," he said, clenching his fist so tightly that his knuckles cracked. His nostrils flared, and he raised his arm as if to slam his fist down on the table. But before his fist landed, he stopped himself, his hand hovering inches above the tabletop. He closed his eyes, taking a deep breath before continuing. "You're the one with a reputation, not Theodore. Think about it, at least," he suggested before standing.

"Where are you going?"

"I have affairs to attend to. My men will bring your dinner." He glanced at the fireplace. "I'll send for more firewood."

The sweet scent she'd been trying to pin down wafted into the air. It teased her senses like a distant memory dancing on the edge of her mind. She craved more of it.

"And blankets," she added, shoving the craving away.

"And blankets," Hawke repeated as he strode to the door,

his back turned and defenses down.

Now.

Lavine's heart pounded in her chest as she slipped the wood shard into her palm and crept closer. Her eyes locked on Hawke's unguarded neck. The thought of killing him now was both tantalizing and terrifying. Every muscle in her body tensed, primed and ready to strike.

She raised her weapon.

"Tread carefully, little assassin," Hawke whispered, "for you have a tiger by the tail and its fangs are no stranger to flesh."

Lavine froze, her blood running cold as his threat sank in. The thrill of the kill turned to ice in her veins, and a wave of wooziness washed over her as the blood drained from her face.

Hawke's slow, deliberate turn felt like a predator closing in on its prey, his gaze piercing and cold. "You are one wrong decision away from forfeiting my kindness. Follow through, and I will treat you like the prisoner you are. You'll be thrown into the darkest, most unforgiving cell I can find—no light, no warmth, no medical aid. You will be left to rot."

The hairs on the back of her neck stood on end, every fiber in her body screaming for her to retreat. The cold shift in Hawke's demeanor was chilling.

"But..." he continued, his tone softening yet still laced with poison. "Stand down now, and we'll pretend this little encounter never happened."

Lavine took a deep breath as she met his unyielding gaze. She weighed her options, feeling in the pit of her stomach that his threat was genuine, though she sensed he was reluctant to act on it. The wooden shard began to feel heavy in her hand. Slowly, she extended it toward Hawke, placing it carefully into his open palm.

His eyes followed her movement, and the faintest hint of satisfaction flickered in his gaze. "Wise decision." As he moved toward the door, he glanced back at her. "Rest well," he said, though it was more of a command than a genuine wish.

The door closed, Hawke and freedom disappearing behind it.

How am I supposed to kill someone like that?

She paced in front of the glass wall, stealing glances at the falling snow outside. Seeing that killing Hawke wasn't feasible in her current state, and with no means of escape, she shifted her focus to finding Mundicar.

"Maybe I can use this to my advantage," she wondered aloud. "He seems inclined to make conversation, so he might let something slip."

But she also grappled with his request for help, uncertain whether it was a ruse or if he was genuine.

Lavine had to admit that Hawke was easy on the eyes, especially when he wasn't covered in dirt and blood. When he wasn't being callous or cold, he had an unusual sort of charm to him. His tall frame and sturdy build made him alluring, and he carried himself with the power and grace that one would expect from a king. Yet he could move with a surprising and vicious speed in combat.

I'm going to have to stay on my toes.

The soft click of the door interrupted her thoughts. As the door swung open, Lavine recognized the man who had entered. "You were there, in the forest."

With an armload of firewood, he replied, "The one you refused help from? Yeah, that would be me." He dipped into a mocking curtsy, a cocky grin stretching across his face.

Presuming he was a member of Hawke's Royal Guard, given his similar armor and the snarling drake emblem on his chest plate, Lavine decided to dig for any information she could get.

"How're the stitches?" he asked, setting logs into the fire.

"Itchy."

"Good, that means they're healing."

"I know what it means," she shot back, placing her hands on her waist.

He smiled, adding more logs to the fire before standing and brushing the dirt from his hands. He was tall and bulky, though smaller than Hawke. His hair and eyes were the same brown as the oak trees back in Marella. Lavine had yet to encounter a man of average height in this castle.

I guess the men here are a different breed altogether.

"If Hawke would just give me some vindeca, it wouldn't be itchy."

"We haven't been able to import the healing water in years."

Every day, she had asked Hawke for healing water, and every day, he had refused. She thought he was using her injury as an advantage, ensuring she'd have difficulty harming him. She had considered revealing the vial that she had hidden in her boot, but feared he'd take it from her.

"How do you heal yourself when injured?"

"Our bodies heal on their own. It just takes some time."

"Well, yeah but…"

Marella, the only producer of the healing water, had cut off all trade with Navaria years ago, and she had never considered the impact it must have had on civilians. It stirred something inside her that made her squirm, and for a moment, she felt uncomfortable in her own skin.

Trying to distract herself, Lavine's gaze drifted to the sword strapped to the guard's waist. He seemed much less of a threat now compared to when she had first encountered him in the woods.

"You're one of Hawke's personal guards," she said, her tone shifting as she refocused on him.

"Calix, at your service," he said with a flourish, tucking one leg behind the other.

"Why are you doing servants' work?"

Calix ruffled his brown hair and tucked a lock behind his ear. "You being here is already risky, and we can't let the court learn your true identity."

"So people know I'm here?"

"Oh, they know." Calix stood, a sly grin creeping across his face. "They just think you're a harlot."

"What?!" Lavine exclaimed, taken aback by the outlandish lie and unsure if she should be flattered or insulted.

"You could easily be trying to seduce His Majesty for your own gain." Calix shrugged, holding back a chuckle. "That's the story we're going with."

Unlike Malric, Hawke wasn't known for being popular with women, and she doubted he had time for romance. Still, the lie was odd but not unheard of in his court. She was certain Malric had bedded half the court purely out of boredom.

"Hawke said you'd bring more blankets," Lavine said, changing the subject.

He nodded as another guard, identical to Calix, entered with an armful of wool blankets. The new guard set them on the bed and stood beside his brother. It was scary how similar they were: the same bouncy brown hair and handsome, angular faces. The only way she could tell them apart was the stubble on Calix's face.

"You have a twin?" Lavine asked as she glanced between the two. "What's it like?"

Calix shrugged. "It has its moments."

"Do you ever wish you were different?" Her eyes flickered, studying their expressions.

"Sometimes," Calix admitted. "Having someone who knows you inside and out is both a blessing and a curse."

His twin shot Lavine a brief, indifferent glance before his attention shifted toward the door.

"Must be handy in a fight," Lavine remarked, her tone light but probing.

He met her gaze with a look that clearly ended the conversation, offering only a curt nod before striding toward the door.

Calix smiled. "Jesper doesn't really care for newcomers."

"Same here," Lavine said, then paused. "What business does Hawke have so late at night?"

"That's not something I'm at liberty to discuss," Calix replied. "Stay warm. I know you're accustomed to tropical weather." He dusted off his pants and exited the room without another word.

Lavine approached the fireplace and ran her fingers along the mantle for the umpteenth time, searching for anything that might unlock the door. After hours of fruitless searching and a brief nap, she paced by the glass wall for another hour. The door finally opened again.

The guard with orange hair entered, carrying her dinner. Lavine glanced out the glass window and saw that the sun had set. She turned back to the guard.

"Where's Hawke?"

He set the tray on the table and took a seat. "Taking care of personal business."

"And that is?" Lavine asked, sitting down and starting on the fresh stew.

"It doesn't concern you," he replied curtly.

This guard appeared to be in his early twenties, smaller than the rest of Hawke's men, with a boyish face. Although, he seemed timid. She could tell that beneath the regal uniform and sword, he was naturally shy, and he struggled to meet her gaze—something Hawke would do unflinchingly. He might let something slip, even if he didn't know it.

"You seem like a decent guy," she said, tilting her head slightly. "What's your name?"

He didn't answer right away. His eyes stayed fixed on the polished oak table, his jaw working as if chewing over whether to speak.

Finally, he murmured, "Wesley."

"Wesley," she repeated, testing the name. "Doesn't sound like someone who'd throw in with a man like Hawke."

He glanced up, his expression unreadable. "You don't know him."

"I know he has quite a reputation."

"And that's all it is... a reputation," Wesley said. "He's not a monster."

She leaned in a little. "You say that like you know him personally."

"I do." His voice was steady. "You don't know the first thing about Greyson."

That caught her off guard. "He lets you call him that?"

"He's like a brother to me."

134

"A brother who hands out black eyes?"

His brows drew together. He tilted his head, almost offended. "Greyson didn't do this. He's never laid a hand on me."

That surprised her more than it should have. Hawke didn't strike her as the type to spare anyone, especially not the men who failed him.

"Then who did?" she asked, watching him carefully.

Wesley hesitated. His fingers tapped once against the table's edge, then stopped. "Doesn't matter."

"I think it does."

He shook his head. "You're digging because you think you'll find something to use. I get it. But don't assume everyone around him is there because they're scared."

She studied him for a moment, then leaned back. "Fair enough."

Still, the look in his eyes wasn't fear. It was loyalty. And that would be harder to crack. *Better to have every angle covered,* she reminded herself.

Wesley moved to leave but paused in the doorway and looked back at her. "I know what the world thinks of Greyson. I used to have the same opinion, but he's not who you think he is."

"Then tell me who he is, Wesley."

"If I did, you wouldn't believe me."

She didn't argue. Gavriil always told Lavine that you could lead a horse to water, but you couldn't make it drink. Wesley turned away, his footsteps fading. The door shut behind him with a soft thud, the click of the lock ringing loud in her good ear.

Lavine resumed her pacing by the glass wall, trying to make

135

sense of what she thought she knew and what she was seeing with her own eyes. The High Council, the Academy, and the *history books* had taught her that Hawke and his ancestors were barbaric and merciless. But the man she had met was quite the opposite.

The situation had grown increasingly complicated and confusing. Lavine rubbed her temples, her mind spiraling. The High Council explicitly warned that he was ruthless and wouldn't hesitate to kill on sight. Yet, she was still alive because of him. After spending nearly a week in his company, she was still alive and being well cared for. The growing doubts clawing at her mind were unwelcome. She shook her head, trying to physically dislodge the thoughts from her mind.

What am I doing? I'm supposed to kill him and find out what Mundicar is.

Glancing out into the darkness beyond the glass, she saw the courtyard torches glowing faintly three stories below. A sudden movement caught her eye. She strained to see what had darted across the courtyard below. The figure shifted toward the kitchens, cloaked in black and slipping out of sight.

Certain that fatigue was messing with her vision, Lavine decided she would try, really try, to escape the room tomorrow. The rest she had been getting was slowly restoring her strength and tonight would be the first time she went to bed without feeling utterly drained. She peeled back the thick blankets and let the warmth of the crackling fire, and the soft mattress pull her down into sleep.

17

Greyson

G reyson's skin felt numb. And for once, it wasn't because of the cold. Snowflakes fluttered and swirled around him, settling on his shoulders and hair. He slipped through the rear courtyards as the gentle snowfall blanketed the pathway.

"She tried to *kill* me," he muttered under his breath.

It should have made him angry, but he was tired of being angry. He was tired of the cold, the death of his people, General Eden, and of his bloodline. He wondered what his life might be like if he vanished into the night, journeyed through the mountains to see what lay beyond. Was there a village where no one knew who he was? Could he live a normal life, knowing that Eden would take his place and sweep over the south without hesitation?

I can't abandon the throne.

Greyson weaved through the outer courtyards, slipping out the south gates and onto the dark cobblestone path that led to Hallowmere Street. It was home to high-ranking officers and members of the court—people who could afford to lose a little. He doubted they even noticed anything was missing.

He ducked behind the first grand house on the left and began his quiet work of slipping through kitchens one after another, stowing bread, fruit, cheese, and meat into a burlap sack.

Once his bag was full, Greyson vanished into the cloudy night. His boots hit the pavement without a sound as he cut through a patch of forest, emerging on the far side into the outer city of Beckinsdale. He crept through the dim streets, turned a corner, and approached the first house on his list.

Slipping in through an unlocked window, he moved quickly and quietly, placing the spoils on the table. And one by one, house by house, he delivered the rest, vanishing just as silently as he'd come.

When the last house was stocked, he lingered on the empty street, the quiet pressing in. His thoughts drifted, uninvited, to Beckett. Their last encounter replayed in his mind: the tension, the near scuffle, the way her eyes had sparked with fire and conviction as she held that wooden shard up.

There had been something in that moment. Something more than admiration, more than curiosity. A thrill had taken root, a sharp pulse of excitement at the closeness of danger. At death. At her.

A deep, guttural growl came from a dark alley. Greyson's heart leaped into his throat, his head spinning to find the source, acutely aware that he was unarmed. Yellow eyes glinted as he slowly backed away. A large, mangy dog emerged from the shadows, baring its teeth.

Greyson dared a quick glance to his right and spotted a mineral refinery with high concrete walls within sprinting distance. The dog lunged. Greyson pivoted and sprinted toward the wall, not daring to look back. His bones screamed as he slammed into the concrete and scrambled up the wall. Behind him, the jaws of the beast snapped at his heels.

Once on the other side, Greyson slumped to the ground, gasping for breath and clutching his chest as the rabid dog snarled through a crack in the wall.

It's definitely time to call it a night.

He steadied his breathing, coaxing his heart to return to a normal rhythm. The surge of adrenaline brought back memories of the only other night he had felt this shaken—when his father's rough hands had jostled him awake in the early hours of the morning.

"Get up! Your mother is dead."

Pushing himself back onto his trembling legs, he shook off the memory and turned toward Beckinsdale Castle.

With sunrise only hours away, Greyson slumped onto his settee. Slamming into a concrete wall made unlacing his boots a painful ordeal. His chest ached as he struggled to slide off his cloak, and his back popped as he rolled his shoulders. Before allowing himself to get too comfortable, he stood and lumbered to his bedchamber.

* * *

He carefully removed his shirt and examined himself in the mirror. Seeing no cuts or open wounds in the firelight, he dragged himself across the room and collapsed into bed. The faint crackling of the fire lulled him into the cusp of sleep.

Just as Greyson was slipping into unconsciousness, a muffled scream came from the next room. He bolted upright, scanning the surrounding darkness. He listened, convinced it was just his imagination, when the scream came again, louder and more intense.

"Beckett?" He sprang out of bed, his feet hitting the cold stone floor.

He bounded across the room in a few strides, slipped behind the tapestry near the fireplace, and found the doorknob of a hidden passageway. With a swift push, he opened it and ran through. Emerging from behind the second tapestry, he found Beckett thrashing in her sleep, screaming and clawing at her throat.

"Wake up," Greyson cried as he clambered onto the bed and pried her hands away from her neck. "It's just a nightmare."

She continued to thrash, her panicked eyes open but glazed over. He held fast to her forearms, preventing her from digging her fingernails into her throat.

"Wake up!" he shouted. "You're safe!"

Beckett came to and froze, looking wildly around the room.

"Hey, look at me. Focus on me," Greyson said softly. "Breathe. It was just a nightmare."

Slowly, her trembling subsided as she struggled to control her ragged breaths. Her eyes met his, confused and teetering on the edge of tears.

"They were here," she gasped. "They were here in this room."

Greyson shook his head. "I killed them. They can't hurt you, Beckett."

She took a deep breath, trying to calm herself when her gaze drifted to his bare chest and then to his hands, still wrapped gently around her forearms.

"You can let go now," she whispered.

Greyson, realizing he was still straddling her, let go and shuffled off of the bed.

"I-I'm sorry," he stammered as he awkwardly stepped away. "You were scratching at your neck."

Beckett's gaze remained fixed on him, her eyes darting between his bare chest and the key hanging from his neck. Greyson's face burned with embarrassment as the silence stretched on. He wished for the darkness to swallow him up.

"Your wound," Greyson motioned. "I need to see it."

Beckett pulled the blankets up to her chest. "Why?"

"You may have ripped your stitches." Greyson moved to the other side of the bed and lit a candle. As he did so, Lavine pulled the blankets up further, still baffled.

"Don't make me bring Sterling up here at this hour," he said.

She mulled it over a few seconds more. "Fine." She pushed the blankets down and lifted her shirt, allowing Greyson to pull back the bandages.

He eased himself into a squat beside the bed, his calves protesting with a dull ache as he inspected the stitches lining her side.

"Well?" Beckett's voice was anxious and small.

"It's red and agitated, but the stitches are still in place and there's no bleeding," Greyson said as he carefully reapplied the bandage. "But it is going to scar."

"It wouldn't be my first one," she replied, gesturing to the notch missing from her eyebrow.

"How did you get that?" Greyson asked, his mind racing through a thousand scenarios. A beast, a blade, a bar fight.

"My first day at the Academy," Beckett said with a weak smile. "It was quite an experience."

Greyson, still crouched at her bedside, watched her intently. He waited, eager for her to elaborate, as each of his own scars had its own story.

She chuckled. "I'm not telling you that story, Hawke." Beckett met his gaze, firelight shimmering in her eyes. She smiled warmly, with no trace of her usual smugness or sarcasm. For the moment, she seemed genuinely content, and Greyson felt a flutter of warmth that went beyond mere joy.

"You can call me Greyson," he said softly, his eyes lingering on hers. The awkwardness that had plagued the room had melted away, replaced with something unspoken.

She stared down at him, caught between surprise and confusion.

"How did Crier's Peak get its name?" she asked, eager to change the subject.

Dancing around conversations once again. He stood and crossed his arms. "Have you ever heard the story of the Endless Night?"

Beckett shook her head.

"It goes back as far as my great-grandfather's time as king." Greyson moved to the foot of the bed and leaned against the massive oak column. "There were two villagers who were deeply in love, planning to marry, have children, and grow old together. But the girl's father disapproved of her lover. He boasted about the lover's skill in combat to the king. The country was at war, so the king conscripted the lover into the army, and he was sent to the front lines and killed.

Upon hearing the news, the girl ran into the forest, heartbroken. She cried so long and so hard that her tears blinded her. Lost in the woods, she stumbled upon a snowy peak. Unable to bear life without her lover and enraged at her father, she threw herself from the cliff and died."

"That's very morbid," Beckett whispered.

142

Greyson nodded. "To this day, people throw themselves off of that cliff. No one has ever survived... until you came along."

"I don't know how."

He shrugged. "Blessed by the stars."

A silence followed as they gazed at each other in the dim light. Their breathing seemed to sync, and Greyson felt an unexpected connection with her. He stared deeply into her eyes, searching for something familiar. The faint light of early sunrise seeped into the room.

I've lingered too long.

Greyson turned and walked to the door, not quite eager to leave.

"How did you get all of your scars?" Beckett asked.

So the room isn't as dark as I thought. "I'll share my story if you share yours," he said with a smile, the warmth in his eyes lingering a moment longer before he closed the door behind him.

18

Lavine

L avine woke to a crisp yellow sky beyond the mountains. As she pulled herself out of bed, the bizarre events of the previous night returned to her. The Ice Reapers had invaded her dreams, slicing her open once more. It had felt as real as the first time. And just as terrifying.

Then she saw his face in the darkness, black wisps of hair falling into his eyes. It had calmed her, though she didn't understand why. This man had killed his father to inherit his throne. She could not trust a being who would stoop to that level. But he had come to her in the dead of night. She had been alone one second, and the next, he was there to comfort her.

How did he get here so quickly?

She couldn't recall hearing the door open or shut. Lavine scanned the room.

"There's another way in."

The idea of Hawke coming and going at will disturbed her. How many times had he been in that room without her knowing?

Lavine prowled the room, looking for odd cracks in the wall, anything that indicated a hidden door. Nothing. She searched again, her fingers trailing along the fireplace mantle when her gaze settled on the tapestry hanging from the wall.

It was so obvious she couldn't believe she had missed it. Pulling aside the tapestry, Lavine ran her fingers along the wall and discovered a crack. A faint breeze greeted her flesh. Her pulse quickened. Lavine ran her hand along the opening, its fissure outlining a small door. She pressed against it, and it gave way, revealing a dark passage. She stepped into the cool blackness, walking barefoot over the smooth, cold stone. At the end, she pressed on the wall again but found nothing. Searching further in the dark, she found a doorknob and opened a second door, finding herself behind another wall of fabric.

Lavine peeked out from behind the canvas and found a bedchamber more finely furnished than her own. Plush rugs, a large wooden wardrobe, a grand fireplace, and a polished four-poster bed filled the room. She ventured out, memorizing every detail. The empty weapon display that hung above the mantel confirmed her theory.

This is Hawke's bedchamber.

The discovery gave her hope. There had to be something about Mundicar somewhere in there.

On the opposite side of the room was a single door, and through a pair of doors to the right, she glimpsed a balcony— a potential means of escape. She approached the single door and opened it cautiously, relieved to find it unoccupied. Inside, she discovered Hawke's office, featuring a finely carved oak desk and a set of tall bookshelves.

Now, this is progress.

Another door to her left led into a large antechamber. Lavine entered and ran her hands along the soft settee opposite a grand, ornate fireplace. A large tapestry of a fire dragon hung from the high ceiling. She passed impressive statues, all carved in the likeness of the dragon from the tapestry. At the end of the room was another door. The exit. Lavine rushed forward and turned the doorknob.

Locked, of course.

She returned to the office and circled the desk, rummaging through the drawers. She could hardly contain her surprise when she found her comm in the bottom of the last drawer.

But where are my daggers? Hawke must be carrying them.

She searched for her boots, hoping her vial of vindeca was still tucked inside. While she could manage to climb down from the balcony and escape, she couldn't bear to leave without her blades.

She paused, realizing that escaping now would mean abandoning the mission. Every piece of intel she needed was in this chamber and with Hawke.

This is exactly where I need to be. Maybe killing him isn't the right route.

She considered returning to her chambers with her comm to stash it but quickly dismissed the idea. If he discovered it was missing, he would know she had taken it. Instead, she returned it to the drawer. She glanced out the window, realizing it was just past midday and that Hawke would be back soon with lunch.

Lavine shuffled everything back to its proper place and skittered to Hawke's bedchamber. After one last look around, she slipped behind the tapestry.

19

Greyson

Greyson stared at the text on the pages before him. The ancient language seemed to dance mockingly across the page, each symbol a taunting door he could not pass through. Despite his efforts, the script remained indecipherable. A door with no key. He knew no one who could read this forgotten language, and the frustration of his stalled progress was beginning to boil over.

The words on the page blurred further as he tried to concentrate, but the sound of the study door creaking open interrupted him.

Silas walked in, and the sight of his old friend's return brightened Greyson's mood. The fatigue that had settled on his shoulders in recent days lifted, if only slightly.

"How was your trip?" Greyson asked, abandoning his book.

There was a joy in Silas' smile that Greyson hadn't seen in a long time. "It was wonderful," Silas replied, his eyes sparkling with warmth. "I needed it, thank you. Now, about the King's Banquet…"

Greyson groaned as he leaned back in his chair, the wood

creaking under his weight, ignoring that his behavior was less than dignified. "It's tonight," he said, rubbing his temples in an attempt to alleviate the mounting stress.

"Indeed. All arrangements have been made. All that's left is for you to confirm the seating arrangement."

Silas handed Greyson a parchment. Greyson's gaze skimmed over the neatly written names and their designated positions. Finding that Eden would be seated on his right, his shoulders tensed.

"I know it's tradition to have the Grand General seated next to the king, but is there no way to move him elsewhere?"

"Not without causing a scene."

"Fine." Greyson sighed. "All looks well."

"How are things going with Beckett?" Silas asked, tucking the parchment into his breast pocket.

"We're getting there," Greyson replied, lowering his gaze back to the desk. His cheeks flushed as the memory of his encounter with Beckett from a few nights ago came rushing back. The way her expansive eyes had stared into his. How it had stirred something within him.

Silas' suspicious gaze lingered for a moment, though his expression remained neutral. "I trust you'll find a solution soon."

Greyson nodded, his focus shifting to the scattered half-finished notes and the open book in front of him. He struggled to push aside the lingering thoughts of his recent encounter with Beckett. The pressure of finding answers about Aarth, and the looming feast, only added to the noise in his head. Each time he tried to concentrate, his mind drifted back to Beckett and the way her gentle smile had awoken a sense of joy in his soul.

* * *

The crown sat heavily on Greyson's head, as if it didn't belong there. It felt almost alien, as though it were a burden rather than a symbol of his authority. He made a conscious effort to keep his posture upright, reminding himself not to dip his head too low.

With Silas at his side, Greyson strode to the feast hall with deliberate steps, each footfall echoing off the stone floors. The hall was a grand spectacle, adorned with banners of black and purple that hung from the high walls, their rich colors shimmering in the flickering light of a thousand candles.

As Greyson entered, the lively, festive music that had been filling the room came to an abrupt halt. The hall fell into silence as Greyson was announced, his presence commanding the attention of every guest. Heads bowed in unison. Once the formalities were observed, the music resumed, filling the vast room with a merry melody.

The long oak table, polished to a mirror sheen, was laden with an array of dishes: roasted pheasant, honey-glazed ham, potatoes of every kind, and delicate pastries filled with sweet cream. The air was rich with the aroma of fine wine and the murmur of laughter from the gathered nobles.

At the head of the table, Greyson was seated on a high-backed chair upholstered in deep purple velvet. His crown, studded with blue jewels, gleamed in the candlelight.

Beside him, General Eden sat with a rigid posture. His sharp features were composed with pride and malice. The wound on his head was now unwrapped, the purple bruising now on display for all to see.

"Your Majesty," Eden said, lifting his goblet. "A toast to your health and to many more years of a mighty and prosperous reign."

Greyson forced a polite smile, though it looked more like a grimace, and raised his own wine-filled goblet. "To prosperity," he echoed, though his tone was less than enthusiastic. He took a sip, his eyes drifting over the crowd. The nobles seemed to be enjoying themselves, oblivious to the starving common folk outside.

The amount of people I could feed with this feast.

It made Greyson's stomach churn. How these nobles could stuff themselves silly without a care, while the rest of his people went to bed with pangs of hunger. His grip on the goblet tightened.

"Captain Brandr," Greyson called, his voice cutting through the hum of conversation.

Silas, who had been standing to the side, straightened and approached with a disciplined grace.

"Summon the rest of the Royal Guard."

"As you wish," Silas replied with a nod before he turned on his heel and left.

Eden leaned in, his voice a low murmur. "I trust you're enjoying the feast, Your Majesty?"

"It is a splendid affair," he said, though his gaze was distant. "Silas and Jesper did a marvelous job in the planning."

"Indeed," Eden quipped. "I did want to bring it to your attention that there still are unclaimed lands in the east."

Greyson's eyes narrowed. "And what of it, General?"

"Our military is as strong as ever and we have the means to expand. I've made sure of it."

Greyson resisted the urge to roll his eyes. From his first council meeting after ascending to the throne, Eden had presented seemingly harmless suggestions that advanced his own interests. His proposals consistently favored the nobles rather than the kingdom's welfare. It became clear that Eden's loyalty lay more with his own vision for Navaria than with the overall benefit of the common folk.

Greyson saw through his manipulations. Eden treated him less like a sovereign ruler and more like a tool for his own goals. Aware of these attempts to influence him, Greyson remained resolute in steering Navaria toward a path that truly benefited the kingdom.

Taking a deep breath to mask his growing frustration, Greyson said, "I will consider your recommendation, General. However, we must be mindful of our actions as a kingdom. Expanding our territory is not a decision to be made lightly."

Eden's smirk widened slightly, but he nodded. "Of course, Sire. I trust you will make the best decision for the kingdom." After a long pause, he added, "It's a shame your mother didn't live to see this day. She would have loved it. Josephine was always so..." Eden paused, swirling the contents of his goblet. "... free-spirited. It must have been difficult for your father, knowing that her legs were always wide open."

Greyson's head snapped toward Eden, his eyes flashing with barely contained anger. The heat of fury surged through his veins as he struggled to determine whether he had misheard or if the wine was going to his head. "Excuse me?"

Eden's expression remained indifferent, his tone slightly mocking. "It's merely an observation. I'm sure it was hard for your father to maintain his pride with those rumors swirling. But, as I said, it's a shame she's not around to see the man you've become."

Greyson's fists clenched, his knuckles turning white. "If I

ever hear my mother's name in your mouth again," he said, his voice low and dangerous, "I will spread the contents of your body over the castle grounds."

"My apologies, Sire. I meant no offense. I simply intended to bring comfort to your celebration."

As Eden departed, Greyson's jaw tightened as a wave of rage surged through him. The room seemed to shrink, the walls closed in, and the air itself became traitorous and oppressive. His body trembled with the effort to contain everything.

Where did he get the gall to say such things?

Eden's words struck Greyson in a place he hadn't antic-ipated. The insinuations about his mother stirred deeper doubts within him—about his own sense of worth and the legacy of his bloodline. Was there truth hidden in the venomous words, or was it a cruel attempt to unnerve him?

"Sire, I've notified the rest of the guard..." Silas' gruff voice trailed off as he noticed Greyson's pale face. Concern flickered in his eyes. "Are you alright? Do you feel ill?"

"I'm alright," Greyson replied. "Come, we must greet our guests."

Silas' gaze lingered for a moment longer. He offered a nod and fell into step beside Greyson, ready to support him in navigating the remainder of the evening's festivities.

As they moved through the throng of guests, Greyson kept a watchful eye on Eden as he moved about. Eden, however, never cast so much as a sidelong glance at Greyson.

The general drifted through the crowd with an air of indifference. Each time he passed within view, Greyson's heart seemed to quicken, a knot of unease tightening in his stomach. The mounting anxiety was becoming unbearable as they continued to greet guests, each forced smile and polite exchange adding to his distress.

Just as the ache in Greyson's chest threatened to explode, a flash of mahogany hair caught his eye. The sight stirred a mix of relief amidst the evening's pressure, momentarily easing the tension that had gripped him.

The woman turned, revealing a square face and an upturned nose. It was clear she was not his captured assassin. Yet, the fleeting glimpse of her had conjured Beckett's face in his mind, as vivid as if she were standing right before him. It calmed him, relieving the anxiety that had seized him.

He tried to brush the thought aside, refocusing on the conversation with the lord in front of him. Despite his efforts to remain attentive, his mind drifted back to Beckett, and with it came that inexplicable warmth.

After a break in the conversation, Greyson excused himself and Silas from the lord and made his way back to the table where the rest of his guards had gathered. As he approached, he saw that they were engrossed in lively conversation, laughing over a shared joke, their plates stacked high with food.

"I see you're all having a good time," Greyson said. "I'm happy to see you enjoying the evening."

"You should join us, Sire!" Calix, his cheeks flushed, clapped Greyson on the back. The wine had gone to his head. "There's plenty of food and drink. We've saved a seat for you."

Calix nearly toppled over as he tried to pull out Greyson's chair. Jesper quickly grabbed his arm, steadying him with a chuckle. "Easy there."

"I'm fine," Calix slurred, waving his brother off and reaching for a nearby pitcher.

Jesper, stifling a grin, snatched the pitcher away. "I wouldn't recommend a seventh glass of wine."

Wesley, sitting opposite the commotion, laughed into a slice of pie. "At this rate, we're going to have to carry him to bed."

Greyson took his place at the table, feeling the stress of the evening melt away as he joined in on the lighthearted banter. As he laughed along with his guards, he felt a renewed sense of brotherhood and all thoughts of Eden and his vicious jabs were gone.

20

Lavine

Lavine rummaged through the near empty wardrobe, finding a box. She pulled it closer and gave it a gentle shake, sending a cloud of dust into the air. Lifting the lid, she found black and white glass figures inside. She examined one—a knight on a rearing horse. Another figure resembled a king and queen. At the bottom of the box was a board, checkered with squares.

She brought the old box to the table and spread the checkerboard on it. As she arranged the figures on the squares, she recalled how Gavriil had tried to teach her when she was a child, but she had found it boring and never bothered with it.

"What was it called again?" Lavine wondered aloud.

"Chess." Wesley's voice came from the door.

Lavine jumped. "How are you all so quiet?" She blanched before her attention returned to the board.

"It comes with the job," Wesley said simply, approaching the table. He reached out and rearranged the glass figures to their correct positions. When he finished, Lavine smiled.

"Teach me."

They sat opposite each other at the table. Wesley pointed to each figure, explaining what they were and how they could move on the board.

"White moves first," he said, motioning to her side of the board.

Lavine made her first move, advancing a pawn.

"Good," Wesley said, guiding her through the next move. They traded turns, capturing each other's pieces with quiet focus.

"Checkmate," he announced a moment later, a subtle smile tugging at the corners of his mouth, excitement flickering beneath the surface. He was in his element, and Lavine could feel it. She leaned into the moment, playing along but also unwinding.

Lavine gently knocked her king over.

Wesley chuckled, his shoulders loosening, the tension in his posture easing.

"What's it like in Marella?" he asked, resetting the game pieces and placing the white figures on his side.

"The complete opposite of here," Lavine replied. "It's always sunny, and the air smells of sea salt. The ocean waves cool your feet when you walk on the beach."

Entranced, Wesley's gaze fixed on her as if imagining the scene. "Are there no winters in Marella?"

"No, it gets a little chilly in the winter seasons, but even then, it's not enough to warrant a coat," Lavine explained. She paused, watching him thoughtfully, and realized that Wesley and Hawke had never experienced the warm summer sun on their faces or the sweet scent of wildflowers in a grassy field.

"And the food?"

"Delicious," Lavine continued as the second game began,

each of them taking their turn moving pieces across the board. "Merchants cook on the streets, so the air is always filled with wonderful aromas like lemon, pork, and pepper."

Wesley watched her intently, captivated by her descriptions of Marella.

"Maybe one day I'll take you there," she added.

Wesley shook his head. "Not without Greyson."

"How did you come to serve Hawke?" Lavine asked, her tone shifting, curiosity piqued.

He reached out to move his knight, but his hand faltered. His green eyes, gentle and introspective, locked with hers.

"When Greyson's father still reigned, they took me from a village in the far north when I was fourteen," he began. "I was too young and too weak to serve on the frontlines. The training was brutal, and not only did it nearly kill me, but my fellow soldiers also tried to do the same. Ginger hair," he said, gesturing to his head, "is rare here. I was an obvious punching bag." Wesley paused, his gaze dropping to the chess board. "When it was time for Greyson to choose the last member of his personal guard, he pulled me out of that torment. He made sure I was fed and protected, but he can't save me from everything," Wesley said, his voice tinged with a mix of gratitude and sadness. "He treats me like an equal, like a brother, and I'd give my life for him."

Lavine didn't know what to make of it. It didn't line up with what she thought she knew about Hawke.

Could a monster be kind?

But of course he could be. She'd seen it firsthand as Hawke was the one who had put himself between her and the Ice Reapers. He had offered protection and sanctuary, even though he hadn't known he was shielding his enemy at the time. And when he discovered the truth, he still chose to provide food and refuge. Choosing to be civil even after she nearly drove a wooden spike through his neck.

His behavior clashed with everything the Academy and the High Council had taught her. The dissonance made her uneasy, and a gnawing discomfort settled in her gut, as if the ground beneath her was shifting and she had nothing to steady her.

Game after game of chess followed their conversation, with Wesley winning each time, though Lavine's skills were improving.

"Where did you learn how to play?"

"Greyson taught me," Wesley replied with a twinkle of pride in his eye. The conversations and games continued, and hours slipped by unnoticed.

The door opened, and Hawke walked in before they had a chance to react. "I thought I told you to keep an eye on her?"

Wesley jumped to his feet. "I'm sorry, Your Majesty," he said, his body stiffening into a perfect salute.

"In his defense," Lavine spoke up, rising from her seat at the table, "he was too busy wiping the floor with me."

Wesley's face reddened, and he hunched his shoulders, a sheepish grin tugging at his lips. His gaze softened, a flicker of amusement dancing in his eyes.

Wesley is his soft spot.

"Very well. Get yourself something to eat," Hawke ordered, jerking his head toward the door. Wesley obeyed, throwing a smile Lavine's way before the door closed behind him.

"You're soft on him," Lavine said.

"He's had a difficult life," he replied, his fingers absently fiddling with the chess pieces.

158

"He shouldn't have. Being drafted into the military as a teenager? That's ridiculous."

"I had no hand in that." His head snapped toward her, his face briefly ablaze with anger before returning to a calmer demeanor. Hawke closed his eyes and took a deep breath before continuing. "That was my father's law."

Lavine's pulse quickened at his sudden outburst, fueling her adrenaline. "You're the *king*. Change the law."

The air grew as icy as the weather outside. He stepped closer, his teeth bared. "Do you honestly think I have the final say in this castle? I don't." He was now inches from her face. "Every law must have both the nobles' support and the Navarian military. And take a guess who sits at its head."

"Grand General Eden," she responded.

"Yes, the Wolf of the North, my father's right hand." Hawke's voice was taut with frustration. "If I took the law into my own hands and slaughtered the lot of them, the world would condemn me. And even though I follow Navarian laws, the world has condemned me anyway."

She opened her mouth to retaliate, but he cut her off.

"You dare come here and preach to me about my people when you know nothing of our laws? You came here to kill, not to learn. Your beliefs are confined to the narrow teachings your *academy* has indoctrinated you with!"

Lavine was too stunned to speak. She stood, her mouth in a thin line. Her shaking hands balled into fists, fingernails digging into the flesh of her palm. Staring deep into his eyes. Searching. His words had cut deep. Wanting to argue but not finding a proper defense, she remained silent.

Hawke didn't move, his eyes locked on hers, unwavering, like a challenge, daring her to deny what he'd said. His breath

159

was steady, but the tension in his posture was unmistakable, as though he were ready for a fight, any fight yet, somehow, Lavine could sense the doubt hidden beneath his anger.

Her body felt tight with adrenaline, egging her to dig deeper. But there was something in his gaze that made her pause. She had always been trained to believe in her cause, to see the world in terms of black and white, right and wrong. But standing here now, facing this man, everything felt less certain.

"You're right," she said quietly, her voice almost lost in the vastness of the space between them. "I don't know what it's like to be you, but I do know what it's like to have nothing, to not know when or where your next meal is coming from."

Hawke's brow furrowed, his anger seeming to ebb just a little. Lavine swallowed, her words coming slower now.

"I... I was taught to see this as a war. To fight for the greater good. But I never questioned who that was supposed to be for. I never thought about the lives on the other side. *Your* side."

The air seemed to shift. He didn't immediately respond, and for a long moment, they simply stood there, two people trapped in the same storm, trying to navigate the wreckage of a broken world. Slowly, his expression softened, his gaze flickering to the ground before he looked back up at her.

"I didn't come here to make you feel guilty," he said, his voice less sharp now. "But you need to understand that I'm not my father. I didn't kill him on a whim. There's so much more to it. I just want people to look at me and see *me*, not my father."

Lavine had braced herself for accusations, blame, and anger. But this, this vulnerable crack in his armor, caught her

160

completely off guard.

"I don't know what to do with that information," Lavine admitted, her voice small, almost apologetic.

Hawke met her gaze, his expression softening. "You don't have to do anything. Just understand that some things are far more complicated than they appear and not everything is within reach." His tone had shifted, now carrying something deeper, something almost tender.

For the first time, Lavine saw it. A flicker of rawness, of humanity in his eyes. Maybe she hadn't understood before, but now there was a crack in the walls they'd both carefully built.

21

Lavine

With only sixteen days left to complete her mission, Lavine was growing anxious. A recent fluke in Hawke's schedule had forced her to halt her escapades into the hidden passage, fearing he might catch her. After spending the last few days memorizing his routine, tonight she had a window of opportunity to search Hawke's office. She lurked in the hidden passageway, listening to him pace around his room. He had been pacing all evening.

He does that a lot.

Hawke would leave as soon as midnight struck to attend to his "personal business," giving Lavine a few hours to investigate. His footsteps eventually faded from the room, and she waited a few minutes to ensure he wouldn't return.

Before emerging from her hiding place, Lavine peeked around the tapestry and glanced out the double doors leading to the balcony. A full moon shone through the crisscross of the mountains.

She moved to his bedside table and dug through its contents, finding nothing of interest. She had already given up on finding her daggers knowing Hawke carried them with him. Now, her only concern was locating her boots. Dropping to her knees, she peered under the bed and found only a trunk full of armor and cloaks.

Lavine circled the room, studying the sparse contents. His bedchamber was undecorated. It had a heavy duvet, plush rugs, and other luxurious items one might expect but felt cold and detached. There were no framed photographs, no personal mementos, no signs of life beyond the bare essentials. It felt lonely and impersonal, devoid of character.

As Lavine approached the door to his office, a glint of polished metal caught her eye. She turned to find Hawke's sword mounted on the wall, and her stomach dropped.

He'll come back for it.

Her instincts urged her to leave, but curiosity got the better of her. She moved closer, the firelight gleaming off the sleek white weapon. Lavine wondered how many lives had been claimed by this blade. She lightly brushed her fingers along the elegant hilt, captivated by the exquisite craftsmanship. Without thinking, she gripped the hilt and lifted the sword from its mount. It was lighter than she had expected, though still awkward to wield. She attempted to hold it as Hawke had but found the weapon long and cumbersome. It was nothing like the ease of her daggers.

How could anyone actually fight with something this big?

"You're holding it wrong."

Lavine flinched and dropped the weapon, which clattered loudly on the stone floor. She spun around to see Hawke standing in the doorway. She forced herself to stay calm as he strode toward her, his cloak trailing behind him. He approached, bent down to retrieve the sword, and examined it with a calmness that only heightened her instinct to flee.

If it had been *her* daggers dropped carelessly, she would have been furious and shouted. Instead, he twisted the sword over once more. Frozen in place, she braced herself, certain he would strike her with it. But Hawke carefully gripped the blade and prodded the hilt toward her. Confused, she backed away. Before she could move out of his reach, he extended his arm and grabbed her hand. He placed the hilt of the sword into her grip, his fingers curling around hers.

"When you grip the hilt, your hands need to be spaced correctly," he said, guiding her hand toward the top of the hilt. He then rounded on her, placing a hand on her shoulder and gently nudging her toward the center of the room. Startled by the sudden physical contact, Lavine complied, allowing him to adjust her stance and limbs. Her heart pounded in her ears, her body tense and on edge, bracing for a violent outburst at any moment.

"For a proper stance, you need to align your shoulders with your waist," Hawke instructed, gently pulling her shoulders back. "Your foot stance must be solid." He nudged his boot against her foot, prompting her to adjust. "You don't want to lose balance or be knocked over. Make sure you're holding the sword up and out."

His arms encircled her, bringing with them the scent of smoke and leather as he adjusted her arms from behind. Goosebumps crept up her skin as his warm breath washed the back of her neck. He circled her, inspecting her stance. Lavine hoped he couldn't hear the pounding of her heart.

He circled her again, nodding in satisfaction. "That's a proper stance." He folded his arms, pleased with his work.

Lavine lowered the sword. "It's heavy."

Not once you're used to wielding it." Hawke shook his head. "I've spent years learning proper forms and styles, and years more learning to utilize them in combat."

She handed the sword back to him with a sheepish smile. "I'm sorry."

He tilted his head, his eyes soft and tired. "For what?"

"For dropping it. I shouldn't have touched it in the first place." Lavine crossed her arms, hoping to hide her embarrassment.

His attention shifted to the tapestry on the wall. "You found the passageway."

Her courage returned with the change of subject. "How many times have you been in my room without me knowing?" she asked.

"Not once." He straightened at the accusation.

"You used it a couple nights ago."

"You were in distress," he said, a hint of hurt flashing across his face. "I only used it once, I swear."

"I might believe you," she said, her tone skeptical but softening at his sincerity.

His shoulders relaxed, and the tension seemed to drain from his body. Lavine now noticed the dark circles under his eyes and the weary slump of his shoulders.

Does this man ever sleep?

He walked past her, placing his sword back onto its mantle, his back turned. "Well, Beckett..." he began.

She could take the opportunity to act, but she knew he could easily overpower her. It would be a reckless move, but it was still a possibility. Doubt crept into her subconscious.

I've taken down men much larger than Hawke. Why can't I seem to get an edge over him?

Lavine reminded herself that while most of her targets lacked the skill to fight back, he was different—trained and fierce. The realization stung. She had always prided herself on being the best, yet here was an opponent that could bring her to her knees without breaking a sweat.

"Since you've figured out how to get out of your bedchamber, you're going to be a difficult prisoner to keep." His voice was quiet, and he seemed both overwhelmed and exhausted. Despite his weariness, he could still overpower her in a one-on-one fight.

"What does that mean for me?" Lavine raised an eyebrow. "Are you moving me to an actual cell?"

"You're still wounded. I wouldn't allow it. But…" He paused, his face shifting back to a stone wall. "…if you set foot outside my chambers or yours, you're on your own. If the castle guard or the Grand General spots you, I'll have no choice but to treat you as an actual prisoner. As long as you stay within these walls, you have my protection."

Lavine crossed her arms. "Yeah, I'm not staying here."

"Figures." Hawke sat on the edge of his bed, his gaze drifting to the window through the double doors. Lavine followed his line of sight and noticed that the stars were visible for once. "I have one other offer," he added.

"Which is?"

He was quiet for a few moments. Lavine was about to speak up to remind him she was still there when he looked at her.

"I need your help, Beckett."

"This again?" Lavine threw her hands up. "Hawke, I've already said I'm not telling you why I'm here."

"Call me Greyson," he corrected her as he closed the distance between them. "My people are dying, Beckett. If

I don't get help soon, Navaria will be no more."

"What am I supposed to do about it?"

"More than you think you are capable of. You must plead my case to your council. I'll help you find whatever you're looking for, but first, I need to know what it is."

"Why can't you just speak to them yourself?"

"I've told you about the letters," he said. "I requested to meet with them months ago. And nothing. Not a word."

She had been blindsided yet again. Tallulah claimed Hawke had refused to contact Marella since his ascendancy. The conflicting information churned in her mind, creating a storm of confusion that made her head spin. And then there was the unexpected pull she felt toward him.

Why can't I bring myself to kill this man?

Lavine lifted her head, searching for the feared monster she had been sent to kill. Instead, she found herself drawn to the warmth in his eyes which held a deep, soulful gaze that was hungry for connection.

Because I don't want to, she realized.

The sight of his tousled black hair, the faint trace of something sweet in the air around him, and the intensity with which he looked at her stirred something within her. It made her stomach flutter. She tried to chalk it up to physical attraction, but his actions spoke for him. Despite his burdens, Hawke moved with purpose and hope. The way he behaved as the doting older brother toward his guard. Though there was a deep, bubbling anger in his soul, it only fueled his drive to help his people.

She needed to get a clear picture of the situation. And fast.

"Why did you kill your parents?"

Hawke recoiled as though the question had slapped him.

Darkness flashed in his eyes, only to dissipate just as quickly. He looked away, chewing on the inside of his cheek.

"My mother's death was not my doing," he whispered. He turned his back on her once more and moved to the twin doors, slowly opening them before disappearing onto the balcony.

Lavine hesitated for a moment before she wrapped a blanket around herself, walked through the doors, and found Hawke slouched over the balcony railing.

She moved next to him and looked down, thoughts of escape or assassination forgotten. The night wind tousled his hair, and his tired eyes tracked the stars in the sky.

"What happened?" Lavine asked gently.

"I told you," Hawke sighed. "I'll share my story when you share yours." His gaze met hers, the stars reflecting in his dark eyes.

It couldn't hurt to tell him. What could he possibly do with that information?

"I was orphaned when I was very young," Lavine began. "So young that I don't even remember my parents. I survived by stealing—food, clothes, valuables. Anything I could eat or resell. I was a menace, a talented one at that. Until one day, on Beckett Street, I... picked the wrong pocket. Gavriil, head of the High Council, caught me. He had no children, so he raised me as his own daughter. He gave me the best education possible and got me into the elite Academy." Lavine smiled at the memory. It had been terrifying at the time, but it had paved the way for her success.

"Is that how you got your name?"

Lavine nodded, smiling.

"Where did Harley come from?"

168

"Harley is the name of my first horse."

"And your scar?"

"I got into a fight on my first day at the Academy. I won and kept the scar as a trophy." She pointed to the missing notch in her eyebrow.

"I take it you won't reveal your real name?" he asked.

Lavine laughed, the cold air stinging her lungs. "Absolutely not." She glanced over and noticed a hint of a smile on his face. "Your turn."

Hawke bit the inside of his cheek before taking a deep breath. "My mother was the kindest person I knew, but even as a boy, I knew she was sad. Family life seemed fairly happy, so I'm still not sure what provoked Father into the actions he took. I remember it being a strange night. It changed everything."

"Were you there for it?"

"No," Hawke said. "Just the opposite. I was asleep when my father woke me and told me she had died. And just looking at her body, I knew…" His voice cracked. "That it was my father's doing, and that my mother had suffered. For hours."

"Why did he kill her?"

"Well, that's the real mystery. I don't know. I was only eight and my father forbade me to speak of that night in his presence."

What? Tallulah said he was fourteen. "I thought you were older when that happened?"

"That's the thing about rumors," Hawke said. "They get twisted around by people trying to fit them into their own narratives."

Lavine fought an urge to defend Tallulah, but she couldn't bring herself to argue with him, not while he was emotionally vulnerable. His answers only raised more questions. She decided to press him further. "And your father?"

"That's when my training in the art of swordplay began. He was harsh and unforgiving. I'm not sure if it was anger that drove him or the guilt of killing my mother, but he blamed me."

Lavine struggled to hide her disgust as she leaned on the railing, joining Hawke in his study of the starry night.

"Your scars?" Lavine ventured to ask.

Hawke nodded. "They're all from my father's training. But the silver lining is that his ruthlessness made me a better swordsman. I had to be the best or be killed."

"But you were just a child," Lavine exclaimed, anger rising in her voice. "Why would he risk injuring his heir?"

"That never stopped him. As I grew older, Malric grew crueler and angrier. I learned where all the hidden passageways were and used them to avoid him. Since my mother died, Malric has hated me, and I've never understood why."

"You didn't deserve that, Hawke. None of it."

"The worst part is," Hawke said, taking a steadying breath, "I can remember a time when my father loved me. I remember him telling me grand stories as I sat on his lap in the throne room, carrying me to bed after I fell asleep in his study… he would tell me how proud he was of me."

His voice hitched as he turned his head, hiding his face.

"One day he adored me, and the next, it seemed he wished me dead."

Lavine's heart swelled and something inside her shifted. Once again, the information the Academy had fed her was wrong. She reached out and placed her hand on his forearm.

At her touch, he flinched and backed away. Lavine held his

gaze until he looked away and moved back inside.

Guilt twisted in her stomach. She followed Hawke to his office and found him leaning over a large map on his desk, trying to recompose himself.

"Well?" he asked, changing the subject abruptly. "Will you accept my second offer?"

"You swear you'll help me? No strings attached?"

He turned to her with renewed resolve. "I swear on my sword."

Lavine couldn't argue with that. "I'll agree, but only on one condition."

"Name it."

"I want my gear back. My comm, pack, daggers, boots. All of it."

He stared at her, looking both unsurprised and conflicted. "Deal." Reluctantly, he pulled her weapons from his belt and handed them to her. Then he moved to his desk, rummaged through the drawers, and retrieved her comm and pins. Turning his back to her once more, he trusted her to keep her blades sheathed and fetched her pack and boots from the large wardrobe.

Lavine smiled as she felt the familiar weight of her daggers in her hands. She had missed the twin blades, feeling naked without them. She stuck the pins into her hair, wrapped her comm around her left wrist, and extended her hand as Greyson handed over her black boots.

"I've built quite a reputation," she said, sheathing her blades and crossing her arms. "Aiding me will surely have consequences."

"Oh, I know all about reputations," Greyson said, holding out his hand. "But unlike mine, yours is well earned."

Kace and Ivy would think she had lost her mind. The High Council might accuse her of treason. But she had a weapon to find, and she needed Greyson's help. She extended her arm, and they shook hands.

22

Greyson

The burden Greyson had been carrying lightened as Beckett shook his hand. The tightness and ache in his chest was replaced by a sense of excited wonder and hope. Things just might change for the better.

Beckett rummaged through one of her boots and pulled out a vial of greenish-blue liquid. Greyson's eyes widened in amazement.

"Is that...?" he began, trailing off as the wonder of seeing it washed over him.

"Vindeca," she confirmed.

He stepped toward her, transfixed by the vial. It was the first vessel of healing water in Navaria in at least fifty years, and it had been smuggled in by an enemy.

"I'm ready to be rid of this hole in my side." Beckett uncorked the vial and drank its contents.

"Can I see?" he asked.

She looked at him, puzzled by the odd request. But her expression shifted into understanding. Beckett nodded and lifted the left side of her oversized shirt.

Greyson crouched, watching in amazement as her wound healed before his eyes. The stitches in her skin sizzled and melted away, leaving her skin smooth and unmarred. He had never seen magic like this in his twenty-six years.

This could help so many of my people.

He made a mental note to request the healing water when he contacted Marella.

"This is the first time you've seen vindeca in action, isn't it?" she said.

Greyson nodded solemnly. "We've been without this for generations. Aarth knows we're desperate for relief." He stood and gestured toward the map spread out on his desk. "So, tell me, why were you sent here?"

"When I met up with Theo back in Alain, he told me he had caught wind of a weapon." Beckett moved to examine the map, her hair spilling over her shoulder as she leaned closer. "The High Council sent me to find it."

His mind raced as he scrambled to process her words. He shrugged off his cloak and furs, finding the room too warm. "What kind of weapon?" he asked, his voice barely concealing his unease.

"Theo said it could wipe out entire villages at a time. He called it *Mundicar.*"

Such a weapon existing was almost too much to comprehend. His stomach churned as he grappled with the possibility that this weapon could be real and, what was worse, that the world thought he would unleash it upon them. "But I have no such weapon," he said.

"This changes everything," Beckett replied. Though her eyes were looking at the map, her mind seemed to be elsewhere.

His thoughts descended into a whirlwind. How could

something like this have been created under his nose? How long had this weapon existed? He steadied himself, focusing on the immediate need for clarity. "Tell me *everything* he told you."

"Theo claimed he was turning in a report to his superior when he overheard your Grand General mention 'Mundicar' to another officer."

Greyson's breath caught in his throat. *Of course, Eden was involved.*

The man had defied every decision Greyson had made, so it was no surprise that he might be conspiring against him. General Eden had always been a thorn in his side, challenging his authority at every turn. Greyson's mind raced back to recent meetings and discussions, trying to recall if Eden had let any information slip. He had always suspected that Eden operated on different beliefs, but he had never imagined this level of betrayal. The realization that Eden was behind something this sinister was both alarming and, sadly, not at all surprising.

An idea occurred to him. He moved to his bookshelves and pulled out a fraying piece of parchment. Greyson unfurled it over the map, revealing several rolls detailing the castle's layout, some newer than others.

"Every time Beckinsdale Castle undergoes renovation or repair, new blueprints are created. This is every single record, including the unofficial reports."

He and Beckett poured over the mountain of blueprints, discarding the oldest ones, since they were the least accurate.

Morning light crept into the office, the sun beginning to peek over the mountains and chase the stars away. Pages crinkled as Beckett shuffled through the parchments.

"The dungeon seems like the most likely place to hide a weapon," she said.

"I've been down there recently. There's nothing."

"It still wouldn't hurt to take another look." She continued sifting through the blueprints. "A fresh pair of eyes might help."

Amid the urgency of the situation and mounting panic, Greyson looked around for a sense of comfort. His gaze settled on Beckett, hunched over the desk and absorbed in the most recent castle renovation report. Her eyes were focused with deep concentration, and faint freckles dotted her face like stars. The room felt warmer than usual, and as her head tilted slightly, her hair fell into her face.

"The passageway between our rooms," she said.

"What about it?"

"They're not on any of these blueprints."

Greyson moved to her side. Beckett pointed to their location in the castle. She was correct. He spread out his stack of blueprints across the desk. The same was true for his copies. Digging to the bottom of the stack, he pulled out the oldest blueprint, but once again, there was no record of the secret hall.

"All the other passageways are here," Greyson pointed out. *Why is this specific one missing?*

"Whoever built it wanted it kept a secret," Beckett speculated. "There could be more like it. Wherever Eden is hiding this weapon, it's not recorded on paper."

The door to Greyson's office swung open, and he turned to find Jesper standing in the doorway, panting. "Your M—" Jesper's eyes widened when he saw Beckett, and his hand instinctively moved to his sword. "Sire!"

176

"Stand down, Jesper," Greyson said, stepping into Jesper's line of sight to shield Beckett. "We have an agreement."

Jesper reluctantly obeyed. "Sire, are you sure about this?"

"Trust me, Jesper. Stand down."

He nodded and bowed.

"Very good. Now, what is it you wanted to tell me?"

"Captain Brandr has returned from his scout," Jesper said, still eyeing Beckett. "He's found a new tunnel."

Greyson's stomach lurched. He glanced out the window, only then realizing the sun had fully risen. "Alert the others and have them meet us in the outer courtyards. Brief them on the," he said, glancing back at Beckett, who was still poring over the blueprints, "current situation."

"Yes, Sire!" Jesper said, promptly leaving.

"Oh, wonderful," Beckett rolled her eyes. "I went from 'prisoner' to 'current situation.' I do love promotions."

"I don't have time for sarcasm, Beckett." Greyson grumbled as he moved into his bedchamber.

"You're going to have to make time," she said, following him into the room, "because you're stuck with me."

He crouched beside his raised four-poster bed and pulled out a chest. Digging to the bottom, he retrieved a thick winter coat.

"Here," he said, tossing it to her. "It might be a bit big, but it'll keep you warm."

He moved past her as she slid her arms into the coat sleeves. Greyson made his way to the antechamber door, double-checking his armor. Beckett joined him, having fully made herself comfortable.

"Stay close to me," Greyson said. "Only servants will be awake at this hour, but they're notorious gossips. Walk as if

177

you belong by my side." He opened the door and jerked his head onward. "Ladies first."

Beckett peered over the threshold, her eyes scanning the hall beyond. For a moment, Greyson wondered if she was contemplating making a run for it. She glanced back at him and nodded, then strode confidently into the hallway. Greyson moved alongside her, guiding her past the royal paintings. Out of the corner of his eye, he could see that Beckett held her head high, gliding through the corridor as if she belonged in a castle.

Adaptive.

Servants scurried about, engaged in their early morning dusting. Greyson's stomach was in knots, knowing their eyes and ears were always alert. Even if they appeared too busy to notice a strange girl walking beside him, he couldn't be certain. As they approached a hidden passage, he forced himself to maintain a steady stride, casting another glance at Beckett.

So far, so good.

"Here." Greyson came to a stop, holding back the grand tapestry and gesturing for her to slip behind it. She moved without hesitation. Greyson took a quick glance around before following Beckett into the darkness.

23

Lavine

Lavine dutifully strode alongside Greyson as he marched through the castle and into the courtyards where his guard stood waiting in a semicircle.

"I see you have a shadow," the oldest man said, watching her closely. He was tall, with silver streaks in his black hair and beard, and his deep-set eyes gave him a worn, fatherly look. Despite his age, Lavine sensed there was more strength under his calm demeanor.

"Silas, meet Beckett," Greyson said, gesturing toward Lavine. "Beckett, this is Captain Brandr, the captain of my guard."

"So, you're what all the fuss has been about," Silas said, crossing his arms.

"The one and only," Lavine said with a bow.

"How's the injury?" Calix asked, shifting his weight with a crooked smile.

"All healed," Lavine replied.

After a nod of approval, Greyson explained why Lavine was there, why she was under his protection, and how this alliance would benefit him.

"Alright," Calix replied, not a trace of doubt in his voice. "So what's the plan?"

"We'll investigate the tunnel on our own," Greyson said. "Silas and Wesley will come with me. You and Jesper, guard my door and fill Adelaide in on the situation."

"Yes, Sire!" the men replied in unison. Calix and Jesper quickly moved through the courtyard, heading back to the castle.

The rest of the group moved out of the bustling courtyard and into the surrounding forest. The trees loomed tall and dense, their branches filtering sunlight into patterns on the snowy path.

"Who's Adelaide?" Lavine asked, breaking the silence.

"She's the last member of my personal guard," Greyson replied.

Interesting. "Why haven't I seen her?"

"She's seen by no one. That is her job," Greyson explained.

As they ventured deeper into the forest, the snow grew thicker and more challenging. Walking became difficult. It was like walking through ocean surf with rocks tied to her ankles. Lavine struggled to keep pace with Greyson, each step a losing battle against the deepening snow. Silas led the way, guiding them to the base of the western mountain. There, he motioned to an opening just behind the remnants of a recent avalanche.

"It's just beyond here." Silas pointed ahead.

Silas and Wesley moved in to shift the boulders, heaving them out of their path. Greyson moved in to help, but Silas waved him away and lit a couple of torches, handing one to Greyson.

"Stay close to me," Greyson said, his voice barely more than

180

a whisper.

With torches in hand, the group strode into the dark mouth of the tunnel.

Lavine trailed behind Greyson, with Wesley and Silas on either side. Every step crunched in the semi-darkness. The tunnel was chilly and damp. Water dripped steadily from the cave walls, creating a rhythmic echo.

The cold seeped into Lavine's bones, making her shiver uncontrollably, her teeth chattering. Greyson stopped and glanced back at her, his gaze fixed on her shaking body. Without a word, he handed his torch to Silas and unfastened his cloak. Gently, he draped it around her shoulders, adding a fourth layer to her already amassed clothing. The cloak carried his smoky-sweet scent, enveloping her in a surprising comfort.

As their eyes met, Lavine found herself captivated by the softness in his gaze. He seemed to study her face, memorizing every detail as though he feared he might suddenly go blind.

Silas cleared his throat, drawing their attention. They turned to see him holding out the torch for Greyson, his brow raised. Greyson took the torch from Silas with a nod and continued on in silence, the flickering light casting long shadows as they moved deeper into the tunnel.

What am I doing?

With Hawke towering a full head and shoulders above her, Lavine lifted the hem of the cloak to keep it from dragging on the ground. As she adjusted it, she watched the furs of Greyson's fitted coat shift with each movement. The muscles in his broad shoulders flexed as he adjusted his torch to the right, casting shifting shadows on the walls of the tunnel.

"Do you live on a beach?" Wesley asked, snapping Lavine

out of her thoughts.

"Switchback Beach to be specific," Lavine replied, offering a warm smile, her voice softly echoing in the tunnel. She tightened the cloak around her shoulders. "I could spend hours watching the sun rise over the waves. My favorite moment is when the sun has barely peeked over the horizon. It turns the sky into the most beautiful shades of pink and purple."

Greyson turned his ear toward her. Lavine's heart fluttered at the sight of a wistful smile on his lips.

She continued. "The air is hot and salty, but the breeze and the water cool you off." A thought sprang into her mind. As she walked, she slid her pack off her shoulder and reached into the front pocket, her fingers brushing against familiar objects. She pulled out the pink seashell she had taken from Switchback Beach. It was meant for Gavriil as a parting gift, but she had forgotten. She held it out to Wesley.

His green eyes crinkled in the flickering torchlight. "Is that a seashell?"

Lavine smiled. "It's yours. You can have it."

Wesley took the shell, examining it closely in the torchlight. His face lit up at the delicate, pink hues.

He reminds me of Kace when he was a child.

"Marella sounds like paradise," Wesley whispered to himself.

"If you want paradise," Lavine said with a creeping smile, "try eating a persimmon."

"What is that?"

"A fruit," Lavine explained. "It's sticky sweet, almost like honey. Just thinking about it makes my mouth water."

"I'd like to try that one day."

"I'll make sure you do, Wesley," the words slipped out, but Lavine found she meant them. She had Greyson's attention again. Though his glances were brief, they stirred a warm knot in her stomach.

"You're too trusting, Lavine." Gavriil's chiding voice gnawed in the back of her mind. "What are we looking for?" she asked, silencing her thoughts.

"A legend."

Her eyes darted around the dark, the torchlight revealing dragon scales jutting out of the walls. Realization set in. "You're looking for Aarth."

Greyson nodded solemnly. "From ashes of old and tales untold, the dragon shall rise, mighty and bold. Through fire and storm, they shall forge a bond as fate intertwines their paths beyond—"

"—Together they'll soar, with power unseen, and banish evil into a timeless dream," Lavine finished.

He paused, studying her with renewed interest.

"I know the legends," she continued. "But why are you chasing a doomsday prophecy?"

Greyson looked around at the tunnel walls. "That's not how I interpret it. My kingdom is on the brink of collapse. If Marella refuses to help, perhaps Aarth will."

"This is your backup plan?"

"Other than you," he said, continuing to walk ahead of the party, deeper into the tunnel. "It's all I have, Beckett."

Lavine stopped, her gaze drifting to the ground.

It really is bad if he's resorting to chasing a bedtime story.

She thought about the deal they had struck. Would Tallulah even allow her to pass on Greyson's message? Would she dismiss it? After all, he claimed that they had ignored his pleas for help.

Lavine spotted a drop in the ground just ahead. Without thinking, she dashed forward, panic flooding her veins as Greyson stepped out into the abyss.

"Greyson!" she shouted, her hands clamping down on the collar of his coat as he began to fall. She yanked him backward, sending him tumbling to the ground. His torch fell into the chasm with a faint flicker.

"Dragons above!" Silas cursed, rushing over to pull Greyson to his feet. "Will you pay more attention to your surroundings? I know I've taught you better."

"I've lived this long." Greyson shrugged, a wicked grin hiding under a grimace. "As long as I have you, I'll be okay."

Cocky bastard.

Silas lifted his torch over the wide chasm in the earth. Lavine leaned over the crevasse, peering into the inky blackness.

"How deep do you think it is?" Wesley asked.

"It's a one-way trip, that's for sure," Lavine replied.

Greyson laid a hand on her shoulder, diverting her attention. "You saved me."

"Call us even." Lavine squinted in the dim light of the torch and turned to Silas. "Do you have any more of those?"

Silas lit another torch and handed it to her. She approached the edge of the chasm and threw the torch across. It landed twenty feet ahead, casting light that revealed the continuation of the tunnel. The path stretched on.

"Seems we have a bridge to build," Silas said.

"We'll have to round up the manpower," Greyson said. "It may take a day or two just to gather supplies."

Lavine ran her hand along the wall, feeling the texture of

the sedimentary rock. She withdrew her dagger and drove it into the cave, the crunch echoing through the tunnel.

"Let me take a quick peek first, just to see if it's worth the effort."

Silas frowned. "How are you going to get over there?"

"Simple," Lavine said, removing the cloaks she was wearing and passing them to Greyson.

"What are you doing?" Greyson asked.

Lavine unsheathed her second dagger and twirled both into a reverse grip. She backed into the wall at an angle to give herself enough clearance. She sprang from the wall, sprinted diagonally across the ground, and leaped into the air.

"Beckett!" Greyson cried out.

Lavine soared over the crevasse and drove her daggers into the tunnel walls. Holding herself up, she glanced down into the dark chasm. She pulled her left dagger out and drove it deeper further down the tunnel.

"Are you insane?" Greyson hissed, horrified. "What are you doing?"

"Getting—" she grunted, pulling a dagger from the wall "—a better look," before slamming it back into the rock. She continued the process, shimmying across the chasm, sweat trickling down her temples as she inched closer to the other side.

Finally, she let herself drop onto the pathway, retrieving the still-burning torch. Holding it up, she saw Greyson and his guard watching her uneasily from across the divide.

"I'll see if it leads any further."

"Beckett, I swear, if you're trying to break our agreement—"

"Relax, I'm not running away." Lavine turned and followed the path.

185

She ventured into the darkness, lifting the torch high. Dragon scales, which had been embedded in the tunnel walls, gradually faded from view. As she walked, they disappeared altogether. She wasn't sure how long she'd been walking when the tunnel finally curved.

Am I going crazy, or is the tunnel getting smaller?

No, the walls were definitely closing in on her. The path grew narrower, forcing her to crouch, and eventually led to a crawl space. Lavine felt a sliver of unease but pressed on. Tight spaces she could handle, but the uncertainty of what lay ahead unsettled her. She crawled through the tunnel, fighting to keep her panic at bay as the darkness closed in around her. After several minutes, the tunnel opened into a small room.

Strange, this looks man-made.

At the far end, she saw an old desk. Resting on its surface was a single roll of parchment, tied with fraying twine. Lavine picked up the roll, half expecting it to disintegrate in her hands.

The desk collapsed, the loud crash more disturbing in the small, dark room. Dust erupted into the air, causing Lavine to cough and wave her hand around. She retraced her steps, keeping a wary eye out for the fissure in the ground. When she reached the chasm, Greyson was pacing on the other side.

"I'm back!" Lavine's voice echoed.

Greyson jumped and spun around. "Beckett! I was beginning to worry."

Silas and Wesley, who had been leaning against the cavern wall, joined Greyson.

"I found something." Lavine waved the roll of parchment in the air.

"What is it?" Wesley asked.

"I don't know, but it's very old and looks important." She tucked the parchment into her belt and made her way back across the chasm. The task was more grueling the second time. Sweat trickled down her back, and stray hairs clung to her neck.

Lavine dropped onto solid ground, landing on her backside. Her muscles ached, and her breath came in labored gasps.

"You scared me, Beckett." Greyson extended his gloved hand to her. "Is this how you usually operate?"

Lavine grinned, taking his hand. "Well, the jump was unnecessary, but I'm a sucker for theatrics."

"What is it with you and jumping?" he teased.

Lavine laughed and dusted herself off before answering. "If you don't jump, you'll never fly."

Greyson crossed his arms and looked down at her with a twinkle of admiration. Lavine smiled involuntarily, a surprising surge of happiness fluttering through her. She wiped sweat and dirt from her forehead, handing over the parchment.

24

Lavine

T hankful to be back in the rustic warmth of Beckinsdale Castle, Lavine dropped into a chair as Greyson untied the twine from the parchment, exhausted. It had been nearly two weeks since she had last pushed herself with such a physically grueling task. She fiddled with the comm strapped to her wrist, spinning the outer dial and watching as the compass adjusted itself to true north.

Silas stood by Greyson's side as he carefully spread the ancient parchment across his desk. Greyson's face went pale. Lavine jumped up and rounded the desk to see what he had seen.

"What is it?"

"This," he said, his eyes scanning the parchment, "could reveal Aarth's whereabouts."

Lavine stared at the parchment in disbelief. A magnificently drawn depiction of the Great Drake was centered on it, intricate but faded. The dragon's scales shimmered with an iridescent black. Around the artwork, strange writing was scribed.

"This language," Lavine said, pointing to the ancient text. "I can't read it."

"Because it's been dead for centuries," Greyson replied.

Lavine shifted on her feet, the gears in her mind turning. *Kace.*

Despite his ridiculously stupid behavior, he was insultingly smart when it came to things like this. Graduating with honors in linguistics, he could read dead languages. However, Lavine doubted he'd be willing to help Greyson. Kace and Ivy discovering this strange alliance was guaranteed and it made her nervous. What would they think of her?

On the other hand, there was Gavriil's private library which might hold useful information. But that library was on the other side of the world.

"What now?" Silas asked.

Greyson turned to Lavine, his eyes solemn and steady. "You're my only hope, Beckett."

Lavine's stomach flipped.

"If Marella won't send aid," he continued, swallowing hard, "I don't know what else I can do for my people. My only option would be to seize resources by force, and that's the last thing I want to do."

"The High Council will help. They'll listen to me," Lavine promised. "But first, I need information about this weapon, if it exists. They need to know that you're not a threat."

"Right," Greyson said, turning his attention back to the parchment, rolling and tying it closed. "Silas, I need you to meet with Eden and see what progress he's made with the search—"

Lavine's stomach audibly gurgled. Both men's attention

snapped toward her. "What? I haven't eaten since yesterday!" She folded her arms defensively.

"Have Wesley bring up breakfast," Greyson said.

As soon as they were alone, Lavine approached Greyson's desk, watching him as he studied the parchment. He was hunched over the polished wood, hair falling into his face, his eyes tracking every detail.

"Where do you think he's hidden it?" The low rumble in his whisper made her stomach flip.

Lavine rubbed the back of her neck. "Hmm…"

She made her way to the bedchamber, Greyson's heavy footsteps close behind. Pulling back the tapestry that concealed the secret passageway between her quarters and his, she inspected each section of the old stone. She held her palm over every crack and fissure in the wall. If Greyson used undocumented passageways, then Eden definitely did. The Grand General was cunning. Aside from inadvertently letting information slip while Theo was hidden, he kept his secrets well.

"It'll be in his quarters," she said, the words spilling out as the realization hit. "Whatever Mundicar is, he's keeping it close."

Greyson shifted behind her. "I was afraid of that."

"What are we going to do about him?" Lavine asked. "He can't be in his room when we search it."

"I've assigned a particularly important task for him. Just a little something to keep him preoccupied." A sneer spread across Greyson's face.

"Care to share with the class?"

"He's looking for you, actually."

"You bastard," Lavine laughed. "That poor man is on a wild

goose chase." She knew Greyson was sharp, but she hadn't realized he was also amusingly mischievous. *He'd fit right in with my crew.*

The image of him laughing with her, Kace and Ivy on a beach blanket painted itself in her mind. It was strange how deeply she wanted to see him like that, how much she wished it for him. Since she'd been at the castle, his smiles had been mere apparitions of the real thing.

No, this is Greyson Hawke. He doesn't need your pity.

Greyson shrugged. "I needed him out from under my boots." He turned to place the parchment on his bookshelf. "And you're my top priority right now. He couldn't resist. The real issue is getting past his guard."

"Of course, he has guards stationed outside his door. Can't you just order them away?"

"That would be a bit suspicious, don't you think? We'll have to create a disturbance to get them away from the door."

She leaned against the fireplace as Greyson unbuckled his chest plate, effortlessly removing his armor piece by piece and placing it carefully on a stand in the bedchamber corner. Now in black pants and a snug white shirt, he still seemed to take up the space around him.

"I have something in mind," he said. "And it's worked in the past."

Greyson motioned for her to follow him out into the castle hall. Her pulse quickened. *Finally, some action!*

She trailed him down a massive spiral staircase and through the chilly hallways of Beckinsdale Castle, noting every hall and corridor as she mentally mapped the building.

He carried my dead weight up all of these stairs.

Lavine watched the muscle in Greyson's back shift under

his white shirt. The sight made her body warm and tense, her thoughts drifting to the idea of taking the shirt off. She conjured the memory of him straddling her in bed, his muscular form looming over her in the dark. Biting the inside of her cheek, a rush of heat flooded her body.

Stop it! She scolded herself. *Now's not the time.*

They left the north wing and headed east, navigating through hidden passageways. The castle wasn't particularly tall, with only five floors and the king and queen's quarters at the top, but it was still a sprawling, expansive structure. As they moved, Lavine made mental notes of landmarks, hoping to orient herself if she ever found herself without Greyson.

They came to a long hall lined with suits of armor, with another hallway running perpendicular at the end. Greyson lifted a finger to his lips. They crept down the hall, their reflections shifting on the polished armor. Greyson extended his arm, stopping her from proceeding further, and motioned for her to move against the wall. She obeyed, pressing shoulder to shoulder with him, obscured by a massive marble statue of an ice dragon. Acutely aware of their physical contact, she could smell him—smoke and cinnamon.

"Stay down," he whispered, leaving her in the hiding place. Shoulders back and spine straight, he sauntered down the hall, turning into the right corridor toward what she assumed was the entrance to Eden's chambers.

"Edward, Alphonse," Greyson said, his deep voice sharp and commanding.

"Your Majesty," came two male voices in unison.

"Has the Grand General returned from the city?" Greyson inquired.

"We've heard nothing from him today."

"Find him," Greyson snapped. "I want an update as soon as possible."

"Yes, Your Majesty!" came the response as armor clanged while they marched forward into the left corridor. Minutes ticked by in agonized silence. She wondered if Greyson had forgotten she was there and was searching on his own.

"All clear," he whispered.

Lavine crept down the hall and turned right, rejoining Greyson at a massive arched wooden door. Greyson turned the handle, but Lavine heard the telltale click of a locked door.

"Step aside," she said, motioning him away. She pulled a pin from her hair and crouched by the lock. Greyson shifted, pacing as she fidgeted with the mechanism.

"Relax, this takes time."

"We don't have t—"

Voices came from the next hall, with footsteps drawing nearer.

"Beckett, we need to leave," he urged, his frantic tone making her nervous. The footsteps grew louder, the clinking of armor echoing closer. Her fingers began to shake.

"Almost there."

"*Now,*" he hissed, placing a hand on her shoulder. Racing down the hall, they ducked behind a tapestry just as the newcomers marched in. They slipped into the entrance of a narrow, hidden corridor. In the dim light, his body pressed against hers.

He stared down at her, breathless, their faces inches apart. His chest rose and fell with each breath, and she could feel the subtle tension in his body. Her cheeks flushed as a rush of warmth spread across her skin. Grateful for the single torch that cast a soft glow. Her traitorous stomach fluttered.

193

"That didn't go as planned," she whispered.

He shook his head slowly. "No, it didn't." His eyes drank her in, slowly drifting to her lips.

Feeling the firm contours of his chest against her, she found herself leaning into him. She needed to pull away, but her body seemed unwilling to obey.

"We need to regroup and try again later," he whispered, his eyes dilated and swimming with what seemed like a frustrated desire on the verge of boiling over.

Lavine nodded slowly, her gaze lingering on his lips as she struggled to resist the urge to close the distance between them. Her body ached for his touch, to unleash the flood of these new feelings.

As he leaned in, the world seemed to narrow to just the two of them. Lavine's resolve melted away, and she closed the gap between them. For a moment, everything else disappeared. Lavine felt the warmth of his touch envelop her, her pulse quickening as the kiss deepened.

What would people think?

She pulled away from him and stepped out of the narrow hall, his warmth lingering on her skin.

25

Greyson

For once Greyson's mind was quiet, focusing on one thought. And with it, came two clashing emotions. A soul-lifting joy which was at war with the raging blackness of guilt. He wanted to feel it again. Craved it like the body craved water. But there was a problem that he needed to address.

"I'm sorry if I made you uncomfortable." Greyson whispered in the quiet of his office.

"Not at all," Beckett replied, avoiding his eye. "Getting into tense situations is part of my job."

Her face was a blank mask, but Greyson could see the nervous flicker in her eyes. He moved closer, placing a hand gently on her shoulder and turning her to face him.

"You know that's not what I meant."

Their eyes locked, and just like in the corridor, the charged silence between them seemed to stretch, every heartbeat rattling Greyson's chest.

"If I came on too strong…"

She took a deep breath. "Greyson, I—"

They flinched as Silas stormed in, forcing them to step apart.

"Silas," Greyson said through gritted teeth, a strange tightness in his chest. "You know better than to barge in without knocking."

"My apologies, Sire." Silas glanced between them, his gaze lingering for a moment before he spoke, clearly unhappy. "Marellen scouts have been spotted five miles east of Beckinsdale."

"What?" Greyson and Beckett gaped simultaneously. He wasn't sure if the shock was from the Marellen scouts or from the sheer audacity of this new complication.

Greyson's gaze snapped toward his captain, the sudden rush of frustration and suspicion surging through him like a gust of wind. His fingers clenched around the hilt of his sword, the familiar metal comforting but no match for the growing storm inside him. "Is this your doing?" The words came out sharp, cutting through the stillness of the room like a blade.

Beckett's expression mirrored his own—pale, wide-eyed, and incredulous. "No," she replied, shaking her head quickly. "I have no idea why they're here. This wasn't part of the plan."

Greyson's mind raced, trying to piece together the fragments of information. The air around him felt heavy, and the distant rumble of thunder seemed to echo his rising unease. His thoughts were clouded, but one thing was certain: whatever this was, it had the potential to unravel everything.

"Get the others ready," Greyson commanded, his voice firm but strained. The cold wind whipped through the cracks in the door, tugging at his cloak as he turned toward Silas, who nodded quickly before retreating to carry out the orders. Greyson's mind spun, the ache for a fight gnawing at him.

Why would Marella send scouts now, of all times? The question swirled in his mind, but he shoved it aside, his thoughts scattering like dry leaves in the wind. There was no time for uncertainty.

As he entered his bedchamber, the sight of his gleaming white armor, so familiar and so constant, brought a semblance of calm. The cool metal felt almost like an extension of his own skin as he slid his arms into the plates, the weight grounding him amidst the chaos brewing in his chest. The rhythmic clink of armor settling into place was almost soothing, a ritual he had performed countless times. But even the routine of securing his sword in its sheath couldn't quiet the sense of foreboding that prickled his skin.

Just as he adjusted the final strap, the door creaked open behind him. Becket stood in the doorway, her expression a stone wall.

"I'm going with you," she said, pausing to admire his armor. "I need to know if these scouts really are Marellan and why they're even here."

"Absolutely not," Greyson shot back. The energy between them seemed to shift back to normal. "If anyone realizes who you are, it'll be off with *my* head."

"I can help you. What if it's an ambush? I *know* how the Marellan military moves."

Greyson walked past her and into the office to retrieve his cloak. "No, you're safer here."

"I can handle myself," she argued. "And I'm not giving you a say. I'm coming with you."

Greyson stopped. "Are you sure you can stand on your own? These men are skilled warriors." He didn't doubt her expertise, he could see her skill in her movements and cleverness. Harley

Becket had a reputation for a reason, and he could see the fire in her eyes.

"*Yes.*"

"What makes you so sure? The Ice Reapers nearly killed you at Crier's Peak."

Beckett planted herself in front of him. "I was alone and outnumbered fourteen to one. That's the only reason they managed to get the better of me."

Bravery was always admirable, but stubbornness?

Greyson whipped out his sword and swung at her. Beckett dove to his left, somersaulting past him. He spun around, and she was already back on her feet, daggers drawn. He hadn't seen her unsheathe them.

He swung his sword, but Beckett caught his downward strike with her twin blades. The force of his swing sent her into a crouch. With their weapons locked, Greyson stared down into her hazelnut eyes through the crossed blades, the frost magic in the sword's metal beginning to mist and freeze the steel of her daggers. She shoved his sword upward and kicked his armored chest, sending him back a few paces.

"Very well," Greyson said, satisfied with her reaction. "You can come."

* * *

Greyson marched into the stables, Beckett struggling to keep pace with his long strides. The air was cold and heavy with the smell of musky fur and manure. He glanced down at Beckett, her eyes were wide at the sight of the great elks lining the stalls.

At the end of the stables, his guards, clad in full armor, were preparing their mounts. Silas, holding Jericho's reins, looked up and straightened. "Your Majesty."

Greyson took the reins and stroked Jericho's neck.

"He's beautiful," Beckett said, curious but keeping her distance.

"He won't bite." Greyson motioned her over.

She seemed reluctant, clenching her fists at her side. "I don't want to spook him."

"Jericho is a trained war mount. It would take an act of Aarth to spook him."

After a moment, Beckett approached, her fists unclenching. She reached out tentatively to pet Jericho, her fingers brushing gently against his snout. The elk nuzzled her hand, and a small smile crept onto her face. Seeing her eyes light up, a warm surge of joy filled Greyson, and he wished for her to be by his side always.

After catching Silas' eye, he cleared his throat, summoning the attention of his guard. Wesley and the twins fell in line next to Silas.

"As you know, Marellan scouts have been spotted not far from here. We're going to intercept them and find out why they're here. Until we've identified their intentions, we are not to engage." Greyson's voice cut through the air, firm and commanding, but even as he spoke, a pit of unease settled in his stomach.

"Yes, Sire!" The answer came swiftly from Silas and the others. Jesper's gaze darted to Beckett, still standing just behind Greyson's shoulder.

Calix stepped forward, his boots crunching against the gravel as he approached his mount, adjusting the saddle with deliberate motions. "How will we gain the upper hand if they engage us?"

"Simple," Silas answered without hesitation. "We'll circle around the forest and catch them from behind. They won't see us coming."

Greyson nodded as he considered the plan. But Jesper wasn't finished.

"Are you sure it's a good idea to bring her?" He shifted uneasily on his feet, his eyes flicking over to Beckett again. "She's one of *them*. This could be a trap."

The air seemed to thicken. The group was silent, all eyes now on Greyson. Jesper's distrust of her wasn't new, his suspicion of outsiders had always been a core aspect of him, but the question was still sharp.

"She's none of your concern," Greyson said, his tone clipped, almost a command.

Jesper didn't flinch, but his posture tightened like a bow-string ready to snap. But he knew better than to challenge Greyson openly.

Though Beckett stood further back, Greyson could feel her gaze on him. She wasn't one of them, not really, but there was no denying the growing bond between them. Her reasons for being here, her presence at his side, always felt like a puzzle he wasn't entirely sure he wanted to solve.

Greyson gave a curt nod. "Enough talk. Stay sharp. We can't afford any missteps, not now. Saddle up!"

And with that, the conversation was over, though the tension still lingered. Jesper's distrust would remain, and Greyson knew that. It was a shadow that would persist, especially with Beckett in their midst. But for now, they had a mission. And that was all that mattered.

In the commotion, Beckett looked around the stables.

"Which one is mine?"

"You're not getting one," Greyson said, stepping into the stirrup and swinging himself into the saddle with one fluid motion. "You're riding with me."

"What? No!" She placed her hands on her hips. "I know how to ride."

"And?" He extended his gloved hand toward her. "Step into the stirrup and I'll pull you up."

"I might as well sit in your lap. No, I want my own mount."

"Take my hand, Beckett."

"No," she shot back.

"*Take my hand*. I will not ask you again."

After a few beats of stubborn silence, she huffed. "Fine." And placed her boot into the stirrup. Greyson hoisted her up into the saddle with him. As she gripped the saddle's pommel, her back pressed against his armored chest.

"Well, this is just perfect," she grumbled.

Leaning in, Greyson let her hair graze his cheek, his voice a low and teasing whisper. "You know, I don't recall you protesting this much the last time our bodies were pressed together."

Her body stiffened and her breath hitch. Her grip tightened on the pommel, and though her voice had a sarcastic bite, there was something softer hidden beneath it.

"Oh, really?" Becket retorted. "Maybe I was just better at hiding my discomfort then."

Greyson couldn't help but smile, sensing that beneath her facade there was more than just annoyance. He wrapped his arms around her waist, his hands finding the reins. With a gentle nudge, he spurred Jericho into motion, and the party surged out of the stables. The sudden acceleration pressed

Beckett more firmly against his chest. As they rode, he caught the faint, unfamiliar sweetness of her hair.

The scent of the persimmons she spoke of?

With his guard riding alongside him, Greyson galloped into the sparse pines. They soon approached a campsite with a recently extinguished fire, faint smoke still smoldering.

"We're close," he said, signaling the twins. "There's a clearing about three miles ahead. Flank them and force them through it. We'll double back and wait for them in the tree line. Wait for Jesper's signal before moving in to arrest them. Remember, we kill only in self-defense and as a last resort."

"Yes, Sire," the twins replied in unison.

They spurred their mounts into motion once more, Calix and Jesper heading deeper into the woods while Greyson led Wesley and Silas back around. The race through the pines was swift.

He extended a hand to help Beckett down, noticing her face was pink and windburned. He grimaced, realizing he'd forgotten that she might need a face shield against the biting air. "Don't leave my side," he instructed.

They tethered their mounts to a fallen tree and hiked the remaining quarter mile. As they neared the edge of the clearing, Greyson scanned the landscape, assessing how to block potential escape routes. The hooting of an owl echoed through the air. Jesper's signal.

Greyson pulled Beckett into a crouch behind a cluster of boulders peppered with snow. Silas and Wesley took cover behind thick brush further from the tree line. Footsteps crunched in the snow ahead, drawing closer to their position.

"Stay down unless I give the word."

"But—" Beckett protested.

"They might recognize you," Greyson interrupted. "I can't take that chance."

She pursed her lips. "Okay." Her finger grazed the hilt of her dagger.

Greyson met Silas' gaze through the brush, exchanging a brief nod before standing in unison and advancing into the clearing.

Emerging from the trees was a large group of armored men, their faces obscured by their great helms. Greyson's hackles raised.

These are no scouts.

Vultures were one thing, but an entire company of trained soldiers posed a greater challenge... and raised more questions. As they drew nearer, Greyson squared his shoulders and tightened his grip on his sword. He counted thirty soldiers. The company came to a halt upon seeing him, drawing their swords and cocking their revolvers.

"Settle down," Greyson commanded, keeping his voice steady. "Why have you come?"

"With respect, Your Majesty," the captain replied, a tuft of green and black fur protruding from his helmet, "our business is our own."

"You are in Navaria and in the presence of its king," Greyson declared. Hoofbeats echoed in the distance as soldiers in the rear shifted. "Your business is now mine."

Calix and Jesper charged into the fray, swords drawn. They reigned their mounts to a halt, effectively blocking the soldiers' escape routes. Despite the twins' arrival, they were still outnumbered—five Marellans for each of them. The odds weren't hopeless, but Greyson's stomach twisted with unease. He debated calling Beckett out to talk them down, but that would jeopardize her mission.

"I think not," the captain said through gritted teeth, frustrated at being forced to fight on two fronts. "I was given clear instructions."

"Which were?" Greyson pressed.

The captain gave no answer. With every passing second, the tension mounted as men on both sides grew increasingly anxious and restless. Dread coiled in Greyson's chest.

This is going to end badly. "I give you one last chance," Greyson called out, his voice firm. "We can discuss this matter, whatever it may be."

"I'd rather see your head on a pike," the captain spat back.

"If you will not cooperate," Greyson continued, "you leave me with two options. My men and I kill you," he paused, letting the weight of his words hang in the air, "or you can surrender, and I will spare your life. I assure you, my dungeons are quite lavish."

The captain laughed, his voice muffled beneath his helmet. "But you misunderstand our intentions." He drew his sword, the blade gleaming with the reflection of the snow.

Greyson unsheathed his own sword, with Silas and Wesley following suit. "This is your last chance," he warned. "Surrender now, or—"

A shot rang out.

Greyson deflected the bullet with a swing of his sword. He and his guard surged forward, meeting the intruders in combat. He clashed with the captain, his blade clashing against the enemy's. Two more soldiers joined the fray, and despite Greyson's skill, their numbers pushed him deeper into the clearing, separating him from his guard.

The soldiers took turns swinging at him. Greyson knew

better than to call for help, knowing his guard was likely engaged in their own battles.

He feigned fatigue, and a soldier moved in to take the advantage. Greyson stepped back and thrust his sword through a gap in the soldier's armor, slicing into his side. The man cried out as he fell, ice quickly spreading through his limbs.

Blades continued to clang around him as the captain circled the fight, waiting for a chance to strike. Greyson managed to run his sword through another soldier, but two more quickly took his place.

They circled him like wolves. He kept his blade up, ready to block. Two soldiers advanced, swinging their weapons. He parried one blow and deflected the second. The captain pressed forward with a thrust. Greyson dodged, but the blade grazed his cheekbone, sending a fiery pain radiating through his skull and into his chest. It felt as if his bones, muscles, and sinews might burst into flames.

He grunted in agony, forcing himself to stay upright. His vision blurred from the burning sensation, and his body quaked with pain. A third soldier moved in, his revolver aimed at Greyson's head. He stared down the barrel of the gun.

This is it. This is how I die.

Out of the corner of his eye, Beckett sprinted into the fray, blood splattered across her face. She leaped onto the back of the revolver-wielding soldier, yanking his head back before slashing his throat.

Another shot rang through the air. Greyson swung his sword at the captain, but the blow missed as he stumbled backward. His sword struck a pine tree, becoming lodged in the wood, ice quickly forming. As he struggled to free it, a soldier advanced on him.

Beckett darted in, intercepting the Marellan soldier before he could reach Greyson. She threw her daggers up just in time to block the soldier's sword, the impact forcing her into Greyson. Straining, she pressed her weight against him and pushed the soldier backward. With a swift kick, her boot slammed into the man's chest plate, sending him sprawling.

Wrenching his sword free from the pine, he said, "Thanks," his vision still a blur and sweat rolling down his temples.

"I've got your back," Becket replied.

Greyson adjusted his stance as the captain charged again. He moved to block, but the captain feigned right and struck. The sword bounced off Greyson's chest plate. He barely had time to recover as the assault continued. Their swords collided, dazzling blue sparks flying with each strike.

Gritting his teeth as the burning pain in his face spread to his chest and limbs, Greyson's hands trembled, struggling to keep his sword steady.

The captain closed in, swinging wildly. Greyson's sword was knocked from his hands, and an armored body slammed into him, driving him to the ground. He loomed over Greyson, raising his sword to strike Greyson's neck.

A dagger whizzed through the air, piercing the visor of the captain's helmet. Greyson rolled aside as the sword came crashing down, slicing into the frozen ground and melting the snow around it. The captain's body slumped to the ground.

As Greyson pushed himself to his feet, Beckett sprinted through the trees with a soldier close behind her. Greyson retrieved his sword from the snow, positioning himself as Beckett led the soldier toward him. Anticipating her plan, he readied his blade with a firm, wide stance. Beckett bounded through the snow, maintaining a safe lead. As she approached Greyson's position, he forced himself to ignore the burning pain in his face. She dove through his legs as he thrust his blade forward. The soldier, unable to stop in time, impaled himself on Greyson's sword. Another body collapsed to the ground, his flesh icing over.

"You really should start wearing a helmet," Beckett said, eyeing his bloody cheek.

"You're one to talk," Greyson quipped as he wiped the blood from his face. "You're wearing no armor."

Beckett shook her head as she crouched to retrieve her dagger from the corpse.

"HELP!" Calix cried out, a horrific fear in his voice. "Greyson, help!"

Ignoring his aching, burning body, Greyson sprang into action, his heart pounding in his ears. He burst into the clearing to find Calix slumped over Jesper's body. Blood soaking into the surrounding snow. The last Marellan soldier loomed over them, raising his bloody sword, preparing to strike again.

Greyson jumped in front of the twins, raising his own blade to block the strike. He stepped forward, shoving the soldier back with relentless aggression. The soldier retaliated with a swing, but Greyson pivoted and drove his elbow into the man's face. The soldier's sword flew from his grip as he doubled over. Calix's muffled sobs filled the air and time seemed to slow. Fury surged through Greyson's veins.

"I surrender!" the man cried, scurrying away with blood dripping from his nose and lip. Greyson stalked forward, his grip tightening on the hilt of his weapon.

"Stand down," came Beckett's voice, garbled and distant. "He's surrendering."

With his free hand, Greyson grabbed the man by the coat, yanked him to his feet, and slammed him against the nearest pine.

"Greyson, stop!"

The burning pain in his skin, the sight of Jesper's lifeless body, the death of his mother, the abuse from his father, the world's indifference—it all came flooding into his veins. The helplessness and anger burned deep in his soul. Greyson lifted his blade to the man's throat, his hand steady.

"Spare me, *please!*" the man pleaded, eyes wide with fear.

"*Greyson!*"

He sliced the blade into the soldier's throat, blood spattering Greyson's face. He watched the life drain from the man's eyes and wrenched his sword free. The man's body crumpled to the ground.

Greyson turned, his ears ringing. Beckett stood a few feet away, her mouth moving, but her words were lost to him. He stumbled over to Jesper's body, dropping his sword into the snow. Jesper's head rested in his brother's lap, his eyes open and unseeing. Tears streamed down Calix's face. Greyson placed a gentle hand on his shoulder.

"He was protecting me," Calix said, choking on a sob.

Greyson brushed Jesper's hair from his face. He allowed Calix to take in his brother's face a moment longer, then gently closed Jesper's eyes.

A heaviness settled in the air and in Greyson's chest. He found it difficult to think. This was a new pain.

He instructed Wesley to retrieve their mounts and listened to Calix's pained cries echoing through the forest, tearing at

Greyson's soul.

26

Lavine

L avine watched in horror as Greyson slit the man's throat in a blind fury. The brutality of the act chilled her to the bone. *This is the monster they warned me about.*

Greyson had slaughtered a surrendering man, without mercy or hesitation. The sheer violence of it left her shaken, but she knew she was just as guilty. She had taken lives—innocent lives. It was part of the job: leave no witnesses. But these troops were on her side.

Despite her own sins, she felt it difficult to come to terms with what she had just witnessed, even as Greyson comforted Calix in his grief.

Was this the real Greyson Hawke?

Memories of the past two weeks with him resurfaced: shared meals, their intimate kiss in the dark corridor, the frantic way he came to comfort her when nightmares plagued her sleep. Fighting by his side had been exhilarating. Greyson anticipated her moves as if they had fought together a thousand times before. But the high of combat was waning and her mind was now clear.

She watched as Greyson heaved Jesper's body onto Silas' mount, where Silas cradled it gently. Calix, still in tears, rode closely behind. They continued on without her, their focus on the somber ride, seemingly forgetting their prisoner.

Jesper's elk trotted into the thicket, grunting and attempting to follow the others. Lavine reached out and grabbed its reins. "Shh," she murmured, stroking its neck. "It's okay."

She was about to step into the stirrup when a faint groan came from behind. She whipped around, scanning the thicket strewn with bodies, and spotted movement just beyond the tree line. After tying the elk to a tree, she drew her daggers and crept forward.

As she passed the dozen or so bodies, she checked for signs of life. Nearing the tree line, she spotted a soldier crawling deeper into the forest, his body creating a path in the snow.

"Don't move if you know what's good for you," Lavine whispered.

The soldier froze. "Please," he whispered, "I was only following orders."

"Take your helmet off, *now*."

He obeyed and raised his shaking hands to the back of his head.

Lavine reached out, grabbing his arm and rolling him onto his back. When their eyes met, the blood drained from her face.

"Andy?"

"Beckett?" he gasped, his eyes widening.

Lavine stared down at Andy, her mouth agape. Memories of their shared history at school rushed back: late night study halls, sparring sessions, and their shared love of food. Andy had been meant to join her squad, but he had a change of heart and decided to join the Marellan military.

"Andy? How...?" Her voice faltered, the words tasting bitter in her mouth.

His blue eyes were wide with fear, confusion, and surprisingly, relief. The vulnerability in his gaze cut deeper than any blade could. "What are you doing here?" His voice trembled slightly, a soft crack that betrayed his usually calm exterior.

She took a moment to steady herself, before she forced the words out. "The council sent me here almost a month ago. Why did they send you?"

He shifted uneasily, his jaw tightening as he moved in the snow. "The council is getting impatient. They thought your team had been delayed and couldn't finish the job. They—"

"What do you mean we couldn't finish the job?" Lavine snapped, cutting him off. Her breath caught again, her chest tightening as she turned her gaze to the ground. She needed to get control of herself, but this was different. This wasn't just about military orders. It was about a betrayal, about a shift in everything she thought she believed in. "They sent you *here...* before I even had a chance to finish what I started?" Her words came out sharper than she intended, the hurt and frustration laced with something darker.

Andy looked away. "There were reports that you may have been killed. We couldn't afford to wait any longer. So, they decided to send us in."

Lavine's heart sank, the admission like a dagger, twisting slowly inside her. She'd always believed in the council, in their vision, in their promises. Their ideals had been her compass. But now, the words sounded hollow, like a betrayal she couldn't quite place. *"Impatient."* It was a small word, but one that felt like a slap to the face.

"Impatient?!" The word escaped her lips before she could stop it, bitter and cruel. "That's it, then? The council's impatience outweighs everything? The mission, my work, everything I've done here, means nothing?"

"Beckett, you must understand the bigger picture. The stakes are too high, and the Navarian threat..." He trailed off, seeing the way her expression shifted.

But Lavine was no longer listening. The veil she'd worn for so long, the one that kept her tethered to her loyalty and belief in the council, was fraying. She couldn't ignore the gnawing sensation, the deepening suspicion in her gut. She wanted to cling to the hope that she could trust the council, that they had a grand vision that would bring stability, peace, but how much of that was truth and how much was manipulation?

A flicker of doubt wormed its way into her thoughts, and it was suffocating. *Had they used me? Used all of us?* "There has to be an explanation." Lavine's voice was taut, but her words seemed to hang in the air, fragile as glass. She wasn't sure if she was trying to convince Andy or herself.

"Why are you fighting side by side with Hawke?" he asked.

"He is not who people say he is," Lavine said, her voice a little softer now.

She reached out a hand, pulling Andy to his feet, her grip firm but unsteady, like she was trying to steady herself as much as him.

"It's... complicated."

"How so?" He looked at her as though she'd just thrown him a riddle instead of an explanation. "He just slaughtered my entire company."

Lavine's heart tightened at the bluntness of the words, but

she couldn't afford to back down. "In all fairness," she said carefully, "your company marched into his country and tried to kill him."

Andy grimaced. "Yeah, I guess you're right. But you haven't answered my question. Why are *you* fighting with him?"

Lavine hesitated, glancing around the forest as if the trees might offer some guidance. Betraying her oaths could lead to execution, and her chances of becoming a council member would be zero. Yet, the lives of millions hung in the balance. Andy could deliver a message that could change everything.

"Listen to me," Lavine said after a pause, her voice low and urgent. "I have sworn many oaths to secrecy, so what I am about to tell you is not to be told to *anyone* except for Regent Carter of Kallistar."

Andy's brow furrowed. "Ivy's father? Why not the High Council?"

"I can't say just yet, but they're hiding something. Something bad is about to happen, and Regent Carter is the only one I can trust with this," Lavine said.

Though confused, Andy nodded, his brow furrowing with concern. "So what's the message?"

Lavine hesitated, her gaze flickering across his face. "That's all? You're going to help me?"

Andy's mouth twitched, a wry smile pulling at his lips. "Well, with my captain and comrades dead, I doubt anyone will be looking for me anytime soon. And… call it a favor for an old friend."

Lavine's chest tightened at the mention of his fallen comrades, but there was no time for sentiment now. She knew this was her only chance. "The High Council sent me here to kill Hawke under the pretense that he was about to unleash a weapon on the world. But it's not him." She took a steadying breath, the truth heavy on her tongue. "It's the Grand General."

Andy's eyes widened slightly, but he didn't interrupt. Lavine continued, her words coming faster now, desperate to get everything out before it was too late. "And you want me to tell Regent Carter?" he asked.

"Yes," Lavine said. "And that I may need his help... with *absolute* secrecy."

Andy was quiet for a long moment, his eyes searching hers. He exhaled slowly, his breath a puff in the cold air. "Alright," he finally said, nodding once. "I'll make sure he gets the message, but only because I know it's serious... you've never confided in me before."

With a final glance, Andy turned and began to move through the dense forest, his figure quickly swallowed by the snow-covered trees. She watched him go, her thoughts racing as the sound of his footsteps faded into the silence.

Lavine took a deep breath, her chest heavy with what she had just set in motion. But there was no room for doubt, no time to second-guess herself. She had made her choice.

Now, all she could do was wait. And hope.

Greyson needs to know.

She unfastened Jesper's mount from the tree and climbed up. With a click of her teeth, the elk bounded forward. The cold wind bit at her face as she thought of the trials ahead. The sun was high in the sky, though blocked by an overcast gray. Lavine pushed forward, and Beckinsdale Castle's spires grew larger as she galloped.

Funny how I'm willingly racing back to my prison.

Lavine slipped unnoticed into the servant corridors, making her way back to the royal chambers. She burst into Greyson's antechamber and moved toward his balcony. Afternoon had arrived, and the day's events felt surreal. So much blood. The way Greyson had lost all control. Seeing him like that was hair-raising.

Would I have done the same if that had been Kace, Ivy, or Gavriil?

Something sharp bit at her wrist. She looked down to find her comm shattered, barely hanging on. She could try to fix it, but who she really needed was Ivy.

Hours had slipped past as Lavine recounted the day's events, when she heard Greyson entering his office. She moved into the room and found him slumped in a chair, rummaging through his desk.

Lavine's heart ached at the sight of him, his usual strut, filled with bravado, had vanished. The pangs of sorrow dampened the edge in her voice, for his loss and Calix's, yet her mind struggled to move past the brutality she had witnessed.

"What are you doing?" she asked.

He lifted his head, his eyes on her face, but not quite seeing. "Planning a burning ceremony," he said, his expression and tone defeated.

Lavine hesitated, the two different emotions swirling inside of her grappling for dominance. On the verge of informing him of Andy's assistance, the memory of Greyson's violent act flashed across her vision.

"What were you thinking?" she asked from a safe distance. "You slaughtered that man while he was surrendering."

"He was about to kill an unarmed man, to kill Calix—one of *my* men."

"You're so quick to resort to violence." Lavine threw her

216

arms out, her irritation bubbling to the surface. "This is why the High Council refuses to answer your requests for help! You're too brutal."

"What I did was for a fallen friend, a brother. Don't act as though your hands are clean."

Lavine's heart pounded in her chest, each beat crashing against her ribs like a tidal wave. It seemed that the direness to find Mundicar had taken a backseat to Jesper's death. Combined with the reality of losing the job she had fought years to be considered for, the lack of sleep and rising ache for Greyson was swelling into a raging storm. The pressure was relentless.

"At least I'm not blinded by anger," she said, her voice sharper than she intended.

"Anger? No," he said. "But loyalty? Absolutely."

"Excuse me?"

"You blindly worship your High Council, never questioning their motives. My father, and his father before him, ruled Navaria through deceit and cruelty. And just like them, your leadership is tainted by corruption."

"I don't *worship* them! If anyone is corrupt, it's you and your damn monarchy."

Greyson stood abruptly. "Don't act so high and mighty. Corruption is an ancient song. When politicians get too comfortable, they fester and become power-hungry," he said, rounding his desk and stalking closer. "I would know."

Lavine stood firm, her hands tensing, ready to reach for her daggers if he lashed out.

"The High Council is no exception," Greyson continued. "You're too blinded by loyalty to see it!"

"I was a child living on the streets!" Lavine shouted. "They gave me an education, a career. I owe them my life and loyalty."

"Apply that logic to me."

"What?"

"I saved your skin at Crier's Peak. Are you going to pledge your life to me?"

He paused, letting his words hang in the air. Her mind raced, the sting of his challenge leaving her without a counter attack.

"I thought not. It's called human decency."

"You're one to talk about decency!" Lavine exploded, stepping forward, unafraid if he met her with physical force. "At least Marella tries to help those in need."

Greyson closed the distance between them, his voice dropping to a whisper. "Tell me, then... Why did they leave a child to live on the streets for years?" His eyes locked onto hers, their faces inches apart. She felt his breath on her skin, the sensation bringing her back to their kiss in the corridor. "Why have they allowed my people to starve? Do you not find it odd that your High Council never reached out when I ascended the throne? They knew we were suffering."

"They said you were planning an invasion. That you had killed your own father because you were a power-hungry bastard."

"If you still believe that, then you're blinder than I thought. You're no better than the rest of the world." His eyes pooled with hurt and anger, a storm of emotions rolling over a restless sea. "You're part of the reason my people starve."

The words cut through her like knives, a bitter sting forming in the pit of her stomach. "You're a monster and a fearmonger," Lavine hissed, still hurt by his accusations. "You

don't care about others. You're as heartless as your father."
Back off, Lavine.

But she pressed on, driven by the need to know who the real Greyson was, regardless of whether he might lash out at her.

"Do you think I rejoice in seeing my people drop dead from starvation?" His voice rose, filled with raw emotion. "Do you think I revel in watching them cower before me?"

No.

"Do you honestly believe I would go through the trouble of murdering my father if I didn't think it was best for the world?" Greyson snarled in her face.

Lavine's hand instinctively moved to the handle of her dagger. Greyson's gaze dropped to her hand, anger flashing across his face.

"Do it, then," he challenged. "It's what you came for."

"I—"

Greyson grabbed her wrist, forcing her hand and the dagger up to his neck. Lavine tried to pull away, but his grip was unyielding. He pressed the dagger firmly against his skin.

"Do it," he seethed. "It'd be easy. The world seems to think it would be better off this way."

Her heart pounded in her ears, anger giving way to a mounting panic. The pressure from his grip forced the dagger deeper into his skin, and a droplet of blood began to well up. He didn't seem to notice.

"*Do it!*"

"NO!" Lavine shouted back.

He released her wrist, the dagger leaving a superficial wound. They stood in silence as she sheathed the weapon, her breath coming in ragged gasps. His warm breath still lingered on her face. Lavine stared at him, her resolve wavering but not breaking. In his eyes, she saw her own reflection—hurt, grief, desperation. As his familiar scent washed over her, a lump formed in her throat. She took a hesitant step back, her heart heavy.

"I don't think the High Council will speak to you."

He turned and stormed toward his desk and, with a violent sweep, sent everything crashing to the floor. Ink bottles shattered, and papers fluttered like snow in the wind.

"I have to steal from my court and nobles to feed the commoners," he muttered, still bent over the desk, his head hung low. "I shouldn't have to go to such extremes."

Though filled with heartache and empathy, she needed to cut this tie that held her down. Time was running out, and she had a weapon to find. With Greyson too agitated to assist, she had to make a decision. It would hurt, but it had to be done.

"I'm completing my mission alone from here on out."

Greyson turned his head, his expression paling. He looked more hurt than angry. "We had a deal, Beckett."

Lavine swallowed, praying to the stars that her voice wouldn't crack and that he wouldn't see the tears pooling in her eyes. "I can't keep dancing with you, Hawke. Goodbye." She strode across the office and opened the door.

"Please," his voice hitched. "Don't leave..."

Lavine kept her back turned, tears welling up in her eyes. *Tallulah was right. I never should have crossed paths with him.*

She stepped across the threshold and didn't look back.

* * *

Tears streamed down Lavine's face as she slipped into the hidden passageway. She had been holding back for far too long, trying to hold herself together while everything around her fell apart. The futility of her mission, the fear of failure, and the relentless exhaustion were all merging into a singular, overwhelming flood.

"Don't let them see your tears, they won't take you seriously."

Tallulah had scolded her on graduation day. Lavine had been overjoyed that the Academy had given her a chance at a career. That had been the last time she cried—until today.

She wiped her cheeks and pressed forward into the corridor, struggling to recall the path Greyson had shown her. Running out of time, she needed something substantial to present to the High Council. The dark corridors felt menacing without Greyson by her side.

Greyson.

What she had said to him twisted her stomach into knots. He was grieving the loss of a friend—hurt, alone, exhausted, and desperate. Yet, she had shut him down and shut him out. The guilt was like salt in an open wound.

I broke our agreement. I called him a monster, but what does that make me?

Lavine reached a junction in the passageway and couldn't remember whether to go left, right, or forward. Her chest tightened and a lump formed in her throat. She sank to her knees and let the tears flow freely. Her shoulders trembled as years of repressed emotions poured out.

She thought back to her childhood, starving and hopeless, until Kace had come into her life. Suddenly, she had a little brother to care for, and the stakes were much higher for a nine-year-old orphan. Lavine had embraced the role of big sister and made sure they survived.

She was certain that even if Gavriil hadn't been in a position to adopt two children, he still would have taken them in. Similarly, if Greyson had known who she was at Crier's Peak, he would have protected her regardless.

And Greyson had no one to protect him.

Lavine had never imagined that her life would be so drastically changed at that cliff. She had never been so close to death, nor had she ever been so terrified by it. She had been running all her life. Running through the streets, for her life. Running, running, running. She was exhausted.

She steadied her breath and replayed her argument with Greyson in her mind. She realized how much of what he had said was true, how she had believed what she was told rather than what she saw. He hadn't been malicious, he was simply trying to open her eyes, to make her see reality.

He wanted to avenge a friend, and I condemned him for actions I would have taken as well.

She had seen the hurt in his face—how her words had stolen the breath from his lungs. Her chest felt heavy, as if someone had stabbed her heart with a knife and kept twisting it.

Lavine pictured his face in her mind's eye, his high cheekbones, stubble, his dark misty eyes, his loose black hair. The way he smelled like cinnamon and smoke. There was only one way forward. Whether she wanted to admit it or not, she wanted Greyson by her side.

In that moment, Lavine realized that her anger wasn't about the immediate situation. It was about all the pent-up frustration, the barrier that the world had put between her and Greyson, and the pressure of trying to keep everything together despite the overwhelming odds. Her emotions were raw and exposed, and she was tired of pretending.

Lavine stood and wiped the tears from her face and made her way back to Greyson's chambers.

27

Greyson

Greyson lowered Jesper's body onto a canvas stretcher and kneeled beside Calix on the floor. It was strange to see when a soul was no longer attached to its body, how a man could be alive and vivacious one moment and glassy-eyed the next. Jesper's abdomen was stained with rusty, dried blood, some of which had transferred to Calix. Tears dripped from Calix's eyes onto his brother's cheek as he combed Jesper's hair to the side, just as he had always worn it.

Greyson glanced over at Calix, knowing that each time Calix looked in a mirror, he would see his brother and be overcome with grief all over again. Greyson's heart ached for him.

Sterling kneeled and gently patted Jesper's face with a wet cloth, wiping away sweat, dirt, and the dried blood from under his nose and in the corners of his mouth. She left the room, giving them privacy in their final moments with Jesper's body. Greyson untied Jesper's sword from his belt and handed it to Silas to hold until the burning ceremony.

Adelaide and Wesley quietly entered the room. Adelaide stayed close to the wall, her hood up and her face hidden. Wesley dropped to the floor opposite Calix and Greyson, laying a hand on Jesper's arm as tears welled in his eyes.

Calix's breathing grew strained and uneven. Greyson moved closer and placed a hand on his shoulder. Calix tensed.

"It's okay to let go," Greyson whispered.

After a few seconds of bated breath, Calix doubled over, burying his face in Jesper's shoulder. His guttural, desperate sobs shattered the silence of the medical wing, the sound piercing Greyson's heart and overshadowing the faint burning sensation in his own face. His hair stood on end as he kept a firm yet gentle grip on Calix's shoulder.

Greyson looked around the room, taking in the scene. Jesper's body, Calix shaking with sorrow, Wesley's silent tears. He caught Silas' mournful gaze and noticed Adelaide a few paces away. He wanted to absorb this moment fully, to commit it to memory. He needed this pain to help ground him.

Malric had not allowed Greyson to mourn his mother. He hadn't mourned when the life left his father's lungs. Greyson was determined to allow Calix to grieve freely.

There was a knock at the door. A castle guard poked his head in and informed them that the burning chamber and procession were ready. Greyson reluctantly stood, placing a hand on Calix's shoulder. "I'll be right back," he said.

"Will this be a private ceremony, Your Majesty?" the guard asked as he walked alongside Greyson down the hall.

"Yes."

The guard nodded and dismissed himself, leaving Greyson alone as he made his way to his bedchambers. His limbs felt numb as he meandered through the castle halls. He tried to recall his last conversation with Jesper, but a sour taste rose in his throat when nothing came to mind. Jesper had been an outlier in his guard—cautious and cynical, the opposite of his brother. While Calix wore his feelings on his sleeve, Jesper kept his emotions hidden. But it was clear that he held a fierce love for his twin brother.

Greyson knew Calix would be okay. He'd be wounded for a long time, but he would heal. However, if it had been Calix who had died, Greyson doubted Jesper would have recovered.

"Your Majesty?" a feminine voice called. "Are you alright?"

He turned to see a servant dusting portraits in the hall. Her timid eyes were full of worry and a hint of curiosity. He realized he had been standing at his chamber door, staring blankly at the polished wood, though he wasn't sure how long he had been there alone. Greyson gave a quick nod. "As you were." He opened the door and crossed the threshold into his chambers.

The antechamber was still and uncomfortably quiet. The furniture was dreary, the lifeless steel dragon mosaics staring unfeelingly from the walls. Jesper's death seemed to have drained the joy from the castle.

Greyson moved into his bedchamber, sensing something else was missing, as though he had lost his shadow. He approached the mounted crown on the grand fireplace, its dark blue stones twinkling in the gentle firelight. Taking the crown in hand, he sat on the edge of the bed and examined the silver ringlet. Its intricate arches were dotted with small bits of dragon metal that mimicked sapphires. Thankfully, Navarian traditions required little adornment of the crown; after all, they were a nation of warriors, and a crown would only be a nuisance.

He examined himself in the mirror, never looking at his face. Not bothering to clean the blood from his face or clothes. The wound on his cheekbone was still swollen, with dried blood sealing it shut. Some of it had dripped onto his fur coat. Matted with dirt and dried blood, he was certain it was composed of a mixture of his own, Jesper's, and Marellians'. The faint light from the fireplace glinted off his armor, which was also speckled red.

In the mirror's reflection, something seemed to move behind him, the tapestry shifting slightly.

"Beckett?" he called, turning around expectantly.

He watched intently, hoping she would step out from behind the tapestry. He pulled it aside, finding nothing but the hidden door. His shoulders sagged. A log shifted in the hearth, causing the fire to brighten and cast dancing shadows around the room.

A trick of the light.

If Beckett really did set out on her own, he'd be left with little hope. What he'd have to do to get help for his people, he didn't know. But now was not the time to think that far ahead. It was time to honor Jesper's death. Too much time had already passed. He straightened his chest plate and made his way into the lower levels of Beckinsdale.

A somber air had settled over the castle. The corridors were cleared for mourning. A burning that required the king's presence was rare—it was a high honor. To earn such a tribute, one must have died valiantly or alongside the king. Greyson wished it wasn't one of his own.

The door to the medical wing opened, and four bearers entered. The scene was as Greyson had left it. Calix's puffy eyes looked up, exhausted from crying. His gaze settled on the four men who would carry his brother to the pyre, and fresh tears began to well up and fall. Wesley stepped back to allow the bearers to lift the stretcher.

Calix tightened his grip on his brother, and Greyson crouched opposite him.

"I'm not ready," Calix whispered, his wet eyes pleading.

"And you never will be, and that's okay," Greyson said gently. "He'll always be with you, Calix."

With some coaxing, Silas ushered Calix away from the stretcher and placed Jesper's sword on his body before moving aside as the bearers lifted the body, each corner resting on a shoulder.

Greyson opened the door and led the procession to the burning chamber. Calix followed closely behind, with Silas and Wesley bringing up the rear.

"Keep an eye out for her," Greyson whispered as he passed Adelaide. She nodded and slipped into the hall, disappearing. Greyson continued the somber march into the lower levels of the castle, his head held high, and his heart twisted and aching.

28

Lavine

L avine had taken a wrong turn somewhere. Frustrated, she opened another door, hoping it would lead to the king's wing.

If it wasn't so damn dark in these halls.

Lavine peeked out from what felt like the tenth tapestry in an hour and found a familiar foyer. It was strangely empty and unnerving. She was about to retreat into the corridor when the sound of footsteps grew closer. She waited in her hiding spot, expecting castle guards. Instead, a familiar mess of black hair came into view, still in furs spattered with blood. Greyson wore a crown adorned with dark stones set into a silver base. The stones, which seemed to shift between blue and black, matched the color of his eyes. The crown transformed him from a frightened prince into a sovereign king.

His guard followed quietly behind, heads hanging. Jesper's body was carried by castle guards. After a few seconds, Lavine darted out from her hiding place and crept into the hall, keeping a safe distance and ducking behind any cover she

229

could find as she trailed the procession.

Greyson led his men into a hall to the right. Lavine soon followed, keeping out of sight. As the procession descended deeper toward the dungeons, Lavine began to recognize the portraits and statues lining the walls. The halls were becoming familiar. When she rounded the next corner, she came to a stop.

A familiar hooded figure stood at the far end of the empty hall, an arrow nocked and ready on the bowstring. Lavine's hand twitched toward the dagger at her belt but remained frozen. It'd be no use. The arrow would pierce her chest before she could draw her blade.

"Adelaide," Lavine whispered, slowly lifting her arm to show her open palm. "I'm just looking for Greyson."

"You broke a promise," Adelaide said harshly. "He trusted you."

"I know," Lavine replied, her shoulders sagging as Greyson's hurt expression crossed her mind. "That was a mistake. But I'm back to honor my word."

Adelaide held her bow steady for a few moments longer before shifting slightly and loosing an arrow. It flew past Lavine, the fletching grazing her cheek and stirring a tuft of her hair. Lavine glanced behind her to see the arrow embedded in the creases of the stone wall.

"Betray him again, and I will put an arrow in your skull," Adelaide warned.

Lavine nodded, knowing the threat was made with full intent. Adelaide lowered her bow and turned, her back facing Lavine.

"Follow me," Adelaide ordered, darting down the hall.

Lavine dashed after her, taking note of the torches and

portraits lining the walls as they raced through the deserted corridors. Adelaide's cloak brushed Lavine's shin as she made a sharp right into a short hall that led to a plain wooden door. They slipped into what appeared to be a storage closet.

The dim room, illuminated by a single candelabra, was packed with dusty crates. The low ceiling made the space feel cramped. Adelaide moved two of the stacked crates and pushed them aside to reveal a slender hole in the wall.

Lavine followed Adelaide into the crevasse, shimmying into unknown darkness. A jagged piece of stone scraped her back as the tunnel twisted unexpectedly. Lavine gritted her teeth but made no sound. The tunnel seemed endless, and she wondered just how deep the burning chamber was. From what she recalled from her classes at the Academy, Navarian soldiers burned their dead rather than sending them out to sea. She imagined the smell would be awful.

A light flickered ten yards ahead. Relief washed over Lavine since the darkness had begun to strain her eyesight.

Before they emerged, Adelaide halted. "Stay down," she whispered, crouching and inching toward the light. The tunnel opened onto a crude ledge overlooking a room below. Lavine followed her lead and peeked over the ledge.

The vast room was arranged with two lines of ceremonial chairs, fanning out from a raised stage. To the left of the stage stood a pyre, while a blacksmith waited by a massive forge on the right. A strange scent tainted the air: it was strong, almost like paint.

Kerosene. They must've soaked the wood in it.

A door creaked open. Below, a crowned Greyson led the procession into the burning chamber. Greyson and Calix ascended the steps and mounted the stage, followed by the bearers carrying Jesper, his sword resting on his body. Wesley and Silas, holding a torch, remained below the stage, standing at attention. They were still in their bloody furs and armor.

"Why don't they change into mourning clothes?" Lavine whispered.

"You will always mourn the dead," Adelaide said. "There's no need to change clothes to signify that loss."

The four guards placed the body on the unlit pyre and took their positions behind the blacksmith.

"Jesper Torryn Bellmore perished in battle alongside his king," Greyson began. "He fell honorably while protecting his brother and fellow soldiers." His voice filled the empty cavern with prestige and calm, enunciating clearly, though there were few to witness the speech. Overseeing this ceremony brought all his kingly traits to the surface. Lavine marveled at his deep, commanding voice that also carried warmth and reassurance.

Greyson reached out with both arms and carefully lifted Jesper's sword, holding it with both ends resting on his open palms. He turned to face Calix.

"Calix Weylin Bellmore, the last surviving kin of the fallen. How do you wish to honor your brother's memory?" He approached slowly, extending the sword toward Calix.

Calix stood silent, deep in thought. "Rings, Your Majesty. Five plain rings."

"It shall be done," Greyson said, placing the sword gently into Calix's hands.

Calix examined the sword, turning it over and running his thumb along the grip. He moved across the stage, dazed, and bowed as he presented the sword to the blacksmith who returned the gesture and began smelting the blade.

Calix rejoined Greyson in front of the pyre as Silas ascended the platform, handing the torch to Greyson before returning to his place on the ground floor. Greyson leaned in and whispered something to Calix who then bowed his head and nodded slowly. His hand trembled as he reached for the torch. Together, they approached the pyre.

"May your soul fly high among the stars and your spirit soar with the Great Dragons above," Greyson said.

"Rest well, brother," Calix said shakily as he lit the pyre. The flames spread quickly, the soaked wood exploding with heat. Lavine could feel the warmth on her cheeks.

Greyson dismissed the four guards, and they exited the burning chamber. As the door closed, Greyson beckoned Silas and Wesley onto the stage. They obeyed, taking their places beside Calix. The four of them stood, staring into the fire. Calix broke down, collapsing to the floor and wrapping himself in his arms, sobbing.

Greyson kneeled and wrapped his arm around Calix's shoulders, pulling him into a side hug. Wesley moved to his right, embracing him, while Silas squatted behind them, placing a hand on Calix's other shoulder.

The whole scene made Lavine's eyes water. It was awful yet heartwarming in a strange way, seeing these men come together to comfort each other and seeing how attentive Greyson was to them. Greyson shifted, easing the weight from one leg to the other. He turned to check the door and glanced upward before his gaze snapped back to Lavine. Their eyes locked. His gaze, though tinged with unshed tears, lit up with a bittersweet joy. It was a sorrowful happiness amid the shadows of grief.

"Thank you," he mouthed.

Her breath hitched. It didn't matter that her and Greyson

were from opposing sides. It didn't matter that that they had hurt each other. In the face of everything, Greyson was still moving forward. Despite how the world treated him, he still wanted to save it. Despite the awful things she had said to him, he still wanted her around.

The High Council, the Academy, the world—they're all wrong.

29

Greyson

The chilly night air nipped at Greyson's face, and the fur of his coat shifted in the breeze. He closed his eyes and breathed in the fresh scent of his clothes, allowing the crisp air to clear away the lingering odors of kerosene and burnt flesh. As the clouds parted, the sun began to rise behind the mountains.

It had been four months since his father's death, and he felt no closer to bringing relief to his people. His eyelids were heavy. Blinking away dizziness and fatigue, he struggled to recall the last time he had enjoyed a full night's rest. After months of sneaking food out of the castle, keeping Eden oblivious and occupied, begging for help from the south, fending off assassins, and now coping with the death of one of his own, it was all wearing him down.

He couldn't concentrate, but his mind refused to shut down. Leaning against the balcony guardrail, the absence of his armor made his body feel unusually light. He dropped his head into his hands as a wave of exhaustion hit him.

I can't keep up with all this for much longer.

A rustling sound came from within the room. Light, nearly silent footsteps approached.

"Did you get what you came for?" he asked, his voice sounding muffled to his own ears.

"No," Beckett replied. "I won't be able to manage on my own."

He lifted his head. She stood next to him on the chilly balcony, staring intently.

"You need a proper night's sleep."

"I look that egregious, huh?" He rubbed his eyes. "I'll rest when my people aren't starving. What's our next move?"

"Not so fast." She leaned against the railing. "If we're to work together, I need to understand you and why you do things the way that you do," she paused, her brown eyes searching his face. "Since you brought me here, I've been nothing but confused. The world tells an entirely different story about you, and what I'm seeing doesn't match. I need you to set the record straight."

"Where do I even start?"

"From the beginning."

Greyson sighed and gazed at the rising sun. He closed his eyes, thinking back.

"My father changed the night my mother died. Everything did. He forbade me to cry, to grieve, or even to speak of her after that. The painting in the royal hall is the only piece of her that I have left."

"I've seen her portrait. I see a lot of her in you."

Greyson smiled, steadying himself and taking a deep breath. "After that, my father trained me relentlessly. At first, it seemed like he just wanted an excuse to beat me senseless. There were nights when I'd be so bloody and bruised that my bathwater turned red. Those early years are a bit foggy. I do remember being confused by the sudden shift in his behavior. I did everything I could to get the father I had known back. I quickly mastered sparring and was able to hold my own against him, but that only seemed to make him angrier. By fourteen, I was an expert and had the entire castle memorized—every hall, secret passageway, and servants' corridor. I learned to be a shadow. All the while, Eden was in my ear, pitting me against him and further poisoning my view of my father. I chose the members of my personal guard at eighteen, and from there, my father doubled down on the training."

He glanced over. Beckett was listening, her brows furrowed and her eyes intense and focused, with flecks of green in her irises. His attention was drawn to the missing notch in her eyebrow. The scar was deeper than he had initially noticed.

"A few months after I turned twenty-six, I realized he was getting weaker with age. Even so, he remained a fierce fighter. But I felt like I was finally on even ground with him."

"What made you snap?" she asked, not unkindly.

He gazed out at the horizon, too exhausted to resist the memories. He let them wash over him.

The torchlight flickered gently in the royal hall, casting shadows across the portrait of his family. Greyson stared at his mother, her black curls framing her heart-shaped face. He wondered what she would be like if she were still alive. Would his father have remained the man he once knew, rather than turning into a cruel stranger? Would he still feel so alone? Would his back still be marred with scars and bruises?

A door creaked open, and footsteps thumped toward him. I

237

shouldn't be here, *he thought, pressing himself against the wall to remain unnoticed.*

"We'll simply conscript Haverlisle's youth into our army and put them on the front lines." Malric's voice echoed down the hallway. "They'll make excellent shields."

"I couldn't have come up with a better plan, Sire." Eden replied.

The hair on the back of Greyson's neck stood on end. He glanced to the right. If he stayed close to the wall, he could slip down the next corridor unnoticed. He moved to leave, his hackles raised but caught his father's eye. A flash of anger sparked in the ice-blue gaze.

"Have you nothing better to do than lurk in hallways?"

Greyson remained silent, his gaze fixed on his mother's portrait, urging his heart to slow as his father dismissed Eden.

A hand landed on his shoulder, and he was shoved back against the wall, the edge of a wooden picture frame digging into his shoulder blade.

"I asked you a question."

"I-I was just leaving," Greyson stammered, avoiding his father's gaze.

"Staring won't bring your whore mother back." Malric hissed. "Man up if you know what's good for you."

Greyson's heart raced, his temples pulsing. He clenched his fists, palms sweaty, nails digging into his flesh.

"You're useless and pathetic, just like her." Malric shoved Greyson harder. "I should've killed both of you that night."

The blood drained from Greyson's face. He ceased struggling and lifted his head, meeting his father's gaze for the first time in years. The silver crown glittered atop his father's head. All these years, Greyson had wondered why his mother had been killed and why he had been denied the chance to attend the Burning. Greyson knew that Malric had killed his mother but he never knew why. Now, he no longer cared about the why. In this moment, all that mattered was vengeance.

Eighteen years of anger and hatred that had festered deep in his soul erupted into his veins. He shoved back against Malric, glaring fiercely at his father. Malric stumbled back, his crown askew, shrinking slightly as Greyson loomed over him. Greyson now noticed the deep wrinkles on Malric's face, his graying hair, and his body frailer than it had been years ago. He realized that he was now much taller and sturdier than his father and possessed the advantage of youth. Something in Greyson's mind shifted into place.

"I'd say using kidnapped children as shields is much more pathetic." Blinded by rage, Greyson drew his sword, advancing like a wolf cornering its prey. "I'd say beating your son half to death is pathetic."

Malric drew his sword just in time to block Greyson's initial attack. He stepped sideways, backing down the hall as his son pursued. Greyson swung again, rage fueling every thrust of the blade. Again and again, he struck at his father. Malric continued to retreat, barely managing to block the swift strikes.

In a split second of reprieve, Malric countered. Greyson pivoted, narrowly dodging as the blade slashed past his side. He thrust his weapon again, but Greyson intercepted the strike, maneuvering it from Malric's grip. The sword clattered to the stone floor. Malric flinched as his back hit the wall, trapped with nowhere to go.

"If you're going to kill me," Malric gasped, eyeing Greyson's sword, "make it quick."

Greyson chuckled darkly, a wicked, toothy grin spreading across his face. He hoped Malric was horrified by the monster he had created.

"You don't deserve the honor of dying by the blade."

He lunged forward, dropping his sword and gripping his father's tunic in both fists. He slammed Malric into the wall, causing the crown to fall from his head. He gasped as Greyson's fist connected with his jaw. Blood splattered onto Greyson's knuckles and face.

Malric managed a quick blow, and tears sprang to Greyson's eyes as his nose cracked, warm blood dripping down his lip. Furious, Greyson slammed his head into Malric's. His father collapsed to the floor with a cry of pain. Greyson's boot slammed into his temple, drawing out another anguished cry.

Greyson straddled Malric's back, took a fistful of his father's hair, and slammed his face into the floor. Again and again, the sound of flesh hitting stone ringing in the corridor. Bone cracking. Blood seeping into the stone and rugs. A long, primal scream. At what point Malric's body went limp, Greyson didn't know.

He came back to himself, realizing that the scream he'd heard had come from his own mouth. Greyson stopped moving, his arms aching. His grip loosened on his father's hair, now a bloody, matted mess. Malric's head was bent at an unnatural angle. His face was smashed beyond recognition. The floor was now soaked in his blood.

Greyson stood, trembling as the adrenaline drained from his body. Leaning against the wall, he stared down at his father's corpse, feeling a weight lift from his shoulders. He retrieved his sword and returned it to its sheath. A glimmer of light caught his attention. He glanced over to see the crown resting on a rug further down the hall. Slowly, he approached and picked it up, studying the glittering metal. Placing the crown atop his head, he strode down the hall with his shoulders straight and head held high. He hadn't realized how caged he had been until he broke free.

GREYSON

"Great dragons above." Beckett placed a hand over her mouth, eyes wide as she hung on his every word.

"You have every right to think me a monster," Greyson said.

She stared at him for a long moment. He worried she might find his actions too gruesome and walk away a second time. The thought filled his heart with sadness, but she needed to know.

"You did what you needed to," she said. "And I think, deep down, you do believe that your mother's death was your fault."

A lump formed in Greyson's throat. He swallowed, his mouth dry, and cleared his throat but said nothing.

"You said you didn't know how your mother died," Beckett continued after a few minutes of silence.

"I wasn't ready to share that part of myself," he admitted shyly.

"Weren't you afraid of the consequences of killing the king?"

"There are no repercussions. I displayed superiority in strength, so no one objected, not even Eden. I'm not the first prince to kill his father for the Navarian throne. My great-grandfather did the same to get an early start on bringing war to Beckinsdale. That's why the castle is partially made of glass."

"Honestly, that's my favorite part of Beckinsdale."

A half-smile crossed his face as a slight breeze whipped through the balcony, disheveling his hair. She seemed more understanding than he had anticipated. Of course, the gore didn't faze her—she was an assassin, after all.

"So why not just kill Eden as well? He seems to be much more of a hindrance than a help."

"Killing my father was one thing, I had leeway with the laws of royal succession. But killing someone outside my

241

bloodline, like the Grand General. That would be pushing it too far. There would be riots."

"Who would riot, though? No one seems to like him."

"It doesn't matter." Greyson sighed. "I'm trying to get what I want while staying within the bounds of the law."

"Sounds like you need to overhaul your entire governing system."

Greyson nodded absently. It wasn't a bad idea, but how he would manage to reform a government that was centuries old seemed impossible to contemplate in his state of exhaustion. "I don't know where to go from here," he admitted.

"How about you start with some sleep?" Her voice softened.

The gentleness in her voice made his shoulders sag. So many burdens had fogged his mind, leaving his body numb. It was as if her voice gave him permission to feel himself. Beckett held her hand out to him. Slowly, he reached out to her, placing his hand in hers.

"Come with me." Beckett said.

30

Lavine

Lavine led him inside to his oversized fourposter bed. She pulled back the blankets and gestured for him to sit. He complied, removing his boots.

"I'll wake you tonight," Lavine whispered.

Greyson fell asleep the instant his head hit the pillows. His deep, rhythmic breathing soon filled the room. Lavine studied him as he slept. His hair was tousled and his mouth slightly parted, his cheek pressed against the pillow. In that moment, he looked like any man you'd meet on the street. He had run himself ragged, nearly collapsing from exhaustion. She had slowly begun to understand his past. His drowsiness had lowered his defenses, allowing her a glimpse into his soul.

Lavine reached over to brush a few stray hairs from Greyson's face. *He looks so normal, like someone I'd meet on a beach in Marella.*

Greyson had weaseled his way into her heart, tugging at her soul like the moon pulled the tides. Lavine's eyes traced his face as she grasped for ways to explain all of this to Kace, Ivy, and the council.

From the paintings she had seen, Greyson didn't look much like his father. His face was strong and angular, framed by a well-kept beard, while Malric's was rounder, pudgier, and less appealing. Greyson also seemed to have inherited his mother's black hair. She speculated that he had gotten his height from a great grandparent.

Not wanting to wake him, Lavine quietly moved into the office. Her fingers glided over the old bookshelves, searching for something intriguing.

A familiar title caught her eye on the top shelf. She reached up on her toes and retrieved the book, flipping through its tattered pages. It was the same one Gavriil had in his library. So many legends and bedtime stories had been told from this book.

This book was in near tatters while Gavriil's edition was in pristine condition. Lavine flipped to the end, where *The Legend of the Great Drake* was featured, seeing the story pages from her childhood.

Drawings of Aarth leaped from the pages, comparing his size to that of an average human. The idea that such a being could be so enormous to dwarf even the size of Marella itself. Below the illustration was a hand written passage written in a strange language. Lavine sat at Greyson's massive desk, turning the book this way and that. The language looked oddly familiar.

She opened the bottom drawer and took out the ancient page she had retrieved from the deep tunnels. Lining it up beside the book's pages, she studied the lettering. They were of the same language. Greyson was on to something.

I need to get this to Kace.

With just a few days left, she knew she wouldn't succeed

in completing her mission. For the first time, she wasn't worried about her job. Greyson needed her help and the idea of contacting the Navarian king and ultimately bringing peace to the nations provided a much more appealing end to her career. Tallulah and the rest of the High Council might not take it well at first, given that her task had been to kill Greyson. But it was a risk she was willing to take.

She squinted as the mid-morning sun shone brightly through the window. Lavine stood and stretched, realizing she would need some sleep. With the book in hand, she moved back into Greyson's room. He was still sound asleep. She brushed his hair from his face and smiled, seeing him blissfully relaxed. After stoking the fire, she made her way back to her chambers. Emerging from the hidden passageway, she found a man sitting at the small table.

"Silas?" she asked in surprise.

He stood, his eyes fixed on her. "What do you want with him?" he demanded, advancing toward her.

Lavine stood her ground, unshaken by his scare tactics. She was used to men using their height as a weapon against her.

"What?" she asked, stalling as he closed in, his hand resting on the sword at his side.

"You were sent here to kill him."

"Yes," she admitted, meeting his gaze without flinching. "That was the original plan."

"So why haven't you?"

She rolled her eyes. "If you want him dead, I swear I'll gut you like a—"

"Greyson is like a son to me," he interrupted, his voice tense. "I would give my life for him. He's too smitten with you to remember your original intentions." Silas pointed a finger at her, his voice dropping to a dangerous whisper. "I swear by the stars above, if you do anything to harm him, I will sever your head from your shoulders."

"If I wanted to kill him, I would have done it already," she said through gritted teeth, choosing to ignore the former part of his statement. Despite the heat rising in her cheeks and her heart leaping, she pushed the feeling aside. Pointing toward Greyson's chambers, she continued. "I could have done it just now, while he's dead asleep."

Silas' eyes darted toward where she pointed. Crossing his arms, his expression remained as hard as stone. Lavine kept her gaze locked on his brown eyes.

"Swear that you'll get him what he needs."

Lavine placed her right hand over her heart. "I swear on my blades."

He extended his hand toward her. Lavine reached out and shook it, then followed him to the door. As Silas held the door slightly ajar, Lavine was unable to hold back her question any longer.

"What do you mean, he's too smitten with me?" she asked.

Silas stopped and turned to face her. "I thought you were smarter than that, if I'm being honest."

Ignoring the insult, Lavine studied his face, seeking confirmation of what she already knew. She needed to hear it from someone outside the situation.

"Have you not noticed the way he looks at you?" Silas continued. "How close he keeps you? It's not just to keep you hidden, he genuinely trusts you. If you abuse that trust, my earlier threat still stands."

With that, Silas left her alone, her mind and heart racing. Her cheeks flushed. The truth had become increasingly clear over the past week. Perhaps it was simply her mind playing tricks on her.

Distracting herself, Lavine placed the book in her pack and unbuckled the comm from her wrist, setting it on the table. She retrieved a small screwdriver from her toolkit and began to tinker with the broken device.

For twenty agonizing minutes, she struggled to pop off the screen without causing further damage. The edge of the screwdriver was too thick to fit into the narrow gap between the screen and the electronic base, making her frustration boil over.

Lavine tossed the screwdriver aside and pulled out her dagger. With a frustrated huff, she slipped the blade under the screen of the comm and tried to pry it open. The tip of the blade slipped out of the groove, and in a surge of frustration and fatigue, she drove the dagger into the comm. The blade sliced through the device and stuck into the table beneath it, the screen flickering rapidly before going black.

Cursing under her breath, she shoved away from the table, nearly toppling her chair in the process. She removed her boots and pulled back the blanket, deciding to sleep in her clothes just in case. Despite her exhaustion, her mind raced, and sleep remained elusive.

Her mind drifted back to the small corridor where her body had pressed against Greyson's. The memory made her stomach flip, and her cheeks flushed with embarrassment despite being alone. Romance had never been on her radar: she had always been too focused on her career to consider it. It was a surprise to her fellow students when she denied Andy's advances.

Greyson was attractive, she couldn't deny the fact. His skill with the blade and the genuine attentiveness he showed to those he cared about only added to his appeal. The brief moments of close contact between them had stirred something deep within her—an undeniable physical attraction that sent butterflies fluttering in her stomach. She couldn't ignore how her body responded to him, despite her best efforts to stay focused.

Maybe it's just that. I've never had time for romance, and he's never been that close to a woman.

But the memories of their conversations on the balcony lingered in her mind. They had connected on a deeper level, emotionally. There was no denying it. She feared what the High Council would think. Tallulah's reaction was especially worrisome. The idea of approaching them with Greyson's plea for help was daunting enough, but the added complication of an emotional connection with the enemy made it even more precarious. Tallulah could never find out. If she did, it would be the end of Lavine's career.

31

Greyson

Greyson woke with a start, disoriented and unsure of where he was. He flailed out of bed, stumbling in the dark, feeling as though he had slept through something important. The room was lit by the crackling fire and the pale moonlight streaming through the balcony door.

As he scanned the room, the fog of sleep slowly lifted. Realizing he was in his own chamber, he stretched. The details of a dream slipped away the more he tried to recall them, but the emotions lingered. A sense of safety, comfort, and belonging still clung to him.

It had been months since Greyson had slept long enough to dream. He stoked the fire and lit the candles and lanterns, brightening the room as he tried to shake off the remnants of sleep. The memory with Beckett flickered at the edge of his mind.

He rubbed his face with his arm, wiping the sleep from his eyes, and strode to the exit of his chambers.

"Sleep well?" Silas asked, standing outside his door.

"How long was I out?"

"Since sunrise."

Panic flooded Greyson's body. It had been too long. "Did anything important come up while I was out?"

"Elric and Alphonse have returned from the city," Silas said. "Nothing new from Grand General Eden. They seemed relieved not to have had to tell you in person."

Greyson smirked and folded his arms across his chest. "Thank you. I'm sorry for sleeping so long."

Silas shook his head. "You needed it."

"Where's Beckett?"

"She hasn't come out of her chambers... or yours. So unless there's another way out, she's still here."

Greyson nodded and turned to open his door.

"Oh, I almost forgot," Silas said, pulling a piece of folded parchment from his breast pocket and handing it over. "From Adelaide. A list of more families."

He mentally added this to his long list of tasks for the days ahead as footsteps approached. Calix walked silently, his attention focused on something in his hand.

"How are you holding up, son?" Silas asked.

Calix looked up, disoriented, as if he hadn't realized he'd reached his destination. His somber eyes returned to the object in his palm.

"The blacksmith completed the rings I requested." Calix held up a smooth, white ring with blackish-blue streaks winding through it. He slid the ring on his finger, dug into his coat pocket, and retrieved two more, handing one to Silas and the other to Greyson.

Even in grief, he thinks of others. "They turned out beautifully," Greyson said, examining the ring in the torchlight before slipping it onto his finger.

250

"There's one for Adelaide and Wesley," Calix added. "I'll go find them."

Greyson wondered how long he would have grieved his mother if Malric had permitted it. He imagined he would still be grieving, but the idea was lost on him. *How would my life be different if my mother had never died?*

The question was too painful to contemplate. He couldn't waste time on "what ifs."

Greyson walked down the hall, entered Beckett's chambers, and found her fast asleep. His breath caught at the sight of her—her disheveled hair spilling across the pillow and the blankets tangled around her legs. Her lips, slightly parted, seemed to beckon him. He couldn't resist the pull, his gaze tracing the curve of them, a deep ache stirring in his chest. Fighting the urge to linger, to memorize the quiet rhythm of her breath, he forced himself to approach and gently shake her.

"Greyson?" She mumbled, rubbing sleep from her eyes as she slowly sat up.

"It's almost sunrise," he said, though his stomach twisted at the thought of being with her, alone, just the two of them in the quiet of the early morning.

"Already?"

Greyson reached out without thinking, his thumb grazing her cheek. The touch was fleeting, but it sent a rush of warmth through him, and they held each other's gaze for a moment. A silence settled between them, a silence that Greyson would have gladly stayed in forever, if he could.

Her eyes darted away first, flicking nervously over his face before turning toward the glass wall, where the sun was rising, slowly chasing away a blanket of stars.

251

"It's usually cloudy this time of year," he murmured, his voice quiet in the stillness.

Beckett didn't reply immediately, her gaze fixed on the horizon as the sky slowly transformed, a delicate mix of golds and pinks bleeding into the darkness. She seemed lost in the beauty of it, and for a moment, Greyson allowed himself to get lost in her.

"I had planned to wake you," Beckett said suddenly, stepping away and sitting at the dinner table. "I didn't mean to sleep so long." Her second dagger was stuck through her comm and embedded in the wooden surface of the table. She glanced at him sheepishly. "Sorry, I was having trouble fixing it."

The tension was unbearable. He knew what had changed between them. Although Greyson wished for things to return to normal, he found himself intrigued by the new, strange dynamic they had developed.

"Well, it doesn't look like you succeeded."

Lavine laughed and shook her head. "Is that sarcasm I hear?" She twisted the device in her hands, examining it closely.

"Learned from the best," he replied with a grin.

Her smile faltered, and she squirmed, as if some invisible creature was crawling under her skin. She shook her head and tossed the comm into a trash bin.

"Listen," she began, forcing herself to look him in the eye.

Greyson's heart jumped into his throat.

"I'm sorry for what I said yesterday. I didn't mean any of it. You forced every single insecurity I have out into the open—I felt exposed and like I... like I..."

"Like you needed to fight back," he finished. "It's okay, I understand. I shouldn't have cornered you like that."

"But what you said is true. I *am* blinded by loyalty, and when

252

what you've been fighting for isn't as noble as you always believed... Where do you go from there?" Beckett's voice trembled, her eyes welling with tears. "It's like the house I built brick by brick has been shaken to the ground, crumbling under the slightest hit. It's terrifying."

Greyson's heart ached as he watched Beckett crumble into tears, her emotions unraveling like a spool of yarn. He wrapped his arms around her, feeling her shiver against him as her sobs shook her entire body.

He pulled her in tightly, his warmth pressing against her as he murmured softly, "Not all is lost, little assassin." His voice was steady, though he felt a lump in his own throat.

Beckett clung to him, burying her face in his chest. Her sobs were muffled, but he could feel the wetness of her tears seeping through his shirt. He breathed in the citrus scent of her hair, wishing he could provide reassurance that everything would be okay, but he himself didn't know what lay ahead. She pulled back slightly, her tear-streaked face looking up at him. Her eyes, red and filled with anguish, met his.

"I don't know what to do," she said, her voice cracking. "Everything feels like it's falling apart."

Greyson sighed. "Wherever your destiny lies, it is not with those who undervalue you. I only wish to be at your side when you make history."

She took a shaky breath, a faint smile forming on her lips, and leaned back into his embrace. Her body relaxed against his, feeling as if she let the weight of her sorrow go.

"I'm sorry," she sniffled. "You have an actual reason to be upset."

"Your grief is no less important than my own," he replied

softly.

As they stood there, wrapped in each other's arms, the outside world seemed to fade away. He could only focus on the warmth of her body against his, while every part of him wished to draw out the chaos and pain from her body.

After a few moments, Beckett gently pulled away, wiping her tears with the back of her hand. Greyson noticed her gaze fall to his hand.

"What's that?"

He looked down, finding Adelaide's list still clutched in his grip. "It's a list of families in the area in need of food."

Her head tilted slightly, zeroing in on the parchment. She looked up at him with a smirk. "So that's what your nightly escapades are all about? And here I was worried you were seeing other women," she teased. "No wonder you've been so exhausted."

She was sharp. It was uncanny how quickly she pieced things together. Greyson wasn't surprised she had graduated at the top of her class.

"From here on out," Beckett said, plopping down onto the edge of the bed and starting to retie the laces on her boots. "No more secrets. Neither of us can afford to screw something up because the other person is in the dark."

Greyson leaned against the wall near the window, arms crossed, watching her. "Right. No secrets."

She glanced up at him. "My crew's camped out on the north mountain, by the way. Just waiting for my signal."

"Oh," he rubbed the back of his neck. "Well, in that case… I've been stealing from my nobles to feed people who are the most impoverished."

Beckett paused, one lace hanging from her hand. "Seriously?"

He nodded. "Adelaide does the scouting and figures out who's struggling the most. Then I handle the thieving and dropping off the supplies."

She snorted softly. "You? Personally?"

"Yes, me personally," he said, with mock offense. "I've got the cloak and everything."

She gave him a mischievous look. "And no one's caught you?"

Greyson gave a sheepish smile, stepping away from the window. "Some people have learned that it's me, others simply know me as the Raven."

"You've got more guts than I gave you credit for." She stood. "Alright, Raven. Let's hear it then—who's Adelaide?"

He wasn't quite sure how much he could tell Beckett. There wasn't much about Adelaide that he knew himself.

"She nearly killed me last night so I'm curious." Noticing his confusion, she added, "Who is she to you? She's highly skilled. Is she part of your personal guard?"

"Yes, but only my men and I know about her."

"Why is that?"

"Like you said, she's highly skilled. She's deadly and I needed her as an ally."

"Was she not your ally to begin with?"

Greyson smiled sheepishly, rubbing the back of his neck. "She nearly killed me in my sleep."

Beckett leaned in, eager to hear the entire story.

"She broke into Beckinsdale the night after I killed Malric. I woke up with a knife at my throat. It was dark and I couldn't see her face, but she threatened to kill me without a second thought."

255

"But?"

"But," Greyson continued, "she demanded that I let her work for me instead. She would follow my every command and guard my life, as long as I never saw her face."

"Wait," Beckett exclaimed, her eyes widening. She leaned back, crossing her arms over her chest. "You don't know what Adelaide looks like? And you're entrusting your life to her?"

Greyson shrugged. "I don't know what she looks like, who she is, or where she came from. Hell, I don't even know if Adelaide is her real name."

Beckett chuckled, her gaze drifting to the balcony. "You seem to have a habit of collecting assassins," she teased before her gaze distant and contemplative. She opened her mouth, as if she wanted to say more.

The room was quiet except for the crackling of the nearby fireplace. The scent of burning wood mingled with the faint aroma of citrus.

"I want to go with you," she said finally.

"What?"

"I want to help you gather food and supplies."

He reminded himself that Beckett had lived on the streets during her childhood and had likely stolen for the sake of others as well.

"Tonight," he assured her. "First, we need to get into Eden's office."

She nodded in agreement. "Same plan as last time?"

"No. I doubt Edward and Alphonse would fall for the same trick twice in such a short period. We'll need to create a distraction."

"Maybe I can help with that." A wicked grin spread across her face.

"What are you thinking?"

"You've got the castle on high alert for an assassin, correct?"

"Yes," his stomach twisted as he sensed *exactly* where this was going. "But I don't think it's a good idea to alert the guards to your presence in the castle. That could bring Eden back to Beckinsdale."

"I'll keep my hood up. They won't be able to confirm that it's me."

Greyson thought for a moment. If they captured her, he'd have to play the part of the ruthless king. She'd be placed in a dungeon cell, interrogated, and possibly beaten or tortured. The thought made his stomach churn.

"They won't catch me," she reassured before Greyson could voice his reluctance.

"If they do, I'll be forced to act accordingly. That means treating you as an enemy, which will be rough until I can sneak you out."

"They won't catch me," she repeated, her confidence un-wavering.

32

Lavine

Lavine pulled her face cover over her nose and donned the borrowed cloak, pulling the hood atop her head. She stomped her boot to secure her dagger in its sheath. With her gear in place, she was ready to go.

Greyson walked in, now fully armored and with his sword strapped to his waist. He stopped, drinking in the sight of her, and beamed. "You look positively deadly."

She bowed dramatically. "Thank you. I've worked hard to become so."

"Ready?"

She nodded, her eyes flashing with excitement.

Together, they trotted down the hall toward a concealed corridor, silently winding their way through the passageways, moving as one.

When they reached the hall that Eden's quarters were located, Lavine held up her hand, signaling Greyson to stay hidden behind the tapestry. Without hesitation, she stepped into the corridor. Edward and Alphonse spotted her instantly and gave chase, their shouts echoing through the halls as they called for reinforcements to capture the intruder.

Lavine sprinted down the corridors, deliberately staying within their line of sight. She weaved through the twisting passages, the sweet high of adrenaline surging through her body. As she turned a corner, she dove behind a statue, holding her breath as the guards thundered past.

After a moment, she slipped her way back to Greyson, the guards' shouts growing fainter down the hall. She retraced her steps and used every available cover, statues and tapestries alike, as more guards rushed by in pursuit.

"How'd it go?" Greyson whispered as Lavine slipped behind the canvas.

"They're heading toward the medical wing. We should be fine for now. Stay here. It's better if only I'm seen," Lavine replied. She approached Eden's door, her fingers finding the pin hidden in her hair. She worked on the lock, listening for a familiar *clink*.

Heavy footsteps neared their position, and just as the lock clicked open, she realized the approaching guard was too near for her to slip inside unnoticed. Lavine was nearly out of sight when she glanced back and locked eyes with one of Eden's personal guards.

"Halt!" he shouted, extending his arm. "I've spotted the intruder!"

She dashed back down the hall and took an immediate left into the corridor lined with armor. Slipping behind the tapestry, she collided with Greyson. Without missing a beat, they jogged through the hidden passageway. Greyson reached back, grabbed her hand, and pulled her into a full sprint.

Her heart raced with exhilaration, grinning as he led her through the dark. Her heart was light from the thrill of the high stakes. It reminded her of the days when she and Kace had raced through the streets of Marella, evading a furious merchant they had stolen apples from.

They dashed behind a tapestry in the west wing. Greyson quickly opened the door to a servants' hall, and Lavine stayed close behind, gripping his hand as they raced through a labyrinth of crisscrossing corridors. She felt as though she were floating, caught in a state of adrenaline-fueled euphoria as torchlight streaked past.

Emerging into a large foyer just outside the royal hall, Greyson whispered, "When the coast is clear, we run." He peered out from behind the thick canvas, only to retreat swiftly as guards thundered by. Once their footsteps had faded, they burst forward. They spotted Greyson's chamber door, and Silas looked up in alarm as the two of them came barreling toward him.

"Open the door," Greyson whisper-shouted.

Silas lunged for the doorknob, swinging it open just in time for them to shoot through. The door slammed shut behind them, and they came to a halt. Lavine wobbled slightly to her left, and Greyson reached out, steadying her.

They stood facing each other, eyes wide and alert. After a few beats of panting, a smile spread across his face. A real smile, one that reached his eyes the way the sun rose over the ocean, slow and captivating. Lavine's heart leaped, and she couldn't help but smile in return. His gaze softened as he studied her face, briefly flickering to her lips before meeting her eyes again.

"Beckett, are you okay—"

"Lavine," she blurted out before she could stop herself.

"What?"

260

"My real name," she clarified. "It's Lavine."

Smoke and cinnamon enveloped her senses once again. She could feel the intensity of his gaze and the warmth of his breath against her face. His smile slowly faded, giving way to a more intense expression. A ball of heat formed in her stomach, spreading outward, making her cheeks flush. Her heart fluttered, and she felt herself leaning into him.

Greyson's hand gently cupped the back of Lavine's neck, pulling her closer. Her breaths came in shallow, uneven gasps as their lips met, initially gentle but quickly becoming fervent. Each second heightening the raging fire in her stomach.

Lavine's hand found his armored shoulder, the dragon steel giving off a cooling sensation. His fingers twisted their way into her hair, balling into a fist and pulling her closer with a fierce, almost primal urgency. As their kiss grew desperate, Lavine's trembling fingers fumbled with Greyson's belt, struggling to unbuckle it.

The balcony doors slammed open. Greyson's arm wrapped around her. Amidst the chaos, familiar brown eyes locked onto hers for a split second before Greyson shoved her behind him.

They're going to kill him.

The scrape of a sword leaving its sheath. A gunshot rang out, followed by a metallic clang. The sudden intrusion was disorienting, but Lavine fought to steady herself. She leaped in front of Greyson, hands stretched out toward the intruders.

"HOLD YOUR FIRE!" she bellowed, her voice cutting through the noise as she stared down the barrel of a rifle and into Ivy's eyes. Kace stood beside her, revolvers drawn and ready. Bewilderment spread across their faces.

"What the hell is wrong with you?" Kace yelled. "Do you

realize who that is?"

"Of course I do. It's not what it looks like," she replied, lowering her voice as she tried to defuse the situation. "Put your weapons away, and I can explain."

"We're not stupid," Kace spat.

"Okay, it's exactly what it looks like," Lavine replied.

Footsteps thundered into the room behind her, accompanied by the taut pull of a bowstring and Silas drawing his weapon.

"Stand down," Greyson commanded.

"Your Majesty," Adelaide protested.

"It's all right," Greyson insisted.

The room was alive with lethal electricity. Lavine could think of all the ways that this could go wrong. Her crew were skilled with firearms, but Greyson was lethal in close quarters and Adelaide could drop them all within seconds.

"Trust me," Lavine said.

Ivy and Kace kept their eyes on their surroundings, wary of Greyson and the additional threats. Moments ago, she was concerned for Greyson's life. Now Kace and Ivy's hung in the balance.

They were still aiming their weapons at Greyson. Though he had quick reflexes, Lavine doubted he could deflect all the bullets at once. If they fired, arrows would be the least of their worries. They weren't listening to her, and anger boiled in her stomach.

"I am the captain of this team," Lavine said through gritted teeth. "Put away your weapons!"

Dead silence filled the room for what felt like an eternity. Lavine's gaze shifted from Kace to Ivy, and theirs, from her to Greyson—a silent battle of wills.

There was a slight movement behind her, and she dared to glance back. Greyson had sheathed his sword, with Adelaide and Silas reluctantly following suit. This seemed to appease her crew. Slowly, they began to lower their weapons, though their eyes remained fixed on Greyson.

Good.

Once their weapons were holstered, Lavine lowered her hands and allowed herself to breathe.

"You've got some explaining to do, Beckett," Ivy said.

"Why did you come for extraction?" Lavine demanded, her voice steady despite the lingering anxiety. "I didn't give the signal. I still have two days left."

"Your beacon went out early this morning. We thought you'd been killed," Kace replied. "But it turns out you've been too busy swapping spit with *him*," he added, gesturing toward Greyson.

His accusation felt like a slap to the face. It wasn't entirely untrue, but the insult stung, nonetheless.

"Excuse me?!" She stepped forward, getting in his face. "Do you want to make more assumptions about a situation you know nothing about?"

"I know what I saw," Kace shot back.

"Sure you do."

Kace huffed and stomped closer. "You're obviously too close to the situation to think clearly!" They were nose to nose, yelling in each other's faces.

This was the most explosive argument they'd ever had, and she wasn't sure what had triggered her outburst.

"And since when have you ever thought clearly?" Lavine snapped. The release of the words felt cathartic, even as she questioned why this confrontation had escalated so rapidly.

263

"Since you started salivating over this blood-thirsty dick-head!" Kace shouted, pointing another finger at Greyson.

Lavine clenched her fists, ready to throw a punch when Ivy stepped in, separating them with her arms. "Knock it off, or I'll send *both* of you home in body bags!"

She stumbled backward as Ivy pushed her away. Her eyes remained locked on Kace's, both of them breathing heavily and glaring at each other.

Greyson placed a steadying hand on her shoulder. "Easy," he said calmly. "He has a right to be concerned. I think you've forgotten how unpopular I am."

Lavine pointed at the guns holstered on Kace's hips. "If you point those things at him again, I will break your wrists."

"Lavine," Greyson whispered softly. "You don't have to protect me."

She looked up at him, the adrenaline slowly ebbing away. Confused glances continued to bounce around the room.

"He knows your name?" Ivy asked.

Lavine nodded. "As of thirty seconds ago."

"Have you lost your mind?"

Lavine remained silent, at a loss for words and unsure how to explain the events that had led to this moment. She had anticipated the day would come when she'd need to explain her relationship with Greyson to her crew, but the timing couldn't have been worse.

Lavine opened her mouth to say more, but Kace cut her off.

"I thought you were dead." Kace's angry voice broke. "I thought I'd have to tell Gavriil that you had been killed."

The thought hit her with full force. She couldn't bear to imagine how Gavriil would have reacted to the news of either her or Kace's death. He wouldn't make it.

"I'm so sorry," she said. "My comm broke. I tried to fix it but couldn't. I didn't think much about it."

"When comms are destroyed, they automatically send out a distress signal," Ivy explained. "We pinpointed your last known location and came to retrieve your body... if there was one."

Lavine realized how insensitive she had been and felt the guilt pinpricking her skin. Without hesitation, she rushed forward and pulled Kace into an embrace. He clung to her, taking a deep breath as his emotions seemed to settle.

"I'm so sorry," Lavine whispered again.

33

Greyson

Questions ricocheted around the room as Greyson processed the shock of being the first outsider to learn Harley Beckett's real name. After all, he was an enemy. Beckett's crew had likely heard the same stories about him.

As the adrenaline began to fade, Greyson leaned against the wall, the cool, rough surface grounding him. More relaxed now that the immediate danger had passed, though his heart still raced. Greyson had been so taken aback at Beckett revealing her real name that he barely had time to react to the intrusion. His sole focus had been on protecting her, positioning himself between her and the threat that had burst through the doors. While he had the advantage of armor, she didn't. Nevertheless, she had taken control of the situation, stopping her crew from continuing to fire into the room. But even he had been a bit startled by her command to cease fire.

In the few weeks Greyson had known Lavine, she seemed to prefer the quieter approach. But in this moment, she had transformed into a drill sergeant, shifting into another person entirely. Her stance had been solid, her voice aggressive. This was the Harley Beckett he had heard rumors of—the ruthless assassin who left no witnesses. Greyson was relieved he hadn't been on the receiving end of her wrath.

Greyson's gaze shifted to the newcomers. The woman had dark brown skin, and intricate tattoos of golden water dragons spiraled down her arms, each scale seemingly alive with movement. Her sharp, green eyes glimmered with deadly intensity. Despite her aloofness, she seemed deeply attuned to her crewmates' emotions, her tight curls cascading over her shoulders.

The male, with black hair and green eyes, seemed close to Lavine in age. His attitude and posture were arrogant and conceited, leaving Greyson uncertain of his exact role in this operation. While it was clear that Lavine was the leader, Greyson couldn't discern which of her subordinates might be second in command.

Before pulling away from Lavine's embrace, the male crew member stared daggers up at Greyson, who met his gaze unflinchingly.

How is she going to explain all of this? Explain us?

Lavine stepped to the side, forming a small circle. "This is Kace," she said, pointing to the male she had been arguing with. "Pilot, tracking specialist, and cook. And this is Ivy," she added, gesturing to the girl. "Weapons expert, mechanic, and medic." Turning to her crew, Lavine continued. "Ivy, Kace, this is Greyson."

"*Greyson?*" Kace exclaimed. "You're on a first-name basis with this man? It's worse than I thought!"

"You will call him 'Your Majesty,'" Silas interjected.

"Yeah, no." Kace chuckled sarcastically. "I don't think so,

pal."

The air in the room thickened with tension once more. Greyson could feel the charged atmosphere, fearing the smallest spark would ignite into a flash of arrows and ammunition.

"Easy," Greyson said, turning to Silas, trying to maintain calm. "Fetch Calix and Wesley. It would be best if we were all on the same page."

"This better not be an ambush," Kace said, glaring.

"It's not," Lavine said, annoyed. "Will you please just listen to me?"

Kace stared at Greyson for a moment, his lips pressed into a thin line. "Fine," he said finally. Leaning against the wall with his arms crossed, he added, "Tell me what you have to say to defend the most hated man on earth."

"I would be dead if it weren't for him," Lavine said, her voice rising once more. She had silenced the room, her emotions rattling everyone present. Greyson had never seen her this reactive before. Her usual cool demeanor had become impatient and explosive.

I feel the same way, he thought.

Still worked up from their romantic encounter, there had been no release. The intense emotions, the passion, urgency, and longing, had been bottled up. Ready to boil over one moment and siphoned the next. His frustration mirrored her own, but for once, he managed to conceal.

Silas soon returned with Calix and Wesley. Once everyone was introduced, they settled into Greyson's antechamber. Lavine began her story as Greyson stoked the fire, the flames casting a warm glow across the room.

She explained how she had reached Navaria, being intercepted and captured by vultures in Warith. Greyson's stomach clenched as she described how the Ice Reapers had planned to assault and sell her. By the time she finished recounting how Greyson had rescued her at Crier's Peak, she had their full, undivided attention. Their expressions shifted from anger to concern and disbelief.

"He rushed me to his healer and took care of me, fed me, and he made sure I was warm. Even after figuring out who I was."

Greyson sensed the shift in the room's atmosphere as her crew processed the information. The crackling of the fire was the only sound in the room as he watched her speak. Her crew drank in her every word. Silas caught his eye and gave a subtle nod toward the corner where Adelaide kept watch. Greyson followed Silas' gaze, and they moved together quietly.

Lavine glanced up mid-sentence. Greyson nodded reassuringly, letting her know everything was okay and she resumed her story.

"What's the plan?" Silas asked, keeping his voice low.

"They can help me find Mundicar and get me an audience with the Marellan High Council," Greyson replied.

"With all due respect, Sire, they tried to kill you," Adelaide cut in.

"Yes, but they were trying to protect her," Greyson motioned. "She is their captain, after all."

"Do we really need them? We don't know them, and I don't trust them." Silas' face was grave. "I barely trust Beckett."

"What other options do I have?" Greyson asked. "I can't keep stealing and sneaking around at night." The toll on his mind and body had become too much. He was ready for relief. Greyson turned to Adelaide. "You, more than anyone here, knows how dire things are getting. People are dying. If I don't act soon, there will be an uprising."

Adelaide stood, pausing to think. From beneath her hood, she nodded. "You're right," she said, her voice soft but resolute. "Are you certain they can help us?"

"I trust Beckett, that's all I need right now."

"Then I stand by you and your decision."

The trio returned to the group. Lavine had wrapped up her story and was now answering Ivy's questions about Mundicar and the troop of Marellan soldiers that attacked them in the forest. Greyson's gaze shifted to his guard. Calix was examining a revolver that Kace had handed him, while Wesley looked on with a mix of wonder and focus. His gaze was unwavering, hardly blinking. Greyson followed Wesley's line of sight and discovered the source of his fascination. Ivy.

A small smile crept across Greyson's face as understanding dawned on him. Wesley had shown no interest in romance since Greyson had known him, but now he was clearly entranced. But the smile faded quickly, replaced by worry. The cohesion of his guard and Lavine's crew was rocky and fragile. They were all strangers, thrown together in the same room for less than an hour, with their initial meeting being tense and hostile. They needed to tread carefully.

"There's one more thing," Lavine continued, turning to Greyson. "I ran into someone in Direwoods."

"What?" Greyson asked, his brow furrowing.

"Not all the Marellan soldiers were killed."

Calix's attention snapped to their conversation, his hand fidgeting with the dragon steel ring on his finger, eyes wide with a mix of disbelief and anger.

Greyson's heart sank, a cold knot forming in his stomach. *What now?* He thought, bracing for bad news.

"One of them survived," Lavine went on. "It was Andy, an old friend of ours. He was unharmed and crawling into the woods when I found him."

Ivy furrowed her brows. "So that's what he's been up to."

"The bastard should've died with the rest of them," Calix seethed, his voice low and trembling. Greyson could feel the rage swirling in the air, thick and suffocating.

"That bastard may be an important piece in getting Navaria help," Lavine said. "I've tasked him with getting a message across the sea."

"You're contacting the council?" Greyson's face brightened.

Lavine bit her lip, shaking her head before continuing. "I sent him to Regent Carter."

Ivy shot up from her chair. "You're dragging my dad into this?!"

Lavine turned to Ivy. "He's the only one we can trust right now."

"That's saying a lot coming from you," Kace said, leaning against the wall with crossed arms.

"The High Council knew Navaria was starving and chose to do nothing. I plan to bring this straight to Tallulah. She may throw us out for bringing Greyson into the city, but I promised to help. And come hell or high water, I will give it my all. If the council refuses to help, your dad is our backup plan." Her voice was steely but determined, as if each word was a promise carved into stone.

Ivy's expression softened. She nodded, a tentative smile creeping onto her lips.

"What all did you pass along?" Greyson asked.

"I told him about Mundicar and that we may need his help."

"What about us?" Kace asked, leaving his place at the wall.

271

"What are we to do?"

"We bring Greyson to Marella and plead his case."

"That's a bit too ballsy if you ask me." Kace shook his head. "Are you set on all of this?"

Lavine nodded.

After a long moment, a grin slowly spread across Kace's face, a spark of mischief lighting his eyes. "Well then," he turned to Greyson. "You better start packing. Travel light because there's only room for two extra people."

Lavine's face brightened, joy and excitement illuminating her eyes. But as Greyson watched her enthusiasm, he felt a faint twist in his gut.

Why does she light up for him?

He quickly pushed the thought aside, feeling foolish for even entertaining such feelings. A new goal settled in his mind. When his father died, he had vowed never to compete for someone's love ever again. Yet, he refused to fade into the background of Lavine's attention.

With a glint in his eye, he squared his shoulders and met Lavine's gaze. "Then let's make sure we're ready," he said, his voice steady. "I'm with you until the end."

As Lavine smiled back at him, the warmth in her eyes lingered for a moment longer. A creeping fear gnawed at him, whispering doubts about how the rest of the world would react upon seeing them on their lands. Would they cower or retaliate? The thought tugged at him like a relentless winter wind.

Greyson envisioned a beachside city, its inhabitants with narrowed eyes and armored guards gripping their guns and swords tightly. While his name was a badge of honor in the north, it was a death sentence in the south. Hawke—a family who killed off the ancient dragons and stormed on Marella without warning, leaving a trail of civilian casualties in their wake. Cold sweat prickled at his brow as a knot twisted in his stomach. Despite the overwhelming fear and doubt, he pushed it out of his mind. He could not afford to be fearful of the future. His people needed him, and no matter how unforgiving Marella might be, he had to try. Greyson needed to be ready for the storm that awaited.

With so many battles ahead, what was one more?

He would rise to the challenge, no matter what it took.

34

Lavine

Ivy groaned, rubbing her temples. "We came all this way just to find that Hawke has no idea what Mundicar is?"

"The situation isn't completely hopeless," Kace replied. "Eden was speaking to someone about Mundicar. That's how Theo overheard the conversation. We need to find out who that other person was."

Now that everyone had calmed down after the initial standoff, swapping and examining weapons, asking questions, and conversing for a few hours, Lavine noticed Wesley staring at Ivy. She had only just met him, but Lavine knew him well enough to know that he was infatuated with her. She and Ivy had been friends since their Academy days, and men were not a concern for Ivy: her focus was firmly on her career. Lavine couldn't help but feel a bit worried about Wesley getting his heart broken.

"There's no way to know for sure," Ivy said, completely oblivious to Wesley's gaze. "Theo didn't describe the second voice he heard."

Greyson rejoined the group, seeming to have spotted the

same thing Lavine had. He nudged Wesley, redirecting his attention to the conversation. Lavine moved to meet Greyson amid their crew.

Lavine shook her head. "I have only one lead." She held out her hand toward Greyson, meeting his eye. Lavine placed her hand on his shoulder. "Him."

Kace crossed his arms, shaking his head. "Gavriil always said you were too trusting."

"You don't have to trust him. Trust me. He's not trying to invade Marella or start a war. He just wants to save his people."

"Isn't it your fault the Navarians are starving in the first place?" Kace shot a piercing look at Greyson.

Greyson's expression didn't waver at the accusation. "They were suffering long before I was born," he replied, his voice steady yet strained. "This isn't about me. It never was."

Kace opened his mouth, then closed it, frustration flashing across his face. Greyson shifted, his jaw tightening. Lavine worried more arguments might break out.

"If he's not planning an invasion," Ivy interjected, pointing at Greyson and breaking the heavy silence, "then that means Grand General Eden is."

Lavine nodded. "And he's a much bigger threat to the balance of the world."

"So what's the plan?" Kace asked. "Are we supposed to work with Hawke and his personal league of assassins to find Mundicar, save Navaria, and hold hands while singing around a campfire?"

"I really don't need your sarcasm right now." Lavine's stern expression threatened to be overtaken by a smile. Sarcasm was a good sign. Kace was adapting to the situation, even if

275

he didn't like it.

It would be a long time before Kace warmed up to Greyson and his guard, but they didn't need to be friends to work together.

"I have maps of the castle," Greyson said, leading the way to his office. He caught Lavine's eye and nodded toward the office door. Silas stepped forward, attempting to follow, but Greyson raised a hand. "It's okay."

Lavine turned to the rest of the group. "Don't kill each other while we're gone."

"No promises," Calix and Kace replied in unison.

Lavine couldn't help but smile as she left the room. *Everyone will get along just fine.*

The door shut behind her, and she and Greyson stood in silence for a moment, neither awkward nor entirely comfortable. Greyson turned to face her.

"That was an anomaly I wasn't prepared for, if I'm being honest," he said.

"Neither of us could've been prepared for that." She ran her hand along the bookcase, her fingers grazing the spines of ancient novels. "Where do we go from here?"

"We can go all in on getting into Eden's office."

Lavine shook her head. "I don't think that's entirely reasonable. One or two of us can go in while the others stand guard."

"You're right. It'd be foolish to take unnecessary risks."

"It'd be a shame if everything fell apart now," she replied, crossing her arms.

"Did you mean it?"

"Mean what?" Lavine asked.

"That you'd help no matter what... What was it that you

276

said?" A smile crept across his face. "'Come hell or high water?'"

Lavine smiled. "I meant every word. No matter what happens, I've got your back."

In that moment, she felt her soul drawn to him—a powerful sense of belonging that was different from what she had experienced with Kace and Gavriil. Past relationships had seemed shallow and unimportant, like fleeting seasons in her life. But this connection was deeper, more intense, as if she had finally found a missing piece of herself. With Greyson, it felt like he was family but in a way that transcended friendship, weaving romance with kinship.

Greyson closed the distance between them, their fingers intertwining. An electric tension crackled in the air. As he lifted his hand to tuck a loose strand of hair behind her ear, their eyes locked, the world around them fading into a blur.

"What is this?" Lavine's voice was barely above a whisper, her heart racing at their closeness.

"I don't know," Greyson admitted, his voice dropping. "All I know is that I've never felt this way before."

Their bodies moved closer, like the moon pulling the ocean.

"I know I'm not the ideal choice," he said, his breath warm against her skin. "But I dare to hope that you would choose me, despite the world's reservations."

The intensity and longing in his eyes were intoxicating. Shadows danced in the dim light, and the air crackled with electricity, mingled with the earthy scent of smoke and cinnamon. She held out her hand, inviting him to take it. As he clasped her palm, she guided it to her face. With a steady touch, he ran his thumb across her bottom lip, his gaze sharpening, growing more focused and hungry.

A familiar heat coiled in Lavine's stomach as Greyson's thumb slowly caressed her cheek. He brought his face closer, strands of dark hair falling softly to the sides. Lavine leaned into him, their lips just a breath away from connecting.

There was a knock at the door. They both jumped, Greyson's attention snapping to the door while Lavine's heart raced wildly.

"Your Majesty?" Silas' muffled voice called from outside.

"Be there in a moment," Greyson replied, his voice steady despite the interruption.

As they stood in silence, gazing into each other's eyes, Lavine felt her cheeks flush. "We'll talk about this later," she whispered, hoping she didn't sound as breathless as she felt.

He nodded before stepping away to retrieve the map. Together, they returned to the antechamber, where everyone was waiting. The others met them with curious stares as they joined the group. Ivy caught Lavine's eye with a suspicious look.

Greyson spread the map on a table near the settee where Kace and Ivy sat. Everyone gathered around, their eyes fixed on the crinkled parchment. Lavine and Greyson explained their suspicions about Eden hiding Mundicar in his office, detailing their failed attempts to get inside.

"What if this weapon isn't in the castle?" Ivy asked.

"Then you and your crew will escort me to Marella," Greyson replied, "and arrange a meeting with your High Council."

"I'm worried about what we might find," Kace interjected, turning to Greyson. "But the risk is worth the reward. Still, considering the High Council expects us to bring back proof of a weapon or plan for invasion or war, I doubt they would agree to speak with you."

"We'll cross that bridge when we get there," Lavine said. "If Mundicar exists, we'll find it in Eden's office."

"So, what's our plan?" Calix spoke up, the lure of adventure lighting up his somber eyes. It seemed instead of letting himself grieve, Calix had kept himself busy to prevent him from spiraling into the abyss of his own mind.

Lavine turned to Greyson. "I think it would be best if you stayed out of sight."

"Again?" Greyson blanched. "No, we've been in this together."

"Hear me out. If you're seen helping us, it will complicate things further. Adelaide can create a distraction, and while the guards are busy dealing with her, you and the boys can patrol the halls." She pointed to Kace and Ivy. "We will go into Eden's office and look for Mundicar."

"What's stopping you from getting what you need and then taking off?" Silas asked, his arms crossed.

He still doesn't trust me. Lavine couldn't entirely blame him, though she felt that she had proven herself.

"The High Council sent me here to kill Greyson," she said. "Does he look dead to you? I've fought by his side and saved his life—twice." She paused, daring Silas to challenge her further. He eyed Lavine closely but eventually relented, nodding his approval. Lavine turned her attention back to Greyson. "We've trained for this for years. It's our specialty, and it's the reason we're here."

"Okay. Let's do this," he said.

Moonlight streamed into the room, casting an ethereal glow. The sight of her crew mingling with Greyson's guard, all bent over the table pouring over a schematic of Beckinsdale, felt surreal.

"We rest until sunrise," Greyson said, "and then we move. We've got a fight ahead, and I won't have anyone too weary to face it."

* * *

Ivy traced her fingers along the columns of the massive four-poster bed. "So, this is where he kept you?"

"Until I figured out how to escape."

Ivy's attention shifted to the glass wall. "He knows how to pick a view." Leaning in, she whispered, "You could've done worse, honestly."

Heat crept up Lavine's neck and into her cheeks as she caught Ivy's meaning. She opened her mouth to retaliate, but no words came. Ivy would see right through her denials.

"I'm not blind." A wicked grin spread across Ivy's face. "I saw you two before we came through those doors."

While she couldn't admit it out loud, Greyson held a piece of her heart. He had captured her attention and captivated her world. "This is not a good time," she said, glancing around the room, though only Kace was there to eavesdrop.

"Who all knows?" Ivy asked.

"Everyone who was around that table."

"We need to keep it that way. If we take him to Marella, the council will be on high alert. They can't know, at least not for now."

Ivy moved to the bed and sprawled out, clearly comfortable in its embrace. It could easily fit all three of them. Kace and Ivy were in for a glorious nap.

Kace stood by the glass wall, gazing out at the dark, snow-covered mountains illuminated by the bright moon. "You know Tallulah will refuse to speak with him, right?"

"You don't know that," Lavine countered. "I'll talk to her. She'll listen to me."

"Lavine, think about this." Kace turned to meet her gaze, urgency creeping into his voice. "He's the king of a long line of ruthless conquerors. They wiped out the dragons, and he killed his own father for the throne. That's not exactly a good look."

"I have to try to get to the bottom of all of this. Greyson has been asking the High Council for help since his coronation, and they said no. Why would they say no to helping innocents?"

"And what makes you think they'll change their minds? What could you possibly say to convince them to help?"

Redirecting her frustration, Lavine tightened her grip on the handle of her dagger. She squeezed it and took a steadying breath. She didn't want to fight with him.

Up. One. Two. Three. Down. One. Two. Three.

"I can change their minds," she insisted, keeping her voice as calm as possible. "He needs help. And if I can't change their minds..."

"We'll be exiled," Kace finished. "What about Gavriil? Our family home?"

Lavine crossed her arms. "Kace, this isn't just about us. What about all the people who will suffer from Eden's actions? If we walk away from this, we'll lose everything. At least this way, we'll be ahead."

"Yeah, but you can't just charge in there like a knight in shining armor." Kace ran a hand through his hair. "You have to be smart about this."

"That's what I have you for."

Kace couldn't help but smirk, looking over at her. Lavine knew he was trying to read her and work out how to convince her of seeing reason.

"I agree with Hawke on one point," he said. "You're too close to the situation to think clearly. They're going to throw us out."

"That's where Andy and Regent Carter come into play. If we're thrown out of Marella, he'll take us in and Gavriil will have a safe place to stay."

"And what about Hawke? Do you think they'll take him in?"

"I've spent the better part of a month with Greyson. I've fought by his side, watched him lose one of his own and grieve. Whether or not I'm too close to the situation is irrelevant. Marella has turned a blind eye for too long."

Kace furrowed his brow, glancing away, his expression a mix of worry and doubt. "I never thought Hawke would be the one to shatter your starry-eyed view of the council." He took a deep breath, his gaze dropping to the floor. "I just... I don't want to see you get hurt." His expression softened. "You've been through so much already."

Lavine's chest tightened. Even as children, Kace had followed her blindly into anything and everything. "I won't let that happen," she promised. "I can't stand by and watch innocents suffer. When I look at Greyson, I see what he's trying to do, and it reminds me of when we lived on the streets."

For a moment, it seemed as if Kace was wrestling with himself. But then he stepped closer. "If you're so sure about this, then I'll stand with you."

Lavine felt her heart lighten, overjoyed to have her brother's support. "Thank you."

35

Greyson

Greyson's face was reflected at him as he cleaned his sword, the dark blue streaks popping out from the white blade. The veins in the metal crisscrossed like shattered glass catching the light. It had been years since he had dared to look into a mirror, afraid to see his father staring back at him.

"Greyson," Silas said from across the table, his voice steady. "May I speak freely?"

"Of course."

"Are you certain you want to get mixed up in this? With them?" He gestured toward Lavine's bedchamber. "This could hurt more than it helps."

"You worry over nothing, Silas." Greyson stood, sheathing his sword and securing it to his belt.

Silas moved closer, stepping directly into his path. Greyson looked at Silas' concerned face, his eyes blazing with dismay. "I've watched you grow into a man, watched you become a king, watched you run yourself into the ground to help your people. You're like a son to me." Silas' voice hitched. "I'm proud of the man you've become, and I couldn't bear to see you get hurt. So please, be careful."

A lump formed in Greyson's throat. He swallowed, a strange twinge of pain shooting through his eyes. The last time he had felt that sensation was the night his mother died. He blinked it away, determined not to let his eyes appear wet.

"Thank you for being here all these years." Greyson extended his hand. Silas took it and they shook hands firmly. "You're a fine warrior and adviser."

"Do you think we'll find this weapon?"

"Maybe. Maybe not. We will bring whatever we find, be it a weapon or nothing, to Marella," Greyson replied. "This could be the turning point for Navaria."

"Whatever comes next, I'm with you," Silas said.

* * *

Everyone gathered around the table in Greyson's antechamber, going over the plan once more. A faint light filtered through the window. Dawn was approaching.

"I'll be patrolling the surrounding halls once you three are inside," Greyson said. "When I feel that we've run out of time, I will give the signal."

"What's the signal?" Ivy asked.

Greyson whistled sharply. All heads turned toward him.

"A whistle?" Kace rolled his eyes and sighed. "You people really are from the dark ages." He unbuckled the device from his wrist as he rounded the table. "We'll use our comms. If something goes wrong or we're out of time, just push the panic button."

Greyson stared at the device as Kace extended it toward

him. He opened his mouth to dismiss the plan but hesitated. He couldn't see any downsides to this form of communication. It was soundless and instantaneous.

"It's a better plan." Lavine said. "A whistle could alert more guards and make getting out more difficult."

Greyson took the comm from Kace's grip and buckled it around his wrist. After Ivy transferred her comm to Lavine, they were ready to set their plan in motion.

"We need to move before the servants wake," Lavine said, nodding toward the door.

They made their way out of the royal chamber as one, leading the others into the hall. Greyson strode down the corridor, flanked by his guards. Adelaide slipped away in the opposite direction, disappearing as she climbed out of a window.

Lavine and her crew hung back, staying out of sight as they slowly inched forward while Greyson confirmed that the halls were clear. Once they reached the tapestry, Greyson pulled it back and Lavine ushered Ivy and Kace into the hidden corridor.

Lavine turned to him. "See you on the other side."

Greyson nodded. "Be careful."

His gut twisted as she vanished into the corridor. Sweat prickled the surface of his skin despite the chill in the air. Staring at the spot where Lavine had been moments before, a memory resurfaced.

Greyson woke with a start, his father shaking him awake.

"Get up," his father said, his voice deep and severe. "Your mother is dead."

Believing he was still dreaming, Greyson wiped the sleep from his eyes. A candle flickered nearby, illuminating his father's face, which was as unyielding as a stone wall. It was not a dream. Fear crept into his heart.

"Father, what—"

"Don't speak."

The blanket was ripped from the bed, and a violent tremble coursed through Greyson's body. His father's firm grip tightened like a vise around his arm, sending a sharp pain through his shoulder as he was wrenched from the bed. The sudden roughness of his father's behavior amplified Greyson's fear.

His father dragged him from the bedchamber and into the hall. The moon hung high in the night sky, its light casting beams through the window. Greyson stumbled.

"Father, please, slow down."

His father continued to drag him down the royal hall, seemingly oblivious to his pleas. They came to a stop outside his mother's bedchamber, his father's words echoing in Greyson's mind.

"Your mother is dead."

His mind refused to accept what he had heard. His father inserted a key into the lock, and the door creaked open. He ushered Greyson inside, then instructed him to wait outside the bedchamber door. Greyson obeyed, reality dawning on him. His father had never lied to him. Tears pooled in his eyes as he clutched his father's cloak, seeking comfort before being left alone in the dark room.

"Is Mother really—"

A hand collided with Greyson's face, knocking him to the floor. Tears he had been holding back spilled down his cheeks. Fear and confusion engulfed his mind as his face struck the cold stone. A hand gripped the front of his nightshirt and yanked him up, lifting his feet off the ground. Warm liquid dripped from his nose, the taste of copper seeping into his mouth.

"I will only tell you this once, so listen well," his father said, his tone filled with anger and venom. "Never speak to me about your mother again." His blue eyes bore into Greyson's. "And if I ever see you cry again, I will beat you into oblivion."

His father let go of his nightshirt, dropping Greyson to the floor. A desperate ache twisted in his chest, longing for his father's love, for the deep embrace that once made him feel safe. An urge to cry out for his mother fought its way to his throat, but his father's threat flashed through his mind.

His father had always kept his promises. He watched his father disappear through the door that led to his mother's bedchamber. For a split second, Greyson caught a glimpse of her enormous bed— where she should have been sleeping, where she would let him rest when night terrors woke him, where she read novels and sang him to sleep. She had been there just yesterday.

Bursting back through the door, his father grabbed Greyson's arm. Pain shot through his shoulder as he was yanked into his mother's room, making Greyson yelp.

"Look at what you've done." His father hissed.

Confused and terrified, he peeked over the blankets. His mother's lifeless body lay in the center of the bed. Fresh blood seeping from the corner of her mouth. Her eyes open, a frightened look on her face.

A shiver tore through Greyson's body. Tears welled up and spilled down his cheeks, and his breath quickened. He shook his head and stepped back.

His father's hand clamped onto his shoulder. "Take a long look. This is your fault."

The urge to cry out after Lavine surfaced gripped Greyson, like he had wanted to cry out for his mother that night.

Greyson feared something would go wrong, that he might never see Lavine again, that her blood would be on his hands.

"Sire, we need to move," Silas urged.

Lightheaded, Greyson turned to his guard, studying their faces. He nodded and shook off the feeling. Leading them through the castle, he took in their impressive armor, each member clad in military regalia. Together, they formed a formidable pack.

Greyson led his men into the west hall, positioning themselves by the tapestry he had instructed Lavine to reach. Minutes ticked by in silent agony; he hoped she hadn't gotten lost.

A door creaked, and he sensed movement behind the wall of canvas.

"Is that you?" he whispered.

"Yes," Lavine replied.

"Three minutes."

"We'll be ready."

Silas and Wesley took their positions a few halls down. With Calix at his side, Greyson made his way to the window at the end of the west wing. He unlocked the window and left it ajar, then stepped back, slipping into the shadows.

Moments later, the window opened. Adelaide climbed in, nodding at Greyson before taking off. His heart raced, praying Lavine wouldn't get caught. He and Calix moved a few halls down, waiting for Adelaide to set the plan in motion.

36

Lavine

Lavine and her crew emerged from the safety of the secret passageway, making their way down the hall. They flattened themselves against the stone wall, silent, bypassing the armor displays placed every few yards. An arrow flew from the left, thudding against the stone at the far end of the hall. Guards shouted and rushed past, oblivious to the group's presence.

She waited a few beats before Wesley peeked around the corner.

"All clear," he whispered, quickly disappearing down the hall.

They moved as one, passing the last of the ancient armor. Lavine glanced down the hallway as they approached Eden's arched wooden door. With Kace and Ivy flanking her, she pulled a pin from her hair and inserted it into the lock. A click echoed softly as she pushed the door open. They hurried through the threshold and closed the door behind them.

The room was dimly lit, filled with the scent of leather and parchment. As her eyes adjusted to the darkness, she began to scan her surroundings.

"We don't have long," she said, stepping forward. "An hour at best."

They ventured deeper into the antechamber, careful not to make a sound. Its layout resembled that of the king's chamber, just on a smaller scale. Navigating would be easy. She memorized the look of the room, noting the usual furnishings and decor, the weapons on stands, dragon busts on pedestals, and various hunting trophies.

Lavine split from the group, studying the room more closely. She ran her palm across each wall, feeling for strange breezes through cracks.

They ventured deeper into the chamber, entering the living area. Lavine moved closer to the stone wall, her fingers gliding over its surface. There was something eerie about the room, but Lavine couldn't quite place what was wrong.

They entered Eden's office. In what little light that came in through the window, Lavine could clearly see the state of the room. It was the complete opposite of her own space back in Marella, where clothes lay on the floor and books were strewn about. Everything in this room was neat—obsessively so. Even Greyson's room wasn't this tidy.

She spun on her heel as Kace reached for something on the bookshelf. "Don't touch anything." She hissed, keeping her voice low. "If we move anything, he'll know someone was here."

Kace examined the arrangement of items on the shelf and nodded in understanding. "Great. He's one of those types of people."

"But how are we supposed to search for evidence if we can't move anything?" Ivy asked, approaching the desk.

"If we touch anything," Lavine replied, "we need to put it back *exactly* as it was."

They nodded and painstakingly sifted through the documents on the desk, careful not to disturb anything in the drawers. As they examined each file, Lavine's heart sank. All she found were military records and inventories of supplies in Beckinsdale. She worried she wouldn't find anything worth bringing to Tallulah.

How can I convince the High Council of helping Greyson if there's no proof?

She had two days left and was no closer to finding Mundicar than she was to being on the High Council. After their search of the desk proved fruitless, they began placing the documents back into their stacks, carefully shifting them into place.

If I had documentation of a dangerous weapon that no one knew about, where would I keep it? "If I were Eden," Lavine began, "I wouldn't document a weapon like this. I wouldn't risk someone finding it."

"You are correct, my dear." A man's voice rasped from the shadows.

The trio jumped and spun around. The hair on the back of Lavine's neck stood on end: she didn't need to see him to know exactly who was in the room. Kace and Ivy flanked her, weapons poised. A sliver of fear crept into her chest as she readied her daggers.

"Steady," Lavine whispered, her pulse quickening.

"You're not supposed to be here..." Ivy whispered, her voice barely audible.

"If anyone doesn't belong in this room, it is you three," Grand General Eden said, creeping forward, his tone dripping with amusement. "And you are looking for Mundicar, are you

292

not? Well... here I am."

Lavine froze, her mind reeling. The room seemed to tilt around her, the words echoing in her ears with growing disbelief. *Mundicar?* The weapon they'd been hunting for all this tim was standing right in front of them. She imagined Mundicar to be some kind of enchanted cannon or a dragon-enhanced crystal. This was far worse.

She opened her mouth, but no words came out at first. Her thoughts tangled together in a messy knot. *Grand General Eden?* The Wolf of the North, a name spoken with fear and hatred.

Her mind struggled to piece it together. *It can't be...*

Eden, Mundicar, gave a slow, mocking smile as he stalked nearer. "Tell me. How did you get into Beckinsdale? I'd love to know, seeing as I've been combing every street and alley, every crack and crevice, in search of the famous Harley Beckett."

Lavine said nothing. Her eyes darted to the comm strapped to her wrist. If she alerted Greyson, he would come running in. If she didn't, she and her crew might die here. Not wanting to give Greyson away, she stood frozen, trying to figure out how to get out of this one.

"Not the talkative type, are you?" he said.

The only way out of this is to kill him.

Lavine's heart pounded in her ears. She could make a clean shot. Her grip tightened on her daggers as she prepared to throw one at Eden. Seemingly reading her mind, Kace fired his revolver.

An explosion of ice erupted from Eden's palm, freezing the bullet midair. The ice trail extended further, encasing Kace's revolver. He let go with a yelp, his hand showing the first signs of frostbite. Gripping his wrist with his uninjured hand, he grunted in pain.

"Retreat," Lavine hissed. "Now."

The three of them slowly backed away.

"Do you really think I'm going to let Marella's famous assassin, and her underlings walk out of here alive?" Eden stalked closer, his eyes never blinking as the trio crept backward over the threshold. They had made it into the antechamber; a means of escape was just a few yards away.

With Kace's labored breaths in her good ear, Lavine's mind scrambled for a way to reach the door. Not daring to throw a dagger, she glanced up at the archway. Her eyes landed on a moose head mounted high above on the wall. An idea formed and she looked to Ivy who followed her gaze, instantly understanding the plan. Ivy nodded, ready to act.

Lavine returned her attention to Eden, who now stood in the archway. She held her breath, praying they would have enough time to escape. Ivy jerked her rifle up and fired at the wall. The moose head crashed down just as Eden crossed the threshold.

The three of them darted for the door, not daring to look back. An angry cry of pain erupted behind them. Lavine yanked the door open and watched Kace and Ivy race into the hall. She turned back to see a deep gash on Eden's head, but it didn't slow him down. He staggered forward, closing the distance between them.

Lavine dashed into the hall, slamming the door behind her. Ivy opened her pack and pulled out a small pry bar.

"Where did you get that?" Lavine asked breathlessly.

"Found it," Ivy replied, sliding the hook end under the door. "I need something heavy."

Lavine glanced around the hall and spotted a chest halfway down the corridor. She sprinted to it and lifted the lid, revealing a stash of unused armor.

"Hurry!" Kace yelled.

Lavine began tugging the chest toward the door. With his uninjured hand, Kace helped hoist it onto the pry bar's handle as the door began to ice over.

"Come on, that's not going to hold him for long," he said.

They raced down the hall, weaving past startled servants and alerting castle guards to their presence.

It doesn't matter now. Just get to Greyson.

Ginger hair flashed in her peripheral vision. "What's happened?" Wesley called out.

"What's going on, Beckett?" Silas grumbled, his voice tight with urgency as he darted past multiple corridors, the thumps of his boots in steady rhythm with her pounding heart.

"Eden," was all Lavine could manage.

Silas faltered, his eyes narrowing. "He's here?"

Before she could answer, they turned a corner and Lavine collided with something solid. The impact knocked the air from her lungs in a sharp gasp. She staggered back, her chest heaving as she fought to catch her breath.

"Lavine." Greyson's voice was low and urgent as he placed his hands on her shoulders, steadying her. His touch grounded her, but the worry in his eyes sent a fresh wave of panic through her. "What's happened? Are you okay?"

Lavine struggled to focus, her heart pounding in her ears. "It's Eden," she panted, her words coming out in a rush. "He's the weapon. He is Mundicar!"

Greyson's expression faltered, his eyes widening in disbelief. "What?"

The rush of the moment forced Lavine's words to spill out quickly, stumbling over each other in a frantic rush. "He unleashed a jet of ice from his hand, and it froze Kace's hand. We barely got out of there and he's coming."

Greyson's jaw tightened. He had sent Eden on a wild goose chase not realizing he and Lavine were on one of their very own.

His mind raced, but before he could respond, the unmistakable sound of footsteps echoed down the hallway, growing louder and closer. The tension in the air thickened, suffocating, as though the walls themselves were closing in.

Lavine's chest heaved with shallow breaths, and Greyson could feel the pressure of her panic as it pulsed through her. She was terrified and that scared him. He hadn't realized it before, but now he understood. Eden wasn't just a target anymore. He was the predator, and they were the prey.

Greyson's hand tightened on Lavine's shoulders. The realization seemed to hit him like a cold wave—the game had shifted. He had underestimated Eden. They had all underestimated him. And now, with Eden closing in on them, they had no choice but to fight or flee.

"We need to leave," Kace said, clutching his injured hand to his chest and downing a bottle of vindeca. "Now—"

"I should've known you were helping them," came Eden's venomous voice.

37

Greyson

The hair on Greyson's neck stood on end. He drew his sword, the metal cold and heavy in his grip. Once again, blood dripped down the side of Eden's head.

"You sent me out to look for this assassin," Eden said, his sons, guards, and Navarian soldiers at his heels. "And you've been hiding her in the castle the entire time? If I didn't know any better, harboring and assisting an enemy is high treason."

Caught off guard, Greyson felt as if the ground had shifted beneath him, but he refused to be intimidated. "My business with her is my own," Greyson replied coolly, his heart pounding like a war drum. "I forbid you from harming her."

"Not only are you a bastard king," Eden pointed a finger down the hall, "you're also a traitor to the crown."

"Is that a challenge, *General?*"

Eden reached toward Greyson. Ice shot down the hall. Greyson whipped his sword upward, catching the jagged stream with his blade. As Eden's new magic frosted over the sword, Greyson pulled away, the blade snapping free from the frozen tendril. The ice fell to the floor, shattering against the stone. He had known Eden would one day rise against him, but not like this.

"So you need strange magic to stand against me?" Greyson asked, twirling his sword. "How about you fight me like a man?"

Eden took the bait and drew his sword. "Stand back," he commanded the guards waiting at his heels. "I've been waiting for this for months."

"*Greyson,*" Silas hissed nervously.

"My right to the throne has been challenged," Greyson said. "By the law of Navaria, I accept your challenge. And by that same law, no one is to intervene until there is a clear winner."

Time stood still as they met in the middle of the hall, swords at the ready, circling each other like wolves. Greyson knew Eden was trying to bait him, but he had a plan. Eden struck first. Greyson countered, pushing Eden back a few paces. Shouts and jeers erupted from both ends of the hall, the cold atmosphere charged with tension.

Greyson struck again, the tip of his sword piercing Eden's shoulder. Blood spread from the wound, soaking his tunic. A fierce anger swept over Eden's face as he came back full force, swinging wildly.

Good.

Eden's fury made him frantic and sloppy, and Greyson was ready to exploit it. He blocked every blow, pushing back toward his guard and Lavine with her crew, patiently waiting for another opening. Their blades locked and their eyes met.

"It's a shame you turned out as weak as you did." Eden hissed, sweat mingling with the blood streaming down his face.

"I'm not the one struggling to breathe."

298

Greyson slammed the handle of his blade against Eden's cheekbone. Skin split open. Quickly dodging the fall of Eden's weapon, Greyson's fist struck the wound, more blood spilling from Eden's face. Eden staggered, wiping his cheek and examining the blood soaking into his glove.

"Losing your touch, old man?" Greyson said. "I think it's time to commission a new Grand General, wouldn't you agree?"

Eden shook his head. "Tell that to them." He pointed over his shoulder.

The horde of soldiers drew their swords in unison, the metallic shriek of steel scraping against leather ringing in Greyson's ears, sharp and jarring like the screech of a dying bird. His heart hammered in his chest, but he kept his stance steady, eyes fixed on the men before him.

"You are members of the Navarian army," Greyson said, his voice cutting through the silence. He gestured sharply, his finger pointing toward the rows of soldiers, each face grim and hardened by years of service. "Your duty is to the throne, not the Grand General."

The words felt like they hung in the air for a heartbeat too long. A few soldiers exchanged uneasy glances, the question of loyalty dancing between them. Their eyes flickered from Greyson to one another and then to Eden.

Finally, one of them, a tall man with a scar running down his cheek, stepped forward, his gaze hard but not entirely devoid of uncertainty. "The Hawke bloodline has always ruled with confidence, power, and relentless determination," he said, his voice low but clear, carrying a quiet challenge in its tone. "You don't possess any of those traits. My fellow soldiers and I hardly see you exercising your right as king."

The words struck Greyson like a blow, and he was reminded of his own fragility in the face of a kingdom that demanded cruelty above all else. He could feel the weight of their expectation, the unspoken belief that power was the only thing that commanded respect. It was a moment that seemed to stretch on forever, the tension thickening as every soldier waited for his response.

Greyson's grip on his sword tightened, but he kept his expression even, though inside, the anger and frustration churned. They wanted power. But how could they see that true power wasn't in a sword's edge but in standing firm when everything within you screamed to run? He swallowed, forcing the doubt to the back of his mind.

"You mistake strength for violence," Greyson replied, his voice barely more than a whisper, yet it carried the weight of someone who had seen too much. His eyes held the soldier's gaze, not flinching. "And I can show you the difference."

"I'm afraid it's too late," the soldier replied. "We've chosen our side."

A sliver of panic raced through Greyson. He couldn't fight them all. Vultures were one thing, but trained Navarian soldiers? And now with Eden's strange new ice magic.

He thought back to all the times he had kept to the shadows, shied away from formal events, and chosen to roam the streets at night. It had all backfired; Eden had the entire military in his back pocket. The common folk had always been his top priority, and he'd never questioned the loyalty of his troops—until now. And now, he was paying for it tenfold.

With Lavine, her crew, and his guard, they could hold their own, but they were still vastly outnumbered. So many bodies battling in such a small space made it too risky. Jesper's face flashed across his mind.

I can't lose anyone else.

He needed to get them out of the hall and away from Eden and his men. Greyson backed away slowly, placing his free hand behind his back to signal a retreat. From behind, guns fired.

Ammunition connected with flesh, pinging off armor. Cries of pain echoed around him. Greyson's ear rang as he caught sight of Eden's eldest son collapsing to the stone floor, a bloody hole in his forehead.

Greyson didn't take a second glance. He followed Wesley as they wound through the castle hall. An enraged cry echoed behind them. Greyson urged them to run faster. They flew down a flight of stairs, skipping three steps at a time.

Lavine reached back from the front of the pack and pulled him into the lead. He held her hand as he opened a hidden passage by the main hall. Everyone rushed past him into the dark corridor.

"Get to the tunnel that leads to Crier's Peak!" Greyson yelled. He stopped to look behind him. *Someone's missing.*

Panic surged through Greyson as he tallied the faces in his mind. Who had fallen behind? The hall above began to ice over, a legion of boots barreling down the stairwell.

"Hawke!" Eden bellowed.

Greyson ducked into the corridor, leaving the door cracked enough to see Eden without being spotted.

"You killed my son!" Eden's voice boomed in the massive room. His two surviving sons trailed behind him, one with a bullet still lodged in his shoulder. He begged the storm in his mind to settle as he realized who was missing.

Adelaide.

He wasn't worried about her. She could handle herself and would remain safe as long as she stayed hidden.

Greyson held his breath as Eden circled the room in a frenzy, a strange cold mist emanating from his skin, as if his emotions fueled the magic. Eden paced, frantic and fuming, his eyes darting around the room, trying to gauge where Greyson had fled. When his gaze fell on the cracked door, their eyes locked once again.

Greyson slammed the door shut just as Eden shot a beam of ice straight at him. The door froze solid, and Greyson raced his way back to the group, hoping the others had made it to the end and confident that Eden would be close behind. He couldn't believe how quickly things had spiraled out of control.

A thump echoed from behind, it sounded like metal on ice. A blade sliced through the thin wooden door, and Greyson's heart jumped into his throat. Another jet of ice whizzed past his head, the chill nipping at his cheek. Greyson pushed himself to run faster, his body numb from adrenaline. He glanced back, seeing torchlight flickering not far behind.

He emerged from the corridor and into the outer courtyard, where the others were waiting for him. Sunlight flooded his vision. It was already mid-morning. Greyson slammed the door shut behind him as Silas and the others heaved a bench into place, barring the entrance.

"Where did he learn this magic?" Calix asked, bewildered.

"I don't know, but we need to move," Greyson replied breathlessly, shaking his head. "Eden and his men aren't far behind. Find the river, it'll lead us to the tunnels. From there, we can get to Crier's Peak."

Calix led the convoy, sprinting through the courtyards and

into the surrounding forest. He met Wesley's wide, terrified eyes as they ran.

Keep them safe.

Greyson slowed his gait, wanting to stay at the back of the pack. After a grueling sprint, the frozen river came into view.

"Hawke!" Eden screeched through the trees.

Greyson stopped and spun on his heel, drawing his sword once more. Eden stormed out of the foliage, flanked by his two surviving sons and a handful of Navarian soldiers.

"Face me, bastard king!"

A familiar anger washed over him, the same anger that had surged to the surface the night he killed his father. *No more running.* "I am Greyson Alexander Hawke. This is my kingdom, my throne, my people. For the last time, stand down, Eden."

"With all due respect, Your Majesty, I'm not the one on the run." Eden and his sons drew their swords, a moment of silent tension hanging in the air.

"Whatever happens," Silas whispered from his side, "I'm with you."

Calix's brown hair came into view on his left. "Together in life, together in death." He, too, drew his sword.

Timid footsteps approached from behind, followed by the sound of another sword leaving its sheath.

Wesley.

Greyson's pride in his men swelled. Fear had fled as quickly as it had appeared, leaving only relentless fury in its wake. But one thing still worried him. He pivoted on his heel and locked eyes with Wesley, placing a hand on his armored chest.

"Get them to the river." Greyson shoved him away with all his strength, sending Wesley sliding across the ice. Greyson turned to face Eden. They stood their ground, bracing themselves as Eden charged.

A war cry erupted from Greyson and his guard as they met Eden and his men with the same ferocity. Greyson's sword clashed with Eden's, their eyes locking in a silent battle of hatred through their crossed blades.

"You have no right to the throne," Eden seethed.

"I have as much right as my father."

Two of Eden's men fell to Silas' blade, and gunfire rang out behind Greyson. More soldiers fell.

Eden swung again, pushing Greyson further onto the ice. His mind raced with possible solutions but found none. The sound of rushing water reached him, and he spotted Wesley, Lavine, and her crew near the dip of the waterfall, trapped on the ice and surrounded. More gunfire echoed in the air.

The falls. We went the wrong way.

The realization rattled him to his core. A familiar voice cried out, and Calix dropped to the ground, his body limp, eyes glassy and unseeing, blood spilling from his chest.

"NO!" Greyson and Wesley yelled. Wesley lunged to intervene.

"Stay back!" Greyson shouted, channeling all his strength into countering Eden's relentless strikes. "That's an *order!*"

Silas' cry thundered as he charged in, positioning himself over Calix's body. He battled the remaining soldiers, but he was quickly overrun, swinging and dodging frantically. A soldier knocked his blade upward and slammed the butt of his sword into Silas' face. Blood spilled from his eyes, nose, and mouth. Silas stumbled.

Greyson parried Eden's strike, knocking him aside, desperate to reach Silas.

Silas fell to his knees, a sword driven through his chest. Greyson locked eyes with him, feeling a rush of horror and disbelief. Silas appeared calm, almost peaceful, as he mouthed, "Together in life, together in death." Then he slumped to the ground beside Calix.

Before he could react, Eden's sword came crashing toward him. Greyson blocked, a bead of sweat rolling down his temple. Over Eden's shoulder, Silas and Calix's bodies lay on the bloodied ice, and Greyson's mind froze, shattered by the sight.

I was supposed to protect them. "How could you do this?" Greyson asked, his voice foreign to his own ears.

A grin spread across Eden's face as he chuckled mercilessly. "Anything to dethrone a false king."

"I am a son of the mighty Hawke bloodline. I hold the sole right to the Navarian throne," Greyson said through gritted teeth, his head pounding.

"You are a bastard prince. You have not a drop of Hawke blood in your veins thanks to your mother!"

Greyson's heart skipped a beat. "How dare you insinuate—"

"Your mother failed to produce a son." Eden snarled. "Four girls. *Four girls* preceded you in birth. All of them were slaughtered within hours."

The blood drained from Greyson's face. He couldn't believe what he was hearing. His stomach churned, dizziness sweeping over him.

I had sisters? "What are you saying?"

"Your whore of a mother saw my three perfect sons and begged me to help her produce a male heir," Eden began, his voice chillingly calm. "I agreed, but only on the condition that Malric would never know and that I would continue to be your right hand when you came to power. I had hoped to rule through you, keep you as a puppet while I held the true power. But you refused to cooperate, thinking you could control things on your own. But it seems you are incapable. Now, my powers are fully developed, and I no longer need you. The time has come for me to take what's mine."

Greyson's shoulders sagged as he lowered his sword, stepping back. His mind was a storm, pieces of a scattered life clicking into place. It all made sense: why his father had suddenly hated him, why Eden so desperately wanted to be at his right hand. His thoughts drifted to Eden's comments during the King's Feast.

No.

"But one night," Eden continued, reveling in Greyson's confusion, "somehow Malric figured out that you were not his. He never discovered who fathered you... and Josaphine died before he could beat it out of her."

"You're lying," Greyson said, his voice barely above a whisper. His mother's face emerged in his mind, bloodied and broken. He couldn't stand the thought.

"Have you looked in a mirror lately?"

Greyson had avoided mirrors since his mother died. He couldn't bear to see his mother's features hidden in his own.

"I had hope for you, boy," Eden continued. "You were meant to be a means to control the people. I couldn't wait to watch you grow into something fierce. But as you grew older, it became clear you took after your mother."

Eden reached out and snatched Greyson's wrist. A burst of pain erupted as ice crystallized on his armor, the cold seeping into his flesh. Greyson dropped his sword, backing away as his breath hitched, holding Eden's tense stare, filled with rage and disgust.

It was too much. His mind reeled as he took a step back. His boot slipped on the ice, and he stumbled. Eden swept his leg outward, catching Greyson behind his knee with the toe of his boot. A sharp pain jolted up Greyson's spine as he hit the ice, a cracking noise echoing as the surface of the ice began to fracture, veins shooting out around him. The sound of rushing water became deafening.

"You're a disgrace to my bloodline. A waste of blood and bones." Eden pointed the tip of his sword toward Greyson's throat. "Malric should have killed you as well."

Ice streaked down Eden's sword, the blade glistening with jagged frost. A numbness washed over Greyson, shattering his world into pieces. He felt his body freeze, a deep, unsettling fear coursing through him as Eden swung his weapon.

In that moment, Greyson's mind settled, accepting his demise. Welcoming death, begging to be rescued from the world he suddenly found himself in.

An arrow struck the back of Eden's helm, falling limply on the ice. Another whir filled the air as a second arrow was loosed. Eden cried out, stumbling back a few paces with an arrow embedded in his shoulder blade. A cloaked figure appeared beside him, and a thick boot connected with Eden's chest plate. He fell. Eden's remaining sons scrambled to tend to their father.

My half-brothers. My father.

A pair of hands latched onto him, dragging him toward the falls. Whatever came next, Greyson was ready to succumb. A handful of Navarian soldiers still standing charged at them, and he thought he heard his name, though it was distant and muffled.

"Get up!" someone yelled.

Suddenly, he was on his feet, running, his hand enveloped in someone's grip.

His feet left solid ground. They tumbled over the falls, plummeting hundreds of feet into the freezing water. The rush of cold stole his breath, the current yanking him under while his lungs screamed for air.

38

Lavine

Lavine couldn't believe what she was hearing. *He's not Malric's son.* "Great dragons above," she whispered incredulously, her voice barely audible over the rushing water of the falls. She couldn't believe what she was witnessing.

Just yards away, Lavine had heard everything. Grand General Eden knocked Greyson off his feet. Eden, steadying himself, put his helmet back on and lifted his sword, frost magic crackling along the blade. Unarmed and vulnerable, Greyson was seconds away from death. She needed to get him out of there.

"Greyson!" Wesley lunged forward.

"No," Ivy urged, grabbing his arm. "You can't help him."

Wesley watched, frenzied and desperate to reach Greyson. They couldn't let him intervene. He'd be killed as well. Lavine's mind raced with possible escape routes.

The forest or go back to Beckinsdale. She couldn't see a way out without Eden following them. Panic bubbled in her chest as she focused on the sounds around her—the roaring water just feet behind.

The falls.

It was risky. If the fall didn't kill them, hypothermia would. But it was their only chance; they just needed to reach Greyson.

He was on his backside, frozen in place, at the mercy of Grand General Eden.

"We'll have to jump," Lavine said, glancing at Kace.

"Are you crazy?"

"It's our only chance. But first I need to get Greyson."

Kace sighed, scanning their surroundings. "Okay, but we need a distraction."

Lavine drew her dagger, aiming for the gaps in Eden's helmet. She doubted she'd get it back, but Greyson needed her. She studied the field one last time.

A lone figure sat perched in a tree to their left, wearing a familiar black cloak. An arrow loosed, striking Eden in the shoulder and distracting him long enough for Lavine and Kace to race the short distance to Greyson. They grabbed his coat, dragging his dead weight backward.

"Greyson, you need to get up," Lavine shouted, pulling him toward the falls. "We don't have much time."

In a daze, he didn't seem to hear her. Panic flooded her body.

"Greyson," she pleaded. *"Get up!"*

Finally, he came to and stood. She gripped his wrist like a vise and dashed toward the others as they jumped.

Lavine hit the water, slipping below the surface. The freezing shock knocked the breath out of her. Reflexively, she inhaled, choking on the cold liquid as her body tumbled and was tossed by the current. Greyson's hand was ripped from her grip.

Not knowing which way was up or down, she opened her eyes. The churning water was white and hazy. Kicking her legs, she fought to break free from the water's grip. Sunlight filtered through the water from above, and she swam hard against the current.

Lavine gasped as her head broke the surface, coughing as her lungs demanded air. Her wet hair tangled around her neck and she twisted around, searching.

"Kace!" she yelled, her breathing uneven and frantic. "Ivy! Gr—"

A mess of curly black hair emerged from the water, coughing up liquid.

"Kace!" Lavine swam toward him, mentally thanking Gavriil for the endless swimming lessons. "Are you okay?"

"Yeah," he replied, wiping water from his face. "I'm fine."

Ivy emerged a few feet away. "Where are the other two?" she asked.

Lavine's lips quivered, her teeth chattering. She whipped her head left and right, waiting for Greyson and Wesley to surface. Seconds passed. Silence. Panic crept in.

"Their armor!" Lavine shrieked. "They must have sunk to the bottom!"

"Dragons above!" Kace cursed before diving under.

Lavine and Ivy sucked in a breath and followed. The water was clear just below the surface as they swam down toward the falls. It darkened near the base, the restless water churning around them.

Lavine spotted two unnatural white glints yards below. Kicking vigorously, she saw Wesley at the bottom of the lake, trying and failing to get to the surface. She grabbed the collar of his tunic and pulled, his armor weighing down his small frame. With all her strength, Lavine pushed his body upward. Kace and Ivy hooked their arms around him and swam to the surface.

Lavine pressed on to Greyson, grabbing his chest plate and tugging him toward her. His mouth was open, his body suspended helplessly. Her lungs burned, demanding air as she kicked her legs frantically.

Greyson's eyes slowly opened, and he gazed at her.

Please try.

As if he read her mind, he shook his head weakly and closed his eyes, air escaping his lips.

"No!" she tried to scream, but the water muffled her voice, bubbles racing upward to the surface. Desperate, Lavine moved behind Greyson, tucked her arms under his, and kicked furiously. Her heart pounded in her ears, her lungs threatening to take in a breath. Her vision blurred and she closed her eyes.

A couple of gentle hits to her face jolted her eyes back open. Kace's blurred face came into view as he pulled her toward him.

Kace placed his hands on her cheeks and brought his mouth to hers. Confused, Lavine flailed in the water. His lips touched hers and air entered her mouth, filling her lungs. Understanding, she stilled. Kace nodded to Greyson, and they each took an arm, swimming upward.

They breached the surface, her lungs burning as they welcomed the cold air. Together, they made their way to the bank, where Ivy had propped Wesley against a tree. Lavine and Kace heaved Greyson onto the land, tugging him through the snow.

"Is he okay?" Wesley's weak voice came from behind.

Lavine dropped to the ground and pressed her finger against Greyson's neck, finding no pulse. Her heart jumped into her throat. She placed her palm over his open mouth. Nothing.

"He's not breathing," she said, almost hysterical.

There was a commotion behind her. "Easy," Ivy said.

Wesley was at her side in an instant, unbuckling Greyson's chest plate. As soon as the armor was removed, Lavine pressed her good ear to Greyson's chest. Still nothing.

"Kace, he's not *breathing!*" Tears sprang to her eyes as she frantically brushed Greyson's black hair out of his face.

Kace began rhythmically pumping Greyson's chest, then moved to perform mouth-to-mouth. He repeated this ritual for what felt like ages, and Lavine began to lose hope, sobs jolting through her body.

Water ejected from Greyson's mouth. His eyes shot open as he gagged and gasped for air. Lavine and Wesley rolled him onto his side. Greyson propped himself up on his hands and knees, coughing and shivering but alive.

Lavine sat on her haunches and looked up at the cloudy sky. *Thank the stars.*

39

Greyson

Despite not being able to feel his body, Greyson trembled. He felt like an empty husk, a void. No home, nowhere he belonged. He'd lost Jesper, and now Calix and Silas.

Silas, how am I supposed to tell Becca?

He stared down into the snow melting beneath his hands, feeling only a numbness so deep it threatened to overtake him.

How am I to save a kingdom that is not mine? When it was never mine?

The faces of his subjects flashed through his mind—cold and starving. His friends, slain. Eden would gather his forces and move south, casting a shadow of death and violence. He would launch an invasion with a simple display of his ice magic. Greyson had never dreamed this day would come. He felt helpless, out of options, and unworthy.

Inhaling deeply, Greyson let out a deep, agonized scream from the pit of his stomach, his mind and soul pouring out. Tears streamed down his face, the first he had shed since his youth. Shifting onto his knees, he wrapped his arms around himself and sobbed violently, a lifetime of pain, grief, and sorrow fighting their way to the surface of his soul.

Nausea swirled in his gut as he fell back onto his hands and knees. Dizziness swept over him, making him sway. His mouth filled with saliva, and he closed his eyes, vomiting into the snow. The burning sensation in his throat was a welcome pain.

I deserve this.

Feeling returned to Greyson's body. His throat was now sore, and his wet clothes clung to him as he shivered.

"Greyson." Lavine gently placed a hand on his shoulder. "We'll get Navaria back."

He shook his head. "I'm not worthy of it."

"What are you talking about?"

"You heard him. I don't have a drop of Hawke blood in me. I have no right to the throne."

"You have more right than Eden does," Wesley said, sitting to his left. "You were raised by Malric Hawke."

Greyson shook his head, tears spilling down his cheeks. "I thought I belonged to a long line of kings, but I'm only the son of a usurper." His voice cracked. "This might be for the best. I can't take any more of this."

"You know that's not true." Lavine grabbed his arm and pulled, forcing him to face her. "Eden is the absolute worst thing for your people."

"I've lost so many."

"More will be killed if you allow Eden to continue!" Lavine urged.

"My men—"

"Will have died for nothing if you give up," Wesley interrupted, a hint of anger in his voice. "You may not be Malric's son, but you're still Josephine's. If you've shamed anyone, it's your mother!" Wesley's wrath continued to pour, the anger surprising even Greyson. "She died protecting you, and you're just going to give up?"

Wesley's words struck hard, shame welling in Greyson's chest. He had been beaten down so quickly and lost so many in such a short time. He wished he could melt into the snow and avoid facing what was to come.

"People say you have a heart made of steel." Lavine placed her hand under his chin and lifted his head. "But who has ever said that steel isn't strong?"

Forced to look into her eyes, soft and full of empathy, another sob escaped him.

"I know it feels like everything has fallen apart, but you have to keep moving. I'm not giving up on you, so don't give up on yourself."

Greyson fell into her, sobbing. For a moment, he felt ashamed for behaving the way he was, but Lavine wrapped her arms around him, her embrace tight and comforting. His throat and lungs were sore as she gently stroked his hair, allowing the release of emotion.

He wasn't sure how long he sat in her arms, but the tears began to ebb, and a calmness washed over him, relieving his body of its emotional weight. He sat up and wiped his face, opening his mouth to thank her, when the thundering of hooves echoed in the distance.

"Take cover," Kace called, waving them over to the thick brush just inside the tree line. They scrambled to hide as the hoofbeats neared.

It sounds like an entire squadron, Greyson thought.

It did not surprise him that Eden was already hunting him. He dropped to the snowy ground, pinning his back against a tree, the brush concealing him. The newcomers came onto the bank, trotting by the lake.

Greyson peeked through the brush. His heart stopped at the sight of his chest plate gleaming in the distant snow, surrounded by their tracks. A rider dismounted and approached their cover. Greyson's heart raced and it was all he could hear. He felt as if his chest would explode. Closing his eyes, he braced for the inevitable jet of ice.

"Greyson?" A woman's voice came in a whisper. "It's me."

His eyes shot open. "Adelaide?" He turned to the familiar hooded figure standing in the snow, relief washing over him. "I thought it was Eden and his men." He nodded toward the group of elk tied to the nearby trees, Jericho among them.

"Your means to retreat." Adelaide approached an elk and unloaded a pile of coats, wrapping one around Greyson's shaking shoulders. "You need to leave Navaria and get help. We can't take on Eden alone," she said, continuing to hand out cloaks. All of them were grateful for the warmth.

"I don't know if anyone can." Defeated, Greyson tugged the cloak tighter.

Adelaide stood, silently scrutinizing him from under her hood. Greyson began to squirm under her gaze. After what felt like an eternity, she lifted her hands and pulled back her hood, revealing her face. Greyson's jaw dropped as she stared intently, allowing him to take her in. Her facial features were eerily familiar.

I know her.

Her black curls, heart-shaped face, and a freckle on her left cheek made his heart race.

317

"You look like…" Greyson said, stunned. "You look like my *mother*."

She nodded. "I am Adelaide Winnet Farley, daughter of Malric Alabaster Hawke and Josephine Ann Farley. I am your elder sister."

Greyson's mind was in a fog; he couldn't wrap his head around it. Yet he couldn't dispute her claim, she was the spitting image of his mother.

"How?" Greyson asked. "Eden said Father slaughtered my elder sisters at birth."

"There were four daughters before you, it is true," she began. "The first three were killed immediately. When Malric came to take me from Mother's arms, she begged for one hour, one hour to spend with the last girl she'd give birth to. He granted her request, demanding that I be brought to the executioner when the hour was up. So, she sent one of her guards into town. He brought back a couple who had lost their baby girl. She traded me for the deceased child, and the couple fled the country with me, the money, and Mother's secret. I grew up not knowing who I was until I received a letter."

My dearest Adelaide,

You may hate your parents after reading this but spare them your wrath. You must understand that it was to save you.

My heart ached to watch strangers ride away with you. But I know they are kind and that you have thrived under their roof and from their love. Though I fear for them, as they carry a heavy secret for the rest of their lives.

You see, King Malric ended the lives of your three elder sisters at birth and planned to do the same to you. A son was his only concern. I could not bear to watch a fourth daughter of mine be slaughtered. My heart was already so broken.

On the night of your birth, another couple had lost a child: their little Marianne was stillborn. Malric hadn't even looked at you, disappointed at your being a girl. He couldn't tell the difference, so the scheme went unnoticed.

I held little Marianne in my arms as they rode away with you, fleeing the country to raise you far from your father's reach. Only when they feel you are ready will they present this letter to you.

Please know that I loved you dearly and always will. I hope one day you will find your way back to me. I dream of seeing the fierce and beautiful young lady you have become.

All my love, Josephine.

Greyson's hands were shaking. His mother had smuggled a Navarian princess out of the country and slept with the Grand General—all to have a son.

All of this to bring me into the world.

Greyson's knees wobbled, and he slumped to the ground, the letter still in hand, staring at the written words of his mother.

His brows furrowed as anger washed over him. He wasn't sure who or what he was angry at, but he felt as if his entire life had been a lie, an illusion.

"I understand your anger." Adelaide squatted in front of him. "But Mother, our mother, did so much for both of us. You cannot blame her for her actions. It's Malric who started all of this."

"If you knew you were a Navarian princess and the rightful heir, why didn't you say anything?"

"When I received this letter, I was indeed angry, just as Josephine predicted, but not at her or my adopted parents.

319

I was angry at being robbed of the royal life I was meant to have. I was angry at Malric for not wanting me, and at you for taking my place. I was jealous and swore vengeance."

His anger wavered, curiosity creeping in. "The night you broke in…" Greyson realized.

Adelaide nodded. "I traveled here with the sole purpose of killing you both and taking what was rightfully mine. I arrived a week before your coronation and saw how Malric treated you, the scars on your back, and the way you flinched at every sound. I saw how helpless you were. I stood by and watched as Malric hit you so hard, you blacked out." She paused, a pained look in her eyes. "In that moment, I didn't see you as a threat or a replacement. I saw you as my little brother, and I wanted to protect you."

An uncomfortable silence hung in the air. Tears welled in Greyson's eyes, but he refused to look away.

"I wanted so badly to kill Malric, but you beat me to it. I watched you kill him…" She paused, letting her words sink in. "And I was proud of you. I lingered to observe, wanting to see what kind of person you were without Malric's looming threat. I decided the best way to learn what you valued most was to get close to you."

"That's when you woke me."

"And when you sent me into the night to find those in need, when you became the Raven, I knew you deserved to live and deserved the throne."

So much had happened before he was even born, and he felt punished for it. A storm of confusion, anger, and joy swirled inside him. In a matter of hours, he had been usurped from his throne, learned of his true lineage, and discovered he had half-siblings. His mother had slept with Eden, resulting in his birth.

Bastard king.

Adelaide was the only one with true Hawke blood. An idea formed in his mind.

"By being the eldest living daughter of Malric and Josephine, you're the rightful heir."

Adelaide frowned and shook her head. "This is your fight, Greyson. Your throne. Your people deserve the man who ran himself to exhaustion to help them."

He was ready to hand Navaria over to her, but of course it wouldn't be that easy.

"My people hate me."

"They don't know who you really are. Do you think they'll hate me less? I'm still my father's daughter." Adelaide paused, tilting her head slightly. "They may hate Greyson Hawke, but they admire the Raven."

Greyson shook his head disparagingly.

"Show them who you really are," she urged.

How would they even react?

Greyson doubted that revealing this information would change anything. Becca's gaunt face flashed in his mind, along with her children. Terra, the daughter of Wimborne's late matriarch. Their behavior shifted after learning about his nighttime risks. They had kept his secret and silently supported him.

He made up his mind. He'd go to Marella and seek help from the High Council. No matter what it took or what he had to say. Even if he had the option to hand over his burdens, Greyson doubted he could follow through.

"I'm going to need help." He stood and glanced over at Lavine, standing side by side with Wesley. They were all he had left.

Though he had lost Silas, Calix, and Jesper, he yearned to honor their sacrifice by continuing to fight for them, for himself, and for his people.

Lavine smiled softly, her wet hair clinging to her cheeks. "We started this together, we'll finish it together."

His heart swelled. "Together in life, together in death." Despite feeling lost and afraid, he no longer felt alone.

40

Greyson

Greyson stroked Jericho's white fur, finding comfort in the elk's presence.

"Will you come with us?" Lavine asked.

Adelaide shook her head. "I'm going to keep an eye on Eden and see what he has planned."

"Can't you just put an arrow in his eye?" Kace asked.

"Now that I've made myself known, I doubt he will remove his helmet anytime soon. I won't be able to get a good shot. Not yet, at least." Adelaide stroked the neck of her mount and chuckled. "I think he finally made the connection that I'm the one who ambushed you in the courtyard."

"Wait a minute..." Kace began. Greyson and Adelaide turned to look at him. "You had your own guard attack you? Why?"

Adelaide grinned, mounted her elk, and glanced at Greyson.

"It was my way of getting Theodore out of Beckinsdale," he said simply, untying Jericho from the tree. "I agreed to release him in exchange for information about Lavine."

Kace's eyebrows shot up as he looked at Lavine. "Are you

sure this is a good idea? Theo may have told an entirely different story."

Lavine smiled and shrugged. "You know we're too far into this to turn back."

"We were supposed to kill Hawke, find a weapon, and leave. That was all." Kace grumbled under his breath. "If we're really doing this, then we need to get back to my ship before we die of hypothermia."

"We'll need supplies first," Ivy said. "It's a two-day trek back to *Piper*, and we've depleted our inventory while waiting on the mountain."

Adelaide nodded toward the river. "Wimborne is ten miles downriver. A half hour trip if you hurry. You have an ally there. And one more thing." She finagled with something on the other side of her mount, out of sight. "I snatched this before Eden could get his hands on it."

Out came a glistening white sword with dark blue streaks through it. Shock and relief washed over Greyson: he had given up hope of ever seeing his sword again.

"Thank you." Greyson smiled.

"Don't lose it again." She took off, racing back to Beckins-dale Castle.

Greyson picked up his chest plate, dusted the snow from it, and buckled it back on. "Let's get moving then." He pulled himself onto Jericho's back and looked up: the sun was still high in the sky. "Before Eden comes looking for us."

"You mean when he comes looking for *you*?" Kace countered.

"You shot and killed his eldest son," Greyson replied. "You're also a dead man."

Kace's mouth fell open, the blood draining from his face.

"Do you really have someone who can help in Wimborne?" Lavine asked as she pulled herself onto her mount.

"I hope so," he said. "If she doesn't decide to shoot me first."

"That's reassuring."

After Wesley, Kace, and Ivy mounted their steeds, he urged Jericho forward, racing along the river.

* * *

Their small caravan trotted into Wimborne by mid-afternoon. The little village looked exactly as it had weeks ago. Greyson slowed his mount to a walking pace, not wanting to alarm the villagers.

The residents of Wimborne noticed their presence immediately, more confused than frightened. The news of Eden's mutiny hadn't reached them. He could imagine how strange it must have looked to see Greyson riding in, soaked and without much protection. He and his small party were exhausted and in tatters.

The little village hall came into view. "Terra?" he called as they neared the village center. Greyson spotted movement at the window of the shack. Terra emerged, her hand resting on her mother's revolver, holstered at her belt.

"I didn't expect you back so soon, Your Majesty," she said, scanning the faces of his companions, probably looking for Eden.

When she didn't find the face she was searching for, her attention returned to Greyson.

"What do you want this time?"

"I need your help, Terra." Greyson dismounted.

Confused, she crossed her arms and stared, her brows

furrowed. Terra watched them all as they shivered, their lips blue and clothes still damp. Finally, she nodded toward the door.

"Come in then, your friends as well."

Greyson tethered his mount to a nearby post, Lavine and the rest of his crew following suit. With Lavine and Wesley at his heels, they entered the little shack where a fire was already roaring in the fireplace.

"Make yourselves comfortable," Terra said as she added more wood to the fire. They all flocked to the heat. "Grab some blankets and tea," she said to one of her guards just outside the door. Within minutes, the man returned. The added warmth of the blankets was a comfort like none Greyson had ever experienced.

A hot cup of steaming tea was placed in his hands. Greyson let the warm steam wash over his face; the shivering in his body lessened, but the ache remained. He settled himself at the table, the very same table he and Terra had sat at weeks ago.

So much has changed.

Lavine and her crew settled themselves on the floor in front of the fireplace, huddling together for extra warmth. Wesley sat next to Greyson. He had been quiet since the lake: no doubt the death of his comrades had shaken him.

"I know it was hard to leave Silas and Calix's bodies behind," Greyson said.

Wesley's eyes met his, tears threatening to spill. "I understand, but..." He shook his head. "You died. You were gone. And worse, you almost gave up."

Wesley's words ran through Greyson's mind. He understood why Wesley would be angry and disappointed in him.

"I admit, it was a moment of weakness, and I am truly sorry, but I will see this through. Are you with me?" Greyson held out his hand.

Wesley stared at him for a moment before reaching out to take Greyson's hand. "Together in life, together in death."

Wesley's strength and willingness to adapt were impressive; Greyson was glad to have him at his side.

Terra cleared her throat and sat opposite Greyson. "Now, what is this all about? Why are you all soaked? And where is the rest of your guard?"

"Do you want the full story or a summary?"

"From the beginning," Terra said with a sigh.

"It all started when the High Council of Marella sent an assassin to kill me," Greyson said, nodding toward Lavine.

Terra's eyebrows shot up. "And you're still alive?"

Greyson went on to explain how he had met Lavine and how she was also sent to find a weapon he didn't have. He detailed their failed attempts to investigate Eden's office until Lavine's crew showed up, then spoke of Eden's mutiny and the slaughter of the majority of his Royal Guard, along with Eden's ice magic.

The more Greyson explained, the further Terra's mouth opened. "How did he even get dragon magic?" she asked.

Greyson shrugged.

"He most likely ingested it," Kace said.

"Frost dragon metal is highly toxic. It would've killed him," Greyson countered.

"Not if he consumed it in minuscule amounts over the course of decades. It's like building up a resistance to poison, and it can make you very sick."

This had never occurred to Greyson, and as much as he

disliked the idea, he couldn't entirely dismiss Kace's theory.

"That would explain why his hair turned white over the years and why my sword didn't affect him when I cut him." Greyson mumbled, his mind racing with questions.

Then there was the matter of his lineage. He wasn't sure if he should tell Terra about his actual bloodline.

What would she possibly do? Kill me? Kick me out?

Secrets were his worst enemy at present.

"There's one more thing you should know about. I don't expect you to keep this to yourself because it will come to light anyway."

Terra's curious gaze never left his face. His grip tightened on the cup of tea to keep his hands from trembling. Greyson hadn't fully come to terms with it, he felt ashamed.

"I am not Malric's son."

Terra didn't respond. She just stared at him, bewildered. Greyson continued, explaining how his father had killed his elder sisters and how Josephine had had an affair with Eden to conceive a son. He left Adelaide and her adoptive parents out of it, knowing it was not his secret to share.

"That…" Terra said, dazed, "is a lot."

Greyson nodded. "Malric and Eden calling me a bastard makes much more sense now."

"What do you want me to help you with?"

"All I ask for is supplies so that we can get back up the north mountain to reach their airship. From there, I'll be traveling to Marella to ask for assistance."

"You want to ask for help? The people who sent an assassin after you?" Terra asked. "Do you understand how insane that sounds?"

"What they believe about me is false, and with Lavine and

her crew at my side, they'll have to listen."

Terra thought for a moment before nodding. "I'd rather have a bastard king than a bloodthirsty one."

"So you'll help?"

"Yes."

Terra had her men gather enough dry clothes and food for the group. After they were dressed and packed, Terra said her goodbyes and wished them luck. Greyson shook her hand, thanking her profusely.

"I am doing this for the Raven," Terra said, not unkindly, "not for Greyson Hawke."

Warmed and revived, the five of them saddled up. With a last glance at Terra, Greyson nodded and raced out of the village.

Lavine caught up and rode by his side. He glanced over and they locked eyes. She smiled, her hair flailing behind her in the wind, and he grinned.

On his left rode Wesley, his back straight and head held high. The five of them barreled toward the mountain.

Greyson didn't know what lay on the path ahead, but he was determined to see this through. His people deserved that much. Someone needed to fight for them. And though the rest of the world despised Greyson, it was up to him to save them all.

Whatever it takes.

A Crier's Peak Playlist

1. *Radioactive* by Imagine Dragons
2. *Lifestyles of the Rich & Famous* by Good Charlotte
3. *High Hopes* by Panic! At the Disco
4. *Move Along* by All-American Rejects
5. *Another One Bites the Dust* by Queen
6. *In Too Deep* by Sum 41
7. *A Sky Full of Stars* by Coldplay
8. *Everybody Talks* by Neon Trees
9. *Walls* by The Jonas Brothers
10. *Perfect* by Simple Plan
11. *The Kill* by Thirty Seconds To Mars
12. *I'm With You* by Avril Lavigne
13. *This Is War* by Thirty Seconds To Mars
14. *Into The Ocean* by Blue October
15. *Keep Holding On* by Avril Lavigne
16. *Whatever It Takes* by Imagine Dragons

About the Author

Nicole Cain is a fantasy writer based in Texas. When she's not writing, you'll often find her curled up at home snuggling with her cat, immersed in books, playing video games, or glued to an episode of *Chopped*.

Crier's Peak is her debut novel, inspired by the struggle of separating oneself from the sins of their ancestors. With a passion for fantasy and deeply emotional character journeys, Nicole aspires to craft stories that hit hard and resonate long after the last page.

She is currently working on the sequel to *Crier's Peak* along with several other projects in development.

You can find more about Nicole at https://linktr.ee/author n.c.cain..

You can connect with me on:

🌐 https://linktr.ee/authorn.c.cain

www.ingramcontent.com/pod-product-compliance
Lightning Source LLC
Chambersburg PA
CBHW030408180626
46812CB00005B/1970